STEVEN MOORE

THE SHADOW OF KAILASH

Vinci Books

vinci-books.com

Published by Vinci Books Ltd in 2025

Copyright © Steven Moore 2018

The author has asserted their moral right to be identified as the author of this work in accordance with the Copyright, Designs and Patents Act 1988. This work is a work of fiction. Names, characters, places and incidents are the product of the author's imagination or are used fictitiously. Any resemblance to actual persons, living or dead, places and incidents is entirely coincidental.
All rights reserved. No part of this publication may be copied, reproduced, distributed, stored in any retrieval system, or transmitted in any form or by any means, including photocopying, recording, or other electronic or mechanical methods, nor used as a source for any form of machine learning including AI datasets, without the prior written permission of the publisher.
The publisher and the author have made every effort to obtain permissions for any third party material used in this book and to comply with copyright law. Any queries in this respect should be brought to the attention of the publisher and any omissions will be corrected in future editions.
A CIP catalogue record for this book is available from the British Library.
Paperback ISBN: 9781036706814
The EU GPSR authorised representative is Logos Europe, 9 rue Nicolas Poussion, 17000 La Rochelle, France contact@logoseurope.eu

Printed and bound in Great Britain by Clays Ltd, Elcograf S.p.A.

By Steven Moore

The Hiram Kane Archaeological Thriller Series

The Condor Prophecy
The Tiger Temple
The Feathered Serpent
The Samurai Code
Of Curses and Kings
The Shadow of Kailash
The Oak Island Enigma
Killing Koreana

"Ignoring the challenges before us cannot be justified. When our aim is worthy, it doesn't really matter if we achieve it during our own lives. Our responsibility is to keep pushing forward with determination and to never surrender."

— Lobsang Paljor

Prologue

Mumbai, India

6:19 a.m.

"Move!" barked Azim, the massive overseer, his dark eyes devoid of any compassion. "Move. Now!"

Azim's boss, who Azim knew only as 'The Vulture', watched as his second-in-command raised his hand as if to strike the young woman, who stood at the end of a line of fourteen others just like her. She flinched. It wouldn't be the first time he'd struck her; she wore the welts and bruises to prove it. But not on her face. The men never struck the girls' faces. It was bad form to damage the goods before potential buyers got to see them. Especially, The Vulture knew, in front of him.

They filed out, a procession of withered, frightened and abused young women who not long ago were enjoying drinks with friends in one bar or another, only to have disappeared without warning or trace. The Vulture smiled. He had orchestrated this drill. These were his methods. Thus, he knew not one of these bitches would ever be seen or heard from by their friends or family again.

Of course, the girls hadn't all been acquired together, nor at the same time or place. None of them knew each other, except the two French sisters, and each had gone missing at various stages over the course of the last few weeks. They did, however, share several characteristics in common. They were all young, between eighteen and twenty-five. And they were all pretty. Very, very pretty.

The last place each of the young women had been seen by friends or travel companions was a bar, though not the same one. There was one further common trait they shared; they were all white. After all, The Vulture knew he had to meet his buyers' specific tastes, and only pretty, young, white-skinned girls fitted the profile.

The Vulture looked on, impassive, as Azim shoved them forward, assisted by several of his men. The girls were silent, their distress muted both by fear and the powerful sedatives they'd unknowingly taken with their water. Herding them like cattle up the dank and dingy staircase, Azim threw open the door and led them out. The girls flinched, raising weak arms to shield their eyes, blinded by the sudden burst of dazzling dawn sunlight. It the first natural light most of them had seen or felt in many days, in some cases, several weeks.

In the loading bay an engine stuttered, then grumbled to life, then the shabby truck reversed; its warning klaxon pierced the heavy silence, reminiscent of a woman's desperate scream. The Vulture smiled again, his thin lips curving upward at the ends. The noise mattered little. He owned the dilapidated warehouse, and no one else would be around at five on a Sunday morning in that rundown, forgotten corner of old Mumbai.

One by one the young women shuffled on bound feet into the rear of the truck, too weak and too afraid to resist, some seemingly almost resigned to whatever horrific fate awaited them. Except one woman. She was tall, and her piercing green eyes never left Azim's. The Vulture noticed her, and glancing at Azim, he could tell Azim knew this one was trouble.

Azim followed them in, shoving them forward, himself followed by two leering thugs. The Vulture suspected their filthy imaginations were running wild. But they wouldn't touch the girls. They knew interfering with their boss's inventory would cost them their lives which were forfeit, worthless to him compared to these women, who were priceless to the right client.

Azim glanced now at The Vulture, whose narrowed eyes stared unblinking at his cargo from the shadows. After a moment, and satisfied with his stock, he offered Azim the barest hint of a nod, which the big overseer returned before sliding down the back door of the truck and bolting it shut with a metallic clunk, locking the terrified girls inside with the lecherous henchmen. Azim jumped down from the loading dock, dusted off his suit, and climbed into the driver's seat of a Bentley Arnage 4.4. The rare bronze paintwork on the long, sleek classic car glimmered beneath an already hot sun.

Straightening his tie and smoothing down his bespoke light grey Armani jacket, The Vulture slid down his Gucci shades and descended the steps onto the loading bay and down to his waiting Bentley.

One of his men stepped forward and swung open the back door, and waited as The Vulture climbed in and relaxed into the plush leather interior. The man closed the door gently behind The Vulture as he checked his Rolex.

"Ready, sir?" asked Azim without looking back.

The Vulture caught Azim's eyes in the rearview mirror, then glanced once more at his £15,000, 18-carat Everose gold Pearlmaster 39. The pure gold hands confirmed it was 6:30 am.

He smiled inwardly, though his outward expression oozed cool disinterest. "Yes, Azim. I am ready," he said quietly.

The Vulture closed his eyes and took a deep breath. Then, he leaned forward and patted Azim on his wide shoulder. "It is time to take this meat to market."

Chapter One

Agra, India

For once, Alexandria Ridley appeared to be genuinely lost for words. Quick-witted and incredibly sharp, Kane knew Ridley could hold her own in any conversation and in any company; she was always able to crack a joke in an instant, regardless of the situation. Nothing held Ridley's tongue for long.

Yet, after waiting in the pre-dawn cool of an Indian morning for what seemed an eternity, where she'd chattered jovially over hot chai with Kane and dozens of tourists, she finally stepped through the impressive red-brick archway and gazed upon the incredible vista spreading out before her eyes. Kane watched on as it seemed her breath caught in her throat. Few things silenced Ridley. This view had.

Standing beside her, Kane snuck a sideways glance at Ridley, and offered his trademark wry grin. She looked radiant in that faint morning glow, her near-raven hair shimmering in the pale light and her blue eyes seemingly iridescent. Kane was in awe, not only of Ridley's beauty, but of the stunning vista spread out before them. It was the same emotion he had experienced on his first visit to Agra some twenty years before. On that occasion he had stood spellbound, just as he remained spellbound now. Yet, nothing made Kane happier than seeing Ridley enraptured this way, and he'd never seen her looking as peaceful and happy as she seemed in that moment. His heart swelled, and with his two loves nearby — Ridley, of course, and his most beloved example of architecture, and one that remained the very essence of love just a couple of hundred yards away— Kane himself had never been happier.

The sun had not yet risen fully, but enough light penetrated the complex to cause a wonderfully mystical, almost ethereal ambiance about the place. Ridley glanced over at Kane. His tall athletic figure was silhouetted, but she seemed to be admiring him, something he'd never truly understood. He watched as a single, silvery tear escaped one of her wide blue eyes.

Very gently, Kane wiped that tear from her cheek, and in his strong arms, he embraced Ridley in a hug that meant everything to him and, he hoped, to her too. A drawn out, silent minute passed, neither apparently willing to break the spell, until at last, Kane eased his love away from him. Desperate to reveal the truth in his heart—a truth he felt sure she had always known—but reluctant to say too much, he asked her a simple question. "Alexandria Ridley... are you ready to explore the mausoleum of a fallen princess?"

A simple nod and a smile was a more than adequate answer for Kane. He gently grabbed her hand and led her out from beneath the *Drawaza-e-Rauza*—the Gate of the Mausoleum—and Kane let his mind drift as they wandered among the growing crowd along the narrow, beautiful twin reflection pools. He glanced at Ridley from the corner of his eye as she admired the unmatched beauty of the Taj Mahal before them, a veritable siren in the now golden light of an Indian dawn.

Kane and Ridley were old friends from their university years back in England—the memories of which at times seemed to Kane like decades ago, and at others like yesterday. The pair were on a well-earned holiday in India. Officially they were a relatively new couple. Yet, the way they acted around each other meant that anyone who saw them together almost always assumed they were a married couple. Occasionally, upon discovering that, in fact, they weren't, Kane was told they should be. *Tell me something I don't know*, Kane would think, though he'd keep his dreams to himself.

They had shared many adventures together, some fun, others bordering on the suicidal, and remained loyal and trusted friends to this day. Despite Kane's best efforts, however, he'd never quite managed to convince Ridley they were indeed a perfectly compatible marriage-worthy couple. Kane clung to the hope that this trip to India, especially coming so soon after their last, ill-fated adventure in the mountains of Peru, might be the time to sway the tide in his favour. In his heart of hearts, Kane dared to believe Ridley was thinking along the same lines. He also believed that a dawn visit to the Taj Mahal, one of the most romantic destinations on the planet, certainly couldn't do his chances any harm.

Kane knew the story of the Taj well and as they walked, he relayed it to Ridley. "A little over five hundred years ago," he told her, "cruel fate shattered a Mughal emperor's heart.

Shah Jahan's beautiful and beloved princess bride Mumtaz died suddenly in child birth, much too young, and sadly, only a year into their blissful marriage." Kane felt Ridley's grasp on his hand tighten just a little. He continued: "It was written that the distraught Shah of Agra never got over the death of his alluring wife. Instead, and using his unimaginable grief as inspiration, he went on to build what many scholars have agreed... and you know I do too... is perhaps the single most beautiful, artistically perfect manmade structure ever created."

Ridley paused their walk and gazed ahead at the Taj, now bathed in the most wonderful pink glow as the sun slowly showed its face. "It is hard to argue with," she muttered, and Kane sensed the emotion in her words.

"Of course, the Taj Mahal was to become the princess's mausoleum, and ever since... for several centuries... it has been wowing tourists and visiting dignitaries alike, with its symmetrical magnificence and dazzling artistry. Quite simply," Kane said quietly and with genuine feeling, "it surely remains one of humankind's most astonishing creations. Now, it stands as both a testament to the love the Shah bestowed upon his young bride, and, on a more personal level to me, it demonstrates the ingenuity of what humans can create in the name of love and art."

Ridley glanced up at Kane and offered a smile, though in it he sensed as much sadness as joy. He kept his council, though, and he allowed Ridley to lead him quietly alongside the serene reflection pools. The rising sun warmed their faces and the vibrant yellows, pinks and reds of the ladies' shimmering saris were slowly coming alive in the magical morning light.

The builders of the Taj had used the purest white marble and, inlaid with millions of dazzling jewels and adorned with the delicate script of the Koran in a stylised, flowing font, Kane firmly believed it remained an artistic masterpiece.

As the sun rose, inch by inch, so the Taj began to glow further. If a witness to its beauty didn't know of its earthly provenance, Kane mused, it would be easy to imagine its creators being otherworldly, such was its mystical power. He glanced again at Ridley, who couldn't keep her eyes from it. Kane had witnessed the power of the Taj once before during a mid-nineties backpacking trip with his old friend Evan Craft. They too had been bewitched by the Taj Mahal, and India on the whole, and Kane had fond memories of witnessing all the reactions of those others lucky enough to behold the daily spectacle of magic that morning.

And now, as he glanced at Ridley, it was obvious she felt the same. They approached the first steps up onto the building's main platform, but he steered Ridley away from the swelling hordes of tourists. Some were clearly in awe, while others stood snapping selfies they would post once on Instagram, count the 'Likes', and never look at again. Kane had never quite understood that new phenomenon and was dismayed at tourists who had spent all that time and money to travel to such a special place, and yet, once there, they failed to appreciate the moment. To each their own, he mused, and continued leading Ridley away from the burgeoning masses.

A hundred yards to the east of the main structure, and in the welcome shade of a large cypress tree, Kane pulled off his backpack and spread out a blanket upon which he set the small picnic hamper he'd been toting. It was still early, barely seven in the morning, but already the sun was beating down. From the hamper he pulled some breakfast things and, to Ridley's evident delight, a bottle of chilled champagne. He knew her well.

"What's the occasion?" she asked, though Kane had never needed one.

"Oh, nothing," he said coyly through his wry grin. "You mean, besides the fact we're alive, we're here in this wonderful place together and, well, why the hell not?" Kane knew this would satisfy Ridley, as she enjoyed a breakfast mimosa as much as anyone. He handed her a glass and poured himself one, then relaxed back on his elbows. "She's really something, isn't she?"

"Who's she?"

"The Taj. Obviously female. Nothing male could be as beautiful." Throughout the history of art—without doubt Kane considered the structure before them to be artwork—people referred to inanimate objects such as boats, weapons, even countries, as male or female. Built for a beloved dead princess, the mausoleum had inspired literature and poems and architecture all around the world, and in that peaceful moment, Kane saw in Ridley's eyes and in the awed expression on her beautiful face that she too agreed that the Taj was indeed female.

She remained silent for a while, and Kane settled his eyes on the stunning structure before him. He let his mind drift to the reason they had chosen India for their holiday, and almost nodded off to sleep when Ridley's voice surprised him from his reverie.

"It's visiting places like this when I... well, I'm at my most... you know... spiritual? I'm not really a spiritual person, as you well kno—"

Kane almost choked on his mimosa. "Holy shit, I thought I was king of the understatement?" he stated, and grinned. "My love, never was a truer word spoken."

Chapter Two

Ridley shot him an admonishing glance. "Ha! Very funny," she said, "but you get what I mean, right? It gets me thinking, and questioning human nature, and what brings out the best in people. We've seen some of the very worst of humanity in recent times, haven't we?"

Ridley was clearly referring to the recent tragic events in Peru, which had resulted in several deaths, including children, and one of their closest friends. Kane suspected she had something to get off her chest and allowed her the space.

"Sometimes it's just nice to experience the best of things, isn't it? The best of people, of humanity..." Her voice trailed off but Kane remained quiet, studying her expression, and noticed it change. It was very subtle, from something like despair, to something akin to sly. "I was wondering..." Kane enjoyed the look now in Ridley's eyes, and was amused, suspecting where this was heading.

"Yes? You were wondering?" Kane teased. He wasn't worried. Whatever it was, he was certain it involved fun.

"Well," Ridley said, glancing at him, "I know we planned to head south to the beach in Goa before heading north into the mountains. But..."

"But?"

"Well, how about we change plans? How about we, well... why don't we head north first instead?"

Kane shook his head, fighting hard to conceal his grin.

"You do remember why we're here, don't you?" she asked, a slight frown creasing her smooth forehead.

Of course he did, but he wouldn't let on. He frowned back, and Ridley's heart seemed to sink as she sighed and shifter her gaze back to the Taj Mahal.

Kane had his heart set on a little beach time, catching some sun and surf, perhaps even some scuba diving. Yet, he knew how much going to the mountains meant to her—it meant the same to him— especially for such an important reason.

"Hiram, it's for Ev—" she started, but Kane cut her off, determined to have a little fun at Ridley's expense. It was usually the other way around. She gazed back at him now.

"Come on, Alex," he said, pouting a little, "you know how long I've been waiting to hit the beach, slurping cocktails out of coconuts and eating my way through half the curry in India."

Ridley nodded slowly, apparently defeated. She turned back to gaze upon the Taj.

"But, well... I guess it's possible someone I know might just have the skills to persuade me." That trademark wry grin crept onto his face again, and he laid back, shoved his hands behind his head and closed his eyes, the wry grin slipping away to be replaced with what he hoped was one of pure smugness.

"Hmm, now I get it" Ridley stated from beneath

narrowed eyes. "Like that, is it?" she purred, and slid into the crook of Kane's arm. "Then, Mister Kane, what can I do to change your mind?"

At that very moment a subtle cough made them sit up. A Taj Mahal groundsman walked nearby, a smile in his eyes on an otherwise deadpan face. He didn't look round, but he'd done the trick. Kane assumed what he was thinking: get a room.

Embarrassed, Kane eased himself away from Ridley. "Okay, it's a great idea," he said, keeping his own face deadpan. "After all, there is some phenomenal hiking up in those hills."

In a blur of movement, Ridley jabbed Kane hard in his unprotected ribs; he saw that she understood the nature of his teasing, and leaned back on the blanket and closed his eyes.

Evan Craft, one of Kane's oldest and best friends, and Ridley's friend too, had tragically died a couple of years ago while helping save the life of a young Quechuan man in Peru's Andes Mountains. At the end of what had been an unimaginable series of events, an devastating earthquake had spilled Kane and the boy over the edge of a mile-high cliff. Somehow, Kane had managed to arrest their fall by grabbing onto exposed tree roots, and the boy in turn had clung onto Kane. With the help of Ridley, Professor John O'nians and Evan, they had managed to haul the boy to safety, more or less unharmed. They had then hauled Kane to safety too. But, in what had been an unbelievable twist of cruel fate, Evan had somehow toppled over the side of the cliff and plummeted to his death.

It was a horrific finale to what had been the worst episode of Kane's career, and the second worst of his life at that point. Despite accomplishing the main purpose of the expedition—finding the long-lost Inca city of Vilcabamba, and with it the revered lost haul of Atahualpa's gold—Kane had lost one of his closest friends. Aged just forty, Evan had died in the prime of his life.

Evan had been with Kane on many of his expeditions, both official and otherwise. Kane knew that journeying to Dharamshala in India to attend one of the Dalai Lama's monthly spiritual teachings was the one experiential bucket list item Evan had not scratched off. It's not that Evan was a spiritual man; like both Kane and Ridley, he certainly wasn't. Kane knew Evan had always admired what the much-respected, almost secular Tibetan leader of all Buddhism stood for, and that he had wanted to experience the teachings for himself. In a cruel twist of irony, it had been the acts of two separate religious terrorist factions—the Catholic Eagle Alliance and the pagan Inca Uprising—that had ultimately cost Evan his life. Only Evan himself might have seen the funny side of that particular irony. After Evan's funeral back in England, Kane had made a decision; as soon as the chance arose, he would go himself to visit the Dalai Lama's Tsug-lag-khang Temple in Mcleodganj, and in honour of his friend, he would listen to the words of His Holiness.

"... and you never know, Hiram Kane, perhaps you might become enlightened."

Kane didn't flinch, and pretended to be asleep, so Ridley jabbed him again, snapping him fully out of his momentary melancholy.

"Ow." Kane smiled. "I was just thinking about Evan."

Ridley smiled. "I know you were. I was just saying that even you might become enlightened."

Kane doubted that, though he had himself long admired the Dalai Lama. No, Kane truly believed that if all the world took on board just some of the humanist lessons His Holiness taught, then it would become a much better place. And not just for Buddhists, either, but for everyone, no matter where they came from or what, if anything, they believed in.

Kane turned to face Ridley. His heart ached for the loss of his friend, but at the same time, he sensed it healing from the love he felt both for, and from, Alex. Everything would be alright. Somehow, despite everything, he believed that to be true.

"Sure thing," he said. "Let's go up north early. For Evan."

"For Evan," she replied, smiling, and proffering her plastic cup of champagne.

Over the next half an hour they reminisced about their good friend and his crappy jokes and taste in women as they finished off the tepid bubbly. When the bottle was empty, and the sun had become uncomfortably hot, they packed up the accoutrements of their picnic and dumped the rubbish in a nearby bin.

Kane grabbed Ridley's hand and, joining the bustling procession of tourists and local pilgrims, led her towards the main structure of the Taj Mahal itself.

"Thanks for agreeing to go to Dharamshala early," Ridley said. After a pause, she added, "That's one of the... two... reasons I love you."

"Just two? I could name a doz—"

Before Kane could finish his sentence, Ridley had slipped her hand from his and was soon dodging in and out of the throngs of wide-eyed tourists and pilgrims, seemingly eager to pay her respects to tragic Princess Mumtaz Mahal.

Kane again shook his head, as always, enamoured by Ridley's passion and enthusiasm. He smiled, took a deep breath, and looked up once more at the majesty of the Taj Mahal.

"This is going to be a good trip, Evan," he whispered, and made his way after Ridley, unable to ignore the unbidden and unwelcome knot of apprehension that formed deep in his gut.

Chapter Three

They hustled them through the dark jungle, rocky cliffs closing in around them as branches slapped cruelly at their exposed skin. Kane's hands were bound so tight he unable to free himself despite his desperate struggles. Ridley, Evan and professor John O'nians were alongside him, all shoved viciously into a clearing with a stone floor stained in blood. They were lined up as if before a firing squad and forced to their knees. In front of them stood a huge Incan warrior. Kane looked on in helpless horror as his friend Sonco Amaru was thrown mercilessly to the unforgiving ground before them.

The Incan spoke. "To appease the Earth Goddess Pachamama, I will sacrifice this traitor. He is conspiring against our Inca uprising and denying the Condor Prophecy. He must die." The big man raised his gun, and with dead eyes and a cold smile at Kane, he pulled the trigger. Sonco Amaru was dead—

"Nooooo!"

Kane shot up in bed, sweat pouring from his forehead.

"Hiram? What is it? Are you okay?" asked Ridley.

Kane exhaled the breath he hadn't realised he was holding, then blinked several times before managing a shallow nod. He slumped back to the pillow, now breathing heavily.

"That damn dream again, wasn't it?" she asked, though she didn't need to.

Ever since those traumas deep in the Peruvian Andes, Kane had been having this recurring nightmare, though he told her it changed slightly each time. Sometimes he said it was Sonco who'd died. Other times it was her. In reality, it was Kane's friend Evan who'd lost his life, along with several innocent Quechuan kids. Kane himself never died in the dreams, he told her, and Ridley sensed that was something that pissed him off. Ridley had known Kane long enough and well enough to know that he was taking on far too much of this burden. After all, it had been Kane's expedition to find Vilcabamba, and he'd told her himself he felt responsible that two disparate terrorist groups had used him and his expedition for heinous purposes. Innocent people died, and Ridley understood Kane would carry that guilt with him for the rest of his life, no matter what she or anyone else said to him.

"I'm sorry, Hiram," Ridley said, a deep sadness in her eyes. She looked at Kane. *Poor bugger*, she thought. Kane insisted he could have, and should have, done more to prevent those unnecessary deaths that haunted his dreams. She and others had tried hard to convince him of the noble part he'd played in getting the rest of them out of the mountains alive. She, and they, had failed. "Listen to me," she stated. More firmly than she'd intended. It was only because she cared. "John didn't die. Neither did Sonco. Nor did Professor Waters," she told him, more gently, and paused for a long moment until finally he looked at her. "And neither did I." She smiled, but within the curves of that smile remained a well of sorrow.

Most of their friends had indeed survived. However, five native Quechuan porters under twenty-years-old had died. Howie Hooper, an American Catholic and disgraced U.S. Army veteran, had murdered them while trying to free his detained leader, Angelo De La Cruz. In turn, the leader of the Inca uprising, Yupanqui Atoc, then murdered Hooper who died along with the Eagle Alliance leader De La Cruz, though Mother Nature had played her hand in that grisly death. Although Ridley knew they were all bad men who had done many horrible things, she also knew each one of their deaths had dominated Kane's dreams since.

A combination of human greed and blind faith in flawed religious beliefs had spilled so much blood, yet it was obvious Kane still clasped onto that responsibility. "It was my expedition," he'd say, especially when he'd been drinking to numb the pain, "so I was responsible!" He believed he'd been so obsessed in locating the lost city that he'd missed the obvious signs terrorists lurked in their midst.

Ridley worried he might never get over it. They'd travelled to India as a kind of memorial to Evan. Though she would never tell him, she also hoped that visiting the Dalai Lama might help Kane regain some semblance of peace and, ultimately, with all the inherent goodness and honesty he had in his heart, he might finally forgive himself.

Kane and Ridley stayed a few more days in and around Agra, soaking up the history of that once grand and royal city. They spent many hours wandering the dusty and charismatic back streets, eating as much street food as they dared. With Kane's voracious appetite, they ate a lot, seriously testing out their inner constitutions and the strength of their bowels.

Having witnessed for the first time the delights of India and her people, Ridley nevertheless found it tough. It was her first time in the country, and though she'd spent many months in developing nations around the world, but especially in Asia, and had read plenty about India's immense and devastating poverty, she realised she was far from prepared for the often inhumane reality of real Indian life.

She'd read an article declaring that the top one percent of India's richest people owned more than half the wealth. It was a shocking statistic, but one she easily believed after just a few days in the country.

The plight of the street kids affected her most. Many of them were as good as naked, all bar none dirty and shoeless. The worst of it was that many of the forgotten children were disfigured. Ridley had heard horrific stories about children cast aside by their parents, then, after being rounded up by callous street hustlers, they were deliberately disabled to make them more 'effective' beggars. The infamous 'blinding' scene from the movie Slumdog Millionaire was something Ridley might never have believed if she wasn't now seeing the barbaric evidence for herself.

She knew Kane was somewhat hardened to the pain of it all, having spent a lot of time in India previously, but the level of human suffering all around them was difficult to stomach and she knew he was keeping a stoic demeanour for her sake. They did what they could. They bought the kids food. They bought them clothes and donated their own. They volunteered a few hours in an orphanage, simply spending important time with the kids. They chatted with the children in English, aware that hand gestures and smiles were the language of the streets. They also thanked the volunteer workers for their invaluable service and kindnesses. They offered a lot of smiles, to which kids smiled back, and for a few moments, perhaps, they experienced love. It wasn't much, but at least it was something.

Ridley watched as Kane played with a couple of young lads. It was a simple game of tag, but it brought the three of them obvious joy. After gaining worldwide recognition last year for being the man to finally discover the long-lost city of Vilcabamba, not to mention Atahualpa's gold, Ridley was aware the Peruvian government had rewarded Kane with a staggering sum of money. He rarely mentioned it and avoided talk of his philanthropy at all costs. Ridley had helped him logistically as he promptly used all that so-called reward money to set up the *Kane & Craft Foundation*, a charity which helped the disenfranchised Andean natives in Peru and beyond.

Because of his charitable work in Peru and across the globe, Ridley also knew Kane now had many connections in the international community. She was sure he would call upon those contacts to help set up a similar organisation for the desperate kids here in India.

She knew Kane... and knew he would think it was the very least he could do. Ridley also knew Evan Craft would have heartily approved.

Chapter Four

"Don't you fucking touch me!" she screamed. "I'll fucking kill you."

Azim Alli's expression didn't change. He displayed no outward emotion whatsoever on his rugged, bearded face, his features worn like old leather shoes. He cared nothing for this 'meat', because that's all these girls were to him and The Vulture. Nothing but meat... ready to be chewed up and satisfy depraved appetites. Azim's was not the place to question those appetites. It was a supply and demand business. He was just doing his job. As long as the demand for their meat stayed high—it was always high, and getting higher—they would continue to supply it.

Azim himself knew he worked as just a small cog in a big machine that needed hundreds of operational parts; those parts were humans, and the sum of those parts was a massive, lucrative empire for The Vulture.

At the bottom of that list of essential components were the street kids, the desperate, disenfranchised urchins known in the business as *the spotters*. Young, heartbreakingly poor and almost all of them homeless. Their job—if earning scraps of food or a handful of rupees constituted a job—was to first spot, watch and then follow the right targets: young white women who liked to party. Azim knew there would never be a shortage of white foreign girls partying in Asia's touristic cities. Azim just happened to operate out of Mumbai.

A level up from the exploited street kids came *the feeders*. The feeders worked the bars and clubs. These operatives were a little older than the spotters; young men, streetwise and savvy, usually handsome and adept at conversing in English. They would skilfully isolate the unsuspecting girls or women from their companions. It was easier than it sounded; a well-timed whispered promise was often sufficient; or, entrance to a private club; a dawn visit to an otherwise off-limits temple; even access to the best weed or coke in town.

The feeders had a hundred schemes, but one scheme was usually enough, and it had a high success rate. Most times the young men were wannabe gangsters, survivors working their way up through the ranks. In rarer cases, they were just well-educated young men who sought excitement away from their over-bearing, usually wealthy parents. Either way, the feeders made good money from their work, and most of them had a good time doing it.

After the feeders it was the turn of *the trash collectors*. They were older, uneducated thugs who, after being tipped off by the feeders about their next collection, would swoop in with chilling efficiency and extract the girls with minimum fuss. This they accomplished, often with the help of a bribed bar owner or, more commonly, with the coercion of a generous dose of Rohypnol.

That's when things started to go very badly for those

girls and young women unfortunate enough to get ensnared in the ever-growing world of international sex trafficking. That's when people like Azim Alli and The Vulture entered the game.

"Don't you fucking touch me!" she yelled again.

As Azim looked coldly down at Kayla Stone, his huge face rigid, his eyes unblinking, he sensed the young Australian woman knew she was in deep shit. Azim had said it many times before, but he felt compelled to say it again now in accented English. "I suggest you stop screaming. I promise you... after you meet my boss you will see I am not that bad." He smiled, but it was cold and brief. He had meant what he'd told the girl, though he had no feelings about her predicament one way or another.

Azim's job was to deliver the meat to market. The buyers he traded with there considered him one of the best couriers in all India. Azim the courier. He liked the name. He'd rather be a supplier, like The Vulture, his boss. That's where the real money lay, in the supplying. But Azim knew he was more fortunate than most, in that he had a fair boss who paid him well, and in this profession—because it was a profession—he knew he could provide well for his immediate and extended family, but especially his beloved daughters.

The irony wasn't lost on the big man from Mumbai. He loved his girls and he would do anything for them. He had many times. There had been the odd murder, and plenty of near-death beatings. Azim considered arson a particular specialty. Sure, the girls he delivered as a courier were daughters too. Yes, some mothers and fathers were obviously distraught not knowing what had happened to their daughters for years, possibly ever, hoping for the best but always fearing the worst. And the worst, Azim had learned through his own experiences in the business, was really, really bad.

He didn't care. They weren't his children, and they weren't even Indian. "May I continue to serve my family and my boss," he said often, always adding "Inshallah." *God willing.*

And after Azim's role as the courier...

Then came The Vulture.

Rarely had a smoother, more handsome and more educated man led two parallel lives so brilliantly. His name itself was an unlikely dichotomy. Prabhakar Das. In Hindu, the given name meant 'The Lord'. The family name meant 'devotee'.

From a modest upbringing, Prabhakar had been a prodigious child. After spending a decade in the British public school system in the seventies and emerging from the eighties with two Master's degrees, he exited the nineties with the smooth skin of a plastic surgery addict as a man who now called himself The Vulture. As someone who could slip so easily between both roles, he almost caught himself out on occasions.

In his regular life, Prabhu, as his unsuspecting and loyal family called him, ran a successful recruitment company in his beloved Mumbai. That part of his personality lived up to his surname, Das—no one doubted his devotion to his family. Some of those recruits later become his own proud employees, entering into a vast range of careers across that even vaster city, completely unaware of the man's alter ego. But by night, for he rarely slept, The Vulture became the incarnation of his given name, Prabhakar, The Lord, a man who ruled his operations from on high, and with subtle yet steel fist.

His nightly rides around the city in his Bentley didn't feel like work to him, though he always took it deadly seriously. He would cruise around, his number two Azim at the wheel, and he would inspect his collections of meat with cold-hearted, business-like calculations.

In the course of one night, his spotters may have called out forty or more potential targets. The feeders would then halve that number after more scrutiny. It was after that second round of systematic culling of sub-standard product when The Vulture went to inspect and have the final say.

Presentation was important to The Vulture. If he felt he looked good, powerful, he would be perceived of in the same way, and in this business, he knew better than most that power was everything. Power was life.

Thus, he was always sharply dressed, portraying his self-made wealth for all to see. On his rounds of the bars and clubs, he would have the women pointed out to him, never more than one per night in the same place. He would position himself close enough to the selected women, perhaps at the bar, in order to say hello, where he might even introduce himself and offer a drink. Whether they said yes or no to him was irrelevant. He just needed to see them close up. And after that brief moment—The Vulture never spoke to the girls for more than a minute or two, even if they showed genuine interest in him, which happened often—he would decide whether to add her to his outgoing shipment of inventory, or leave her at the mercy of Mumbai's corrupt, turbulent and dangerous underworld.

The Vulture chose wisely, and understood his innate gift for the selection and procuring process. His wealth provided testimony to that, not that he needed it.

Then, once the night's trash had been collected and the scraps left to the hordes, his girls and young women were delivered by the collectors to The Vulture's premises in a forgotten corner of old Mumbai. In nine out of ten cases, their spirits were broken within the hour.

The Vulture had become a legendary supplier within India's human trafficking industry and his financial rewards had been immense. Yet, Prabhu Das was an ambitious man, and with his network of contacts across India and beyond, and a never-ending supply of quality product, The Vulture was ready to spread his wings.

Chapter Five

Like any other road trip in India, the journey north to Dharamshala in Himchal Pradesh was wild. At a little less than 450 miles, the distance was modest. Modest distances in India, however, are unlike any other in the world. To begin with, the roads are horrendous, more pothole than tarmac, and with shitty wooden bus seats that killed nerve endings and bruised bones, the hours were endless. Then, as if crazy Indian drivers weren't enough to contend with, dodging in and out of traffic and taking mountainous bends on the wrong side of the road, there was the ever-present issue of 'holiness'. Kane was well aware this specifically meant 'holy' cows.

Those sacred bovines, beloved in tradition but far from loved in reality, were, it seemed to Kane, holy in vain. Left to fend for themselves, unfed and uncared for, they subsisted on whatever they could forage. In India, the world's dirtiest country by any stretch of anyone's imagination, this meant that a cow's staple diet consisted of little more than plastic, and in its many wondrous forms. Bottles. Bags. Packaging.

Discarded furniture. Anything disposed of by the billion-plus populace inevitably ended up either choking a river or choking a cow, both dying slow and painful deaths due to the ignorance of its humble, kind yet dangerously uneducated population. And the cows are everywhere. They blocked roads, highways and train tracks, and despite the obvious problems they caused for infrastructure, little is ever done about it. The result? Endless traffic jams, delays and countless accidents, mostly caused by desperate avoidance measures on the part of impatient drivers. The penalty for killing a sacred Indian cow, accidentally or not, was beyond harsh. Being beaten to death by an angry mob was not an uncommon outcome.

Thus, two days and two nights after leaving the hustle and bustle of Agra, it was with exhausted excitement that Kane and Ridley entered the tiny Himalayan foothill town of Mcleodganj. Also known as Little Lhasa, the humble settlement just beyond Dharamshala clung bravely to the steep, dramatic slopes of the mountains and remained home to someone Kane considered one of the most inspirational humans that has ever lived: the venerable Dalai Lama.

Even the usually laid-back Kane felt wired with anticipation, though his excitement was on multiple counts. In memory of Evan, Kane and Ridley had planned to spend a couple of days at the Tsug-lag-khang Temple, listening to one of His Holiness's popular teachings. Surrounding that tiny sloped village, of course, was the magnificently picturesque scenery of the Himalayas. To the north lie the stunning Dhauladhar Ranges, a region known for excellent hiking, and camping above the snow line. Kane had read there was even a tented cafe somewhere up near the top, known as the Snowline Café. Being an avid hiker of world renown, and with the equally outdoorsy Ridley by his side, Kane couldn't wait to get snow on his boots and inhale deeply of the invigorating Himalayan air.

After checking into their cosy guesthouse, Kane and Ridley did what they always tried to do when arriving in a new place: they hunted out the nearest bar. Toasting their arrival in exciting destinations with a few local beers had become a long-standing tradition between them, especially after arduous and uncomfortable journeys, so they wasted no time climbing three flights of stairs to the stunning rooftop of McClo Bar just in time for sunset.

Kane spotted Ridley attempting but failing to stifle a yawn, her blue eyes gleaming in childlike enthusiasm. "Shit, I never thought we'd make it... what a journey," she said, then took a long sip of her large Tiger beer. "Remind me why we didn't fly here?"

"About the longest road trip I've ever taken, I can't deny it," replied Kane, he too yawning and stretching his frame at the same time. "Though if we'd flown we'd have missed out on all the fun." In truth, Kane knew flying to the Dharamshala region wasn't an option unless you rented a private helicopter—or you were the Dalai Lama. Though Kane could afford such luxuries, it just wasn't his style, and he definitely wasn't His Holiness. The thought made him chuckle.

From their rooftop seats, the view was incredible, and if Kane hadn't known better, he could have forgiven himself for thinking he'd boarded the wrong bus in Agra and got off in the Scottish Highlands. Tall *deodar* cedars clung to the near vertical hillsides, and in the distance, below the setting fireball of a sun, dazzling snowy peaks loomed like faraway crystals, throwing spears of orange light right across the valley. It was breathtaking, and just what Kane thought they both needed as he filled his lungs with the clear mountain air. After the stifling confines of the crowded bus and the clogging smog of Agra, it felt like manna from Heaven.

The vibe on the rooftop was predictably lively, as backpacker hangouts tended to be. It wasn't the rowdy buzz of Bangkok bars or the music-heavy vibe of a Filipino beach, though. Rather, it was the hum of enchantment, young travellers sharing stories of their day in the mountains or alive with anticipation about visiting the Dalai Lama in the morning. It was a jovial atmosphere, and one which they and all those around them seemed to be relishing.

"Tell me about the Dalai Lama," Ridley said through another yawn.

Kane grinned, and although he knew their friend Evan knew more about His Holiness, he obliged. "Since 1953, Mcleodganj had been the exile home of His Holiness. After he was forced to flee his Tibetan homeland due to the illegal occupation and oppression of Chairman Mao's communist China, India welcomed the venerated leader with open arms," he said, opening in his own arms to make the point. After a long swig from his bottle of Himalayan, the blue label proudly ensconced with an image of Mount Everest, Kane continued. "In the decades that followed, more and more Tibetans also escaped the torture and persecution of the invading forces and sought sanctuary in this area. Most settled in the nearby bigger town of Dharamshala," he stated and pointed in the general direction of the more famous city, "but many stayed in Mcleodganj. That's how it got to be known by its apt moniker of Little Lhasa. Thus, by all accounts it soon became a small town with a big heart. And as we sit here now, you and me, it is difficult to imagine a more calm and peaceful location anywhere. Only one thing could make it better," he added, and his smile slipped just a little.

Ridley nodded tiredly yet knowingly and raised her beer. "To Evan," she said simply.

"To Evan," Kane repeated and leaned forward and chinked bottles with Ridley, before settling back in his chair and letting his mind drift to memories of his friend, Evan.

Kane endured a few minutes of melancholy, yet it didn't last. They'd only been in the town a few hours, but Kane already felt the welcoming, spiritual influence of the resident Buddhist monks they'd seen down at street level from the roof terrace lifting his spirits, and the tranquillity Kane in that place at that moment felt was like a warm blanket against the descending darkness and chill of a Himalayan evening.

The following morning, nursing gentle hangovers but eager to explore, Kane and Ridley wrapped up against the chill and descended the forested gravel road into town. They passed gangs of curious macaque monkeys, while squirrels and chipmunks darted from tree to tree. Wild flowers adorned the narrow road, and the clear air was laced with fragrant incense burning in hidden forest homes.

Once in the centre of the small town—little more than a modest central crossroads—they each gulped down two cups of delicious, over-sweet chai, then feasted on a breakfast of spicy vegetarian dosas, washed down by yet more chai, poured by a grinning chaiwala, whose smile seemed to be a permanent fixture.

Next they secured their tickets for their visit with His Holiness in two days' time, then set off to explore the town of Little Lhasa. With an open heart and a full belly, Kane was in his element, and glancing at Ridley, he knew she was too.

At the end of a lazy, recuperative day, Kane and Ridley ate dinner then went for the custom couple of rooftop drinks. "Well, we need something to wash down the curry," Kane said, as if they needed an excuse.

Chapter Six

With an eight o'clock start to the Dalai Lama's teachings ahead, Kane and Ridley rose early and headed back out from the guesthouse along the gloomy yet now familiar forest road down into town. They stopped at the equally familiar chai stall and chatted amiably with the chaiwala, their excitement about their imminent visit to the temple most likely obvious to the young tea seller. He'd probably seen it all before, of course, and they soon learned he had occupied that same prime spot selling his chai for years. In fact, he was quite a character, and seemed to have his finger on the pulse of everything that happened in Little Lhasa. He also claimed to know His Holiness personally, but the glint in his eye suggested that might not be the whole truth. Kane listened with amusement as the young man introduced himself.

"My name is Abhay Punyamarthula, but since I'm as thin as a rice farmer's scythe and worth just as little, my friends call me Puny. And since we are now firm friends, isn't it, you may call me Puny too." Puny was a farmer's son, he told them, and though Indian, he explained he had a great affinity with the Tibetan refugees, and that many of his friends were indeed Tibetan. His parents lived in nearby Dharamshala, but Puny had chosen to live in Little Lhasa because, he said, the chai business was booming. Kane suspected Puny simply enjoyed meeting and chatting with the tourists, though probably both reasons were true.

They bid Puny farewell, promising they'd drop by for chai after visiting the Dalai Lama, and merged with the calm yet burgeoning crowds heading slowly towards Tsuglag-khang Temple.

After passing through what Kane thought was fairly lax security for such an important cultural location, they made their way up the stairs to the temple's upper level where they found a spot on the cushioned floor, nestled cosily between wide-eyed tourists and many monks of all ages.

Amid what was an electric atmosphere, everyone seemed to be eagerly awaiting the arrival of His Holiness. It wasn't surprising to Kane who excited the crowd appeared. The Dalai Lama was a man who'd inspired so many millions of people across all faiths with his simple messages of harmony and love for all, no matter where they hailed from. The buzz of the vibe made the hairs on Kane's arms stand on end, and he snuck a sideways glance at Ridley, who seemed as enthused and in awe as the rest of the pilgrims, local and tourist alike, around them.

There were many hundreds of people sitting on that upper floor of the temple, and what struck Kane so vividly was that everyone he saw was smiling. When things had unravelled last year in Peru, the smiles of his friends and colleagues had soon been replaced with anxious expressions of fear, and rightly so as their very lives were threatened.

But no fear had entered this place, and joy permeated the very air around him. It was most welcome.

A hush descended throughout the temple as a whispered rumour circulated that the arrival of His Holiness was imminent. Kane glanced to his left at Ridley, as the whispers fell away into a heavy silence. He'd never seen her more enthused. They shifted on their bums, trying hard to see across the hundreds of heads to where His Holiness would make his much anticipated entrance.

And then, very slowly His Holiness, The Dalai Lama, ascended the steps from the bottom floor and gently took his seat on the dais. Even from his position twenty yards away, Kane saw that the revered leader's own smile was wider than any of those there to listen to his teachings.

The man just radiated goodness and compassion. Kane, and probably everyone else squeezed into that pleasantly crowded space, became spellbound. And then, once the Dalai Lama began his legendary Tibetan Buddhist teachings, aside from his soft yet confident voice, Kane thought he could have heard a pin drop.

Kane was genuinely enthralled, but after an hour of sitting in the same spot, despite the floor cushion, his aging legs had started to protest, and within another thirty minutes, they'd gone completely numb. He enjoyed the translated teachings, but, as they usually did, both his mind and his eyes began to wander. Glancing around him, he admired the attention most others seemed to be paying, admiring too their ability to not fidget, a skill he'd never possessed.

Dozens of Tibetan monks sat spread about the hall; some appeared to be novices, barely more than kids; others were wizened, older men. One such monk, probably in his fifties Kane guessed from his lined face and sparsity of hair, caught his eye. He stood out from the crowd, not because of his crimson and orange robes, which all the monks wore, but because, unless Kane was mistaken, he kept dropping off to sleep... much to Kane's great amusement.

After the latest of his many sleep-induced moments, in which he partook in some gentle, involuntary head-banging, the monk looked around, and happened also to catch Kane's eye. The two men shared a moment and the mischief in the monk's eye left Kane in no doubt about his character. As if he'd been caught red-handed, like a child falling asleep in a primary school assembly, the monk sheepishly raised his finger to his lips, apparently asking Kane to keep their secret. They shared a grin, and the monk returned to his half-listening, half-dozing session.

During the first break of the teaching, Ridley helped Kane off his numb bum and with some subtle groaning from him, they walked around a little to stretch their legs and get some blood flowing back into the joints. Kane then felt a gentle tug on his sleeve. He spun around, delighted and surprised to see the friendly monk. "Hello," said Kane.

"And hello to you too," the monk replied in excellent English. "I hope you will not tell His Holiness I fell asleep?" He chuckled, and it was the laugh of a man apparently fully at peace with the world.

"No, I won't tell him, if you promise not to tell him I nodded off too?" They both grinned. Ridley remained oblivious to the private joke, so Kane introduced them both. "This is my... uh, friend, Alexandria Ridley."

"Very nice to meet you... um?"

"My name is Lobsang Paljor. Lobsang to my friends. You can call me... Lobsang," he said, the glint in his eye a joy to behold as he proffered his hand, which Ridley took.

"Hi Lobsang. Please call me Alex. This is Hiram Kane."

Kane held out his hand and shook with the monk. "Well, I am very pleased to meet you Hiram, and you, Alex. Now, I wonder, would you do me a great honour and eat lunch with me after the teaching is finished? I would very much like to chat with you both."

Before Kane could respond, Ridley answered on their behalf. "Thank you Lobsang, we would love to."

Lobsang grinned and bowed his head a few inches, then turned and disappeared into the throngs of avid pilgrims, most chatting excitedly with their friends or fellow pilgrims. Many were rubbing their bruised posteriors.

Chapter Seven

The Dalai Lama finished speaking at noon, and after a respectful but nonetheless joyous round of applause, the awed crowds slowly moved away and dispersed away from the temple.

"Well, what did you think?" asked Ridley as they made their way out into the sunlight.

"Evan would've enjoyed it. I'm really glad we came."

"But what did *you* think? Do you feel enlightened?" It was a serious question, but was said from beneath twinkling eyes.

Kane paused and flashed his trademark wry smile. "I think I'm hungry. Where's Lobsang?"

Just then Lobsang Paljor emerged from around a corner and beckoned them over, and a moment later they trailed the sprightly monk down the wide and well-worn stone stairs and out into a courtyard. There they found many people gathered, both tourists and Tibetans alike, sat waiting for lunch.

Leading them to a quiet, shaded spot against the outer

wall of the temple sanctuary, Lobsang then stepped away and disappeared for a moment before returning with generous platefuls of rice, dhal and vegetables. Placing down the food, he hustled off and a further minute later returned with the ubiquitous mugs of yak's butter milk.

Grateful for the temple's generosity and of Lobsang's kind request for them to join him, and following his evidently hungry lead, Kane and Ridley tucked into the food with gusto. They hadn't eaten since dawn, and Ridley couldn't stifle a chuckle as Kane's stomach audibly growled in protest. Suitably embarrassed, Kane apologised, to which the playful Lobsang countered with a hearty burp.

Once they'd eaten, Lobsang launched into a story about how he'd come to be in Mcleodganj, and it was quite the wild tale. Kane and Ridley were rapt listeners.

"It got desperate for us in Tibet, our own country. The Chinese soldiers beat us and even arrested us for anything they deemed worthy. It was for simple things, such as singing our traditional songs or displaying our national flags. The government stole our livestock and left us with nothing. It was too dangerous to stay and study, so, in nineteen-eighty-five, I left."

Lobsang paused long enough to refill their cups with yak's milk. Both Kane and Ridley were polite enough not to tell Lobsang what they really thought of the rancid, sickly-sweet and fatty drink. Secretly, Kane considered it nothing more than a heart attack in a cup. Over the top of his large cup, Kane saw the trauma in the monk's eyes, and was once more reminded of just how badly some people were capable of treating others.

"It took twenty-five days of trekking across the mountains to the Indian border," Lobsang continued, "and we could only travel in darkness, surviving on raw tsampa plant and black tea. It was a cold, difficult and dangerous journey... so very cold, so very dangerous... but it was a journey we had no choice but to attempt to make. By luck, or," he said and paused, spreading his arms out, a grin creeping onto his weathered face, "by the grace of the Lord Buddha, "all of group somehow made it all the way here, proud and very relieved. But we were also sad. We had survived, and made it to safety. However, we had left friends and family behind. Many of them are still there." A wistful look entered Lobsang's eyes, but that impish glint soon replaced it. "More yak's milk?"

It seemed as if Lobsang had been chatting for hours, but in reality, only thirty minutes had passed. Kane had been deeply absorbed in the awful but rousing story of Lobsang's escape from Tibet and the shocking hardships he and thousands like him had suffered and were still suffering to this day.

"That's an amazing tale, Lobsang," Ridley said with no shortage of compassion. "I am so sorry you and so many others have had to suffer so much and for so long... it's just terrible. Thank you for sharing it with us."

"I agree... you're a brave man," agreed Kane. "And yet you should never have had to leave your homeland like that."

Lobsang smiled. "It was not bravery that made us leave... it was our duty. It was a much braver thing to stay behind." His smile faded just a little and he looked off, somewhat wistfully across the courtyard, as if recalling those he'd left behind.

Kane wasn't sure he agreed it was braver to stay, but he understood the monk's point. Kane had heard of the Chinese oppression in Tibet, but—and he believed this was likely the case for many westerners—he didn't know enough about it. At least until now. Yet, like he had on so many occasions during all of his world travels, Kane felt helpless to ease their suffering, unable to assist in any way that would actually make a difference. In this case, the Chinese regime was simply too powerful.

Yes, he had assisted many people. He had even created charities, and Hiram and the Kane family had always donated a lot of money to good causes. Kane had volunteered in a dozen countries across four continents, but there was only so much an outsider could do. And Kane knew, when going up against the might of the Chinese government it would take more than a humble Englishman to change the world. *What was it His Holiness said?* Something like... *If you think you're too small to make a difference, try sleeping with a mosquito.* Well Kane understood that logic... mosquitoes were the very bane of his life, and though he didn't like to kill any living creatures, mosquitoes were a definite exception to the rule.

Still, in moments like those Kane wished he were a braver man, brave enough to go to Tibet and do something, although what he could legitimately do, he didn't have a clue. There were organisations that helped refugees, not just in Tibet but all over the world. Many thousands of good and selfless people helped millions of displaced people on a daily basis. The plight of the Tibetans, however, didn't seem to get nearly enough coverage in the media as, say, Syria, and west African states that seemed to be in perpetual civil wars.

Ultimately, Lobsang's revelatory story had struck a chord with Kane he couldn't quite understand. However, until he did, he would blame it on Lobsang's contagious, ever-present smile.

They all rose, and Kane and Ridley said goodbye to the

jovial monk and accepted his invitation to meet sometime for coffee at his favourite cafe in town. *Monks drink coffee?* mused Kane. Little Lhasa was full of surprises.

When they approached Puny, the effervescent chaiwallah, at his usual spot, they were not surprised to find him engaged in conversation with a pair of young hikers. A charmer, definitely, but Kane believed there was no doubt he was a nice young man with a good heart. Kane had a few questions for him, and they waited while he finished chatting with the girls Kane guessed were Scandinavian. Wherever they were from, Puny had them laughing aloud at his jokes.

"A monk stole a sheet of red cloth from my father's tailor shop," he said. "I hope he does not make a habit of it."

Though the girls laughed, as did Kane and Ridley, Puny clearly found his own jokes funnier than his impromptu audience of four. It didn't put him off. "I am thinking of becoming a monk myself."

"Really?" asked one of the girls.

"Yes, why not?" he asked, feigning hurt. "I have all the qualifications."

"And what are they?" Ridley pressed.

"A nearly bald head, a red bath towel, and I have not had a girlfriend in years."

More good-natured chuckles followed all around, and as the girls left, one looked back and said, "We expect more jokes tomorrow, Puny." Then, off they strolled up the hill, chuckling as they went.

"They like me, isn't it so?"

"Everybody likes you, Puny, including us. You, your

jokes, even your chai. Two cups, please, and I have a question."

"One minute, Mister...?"

"Kane, but please, call me Hiram."

"Okay, Mister Hiram, ask me anything you like. If I do not know the answer, I will make one up." He smiled and handed over the chai.

Kane didn't bother to correct Puny in case he hurt his feelings, and asked his first question. "I know Mcleodganj is known as Little Lhasa because of all the Tibetan refugees living here. I wonder, how many live in exile here, and how many more flee Tibet each year?"

The smile remained, but a trace of sadness entered Puny's hazelnut eyes. "Too many. I do not mean they should not come here, of course not. They should not have to leave Tibet in the first place. What the Chinese are doing is bad, Mister Kane. Evil, and most of us do not understand it. Tibetans are peaceful people, and... well, it is just not right."

Kane thought for a few seconds, then surged on. "Okay, but is there anything tourists like us can do? I mean, to help in some way?"

Puny fell quiet for a moment, as if thinking carefully about his answer. At last he spoke, the missing sparkle returning to his eyes. "Yes, Mister and Missus Hiram. I know a man."

Chapter Eight

It was seven when Kane and Ridley arrived at the restaurant that evening for a meeting arranged by their new friend, Puny. They gave their names at the door and were ushered into a booth to be greeted by an affable American citizen of east-Asian descent.

He was a large man with a confident handshake and a deep voice. As he welcomed them to his table like old friends, offering a generous bow, Kane liked him immediately.

"It's so nice to meet you," he said. "Please, take a seat."

Kane and Ridley squeezed into the booth after a round of handshakes.

"And let me say right now, it is a pleasure to meet like-minded people who just want to help. And... you do want to help, don't you?"

"Well, yes. We think so." Ridley glanced at Kane, who nodded. "It's just... well we're not sure exactly what it is you do, Mr...?"

"My name is Mr. Lee, but please, call me Chan."

"Chan, Puny only told us you were the man to see if we wanted to help the Tibetan people." Kane paused for a moment, and Chan Lee sensed his dilemma.

"Go ahead, you can ask," he said, smiling.

Kane smiled too, though he felt somewhat embarrassed. "Forgive me, but you are of Chinese origin, aren't you?"

"I do indeed have Chinese parents," Chan explained, "but I'm an American citizen, born and raised in San Francisco. Yet, it's exactly because of my Chinese heritage that I'm in the perfect position to help the Tibetans, since I don't get harassed by Chinese soldiers at the border crossings as I move in and out of Chinese Tibet." He stopped and spread his hands apologetically. "However, let me take a step back and tell you what it is I actually do. It's a nasty word, one I don't like to use. For ease of explanation, you might say I'm a smuggler of sorts. And the goods I smuggle are people."

Neither Kane nor Ridley hid their distaste at hearing the word smuggler, but both remained silent. Chan smiled.

"I see you find that word as abhorrent as I do. And I understand it comes with many negative connotations, rightly so in this era of human trafficking." He stopped as Kane and Ridley shared another subtle glance. *He'll need to try harder than that,* Kane mused inwardly. Chan Lee continued. "Let me elaborate. What I do is not so much smuggle people. I..." He paused again, the hint of a smug grin on his face as he seemed to choose his next words with care. "I might just as easily say I rescue them. First, I have to arrange it with their families here in India... those families lucky enough to have already made it across the mountains from Tibet. Once I have finalised the arrangements, I then travel to the Tibetan border, sometimes through Nepal, though most times I cross directly from India. Then, and after some serious backsheesh—or in English, bribery—I drive what are often huge distances across Tibet. I then collect the refugees from a designated pick up point, and return, safely bringing those refugees into India. More often than not it is here to the Dharamshala area."

They stared at each other then, Ridley and Kane, Kane wondering why he had a sudden mistrust of Mr. Lee and suspecting Ridley felt that same caution. They didn't know enough yet, however, and were keen to hear more.

"Please, Mr. Lee," said Ridley, "tell us everything."

"It's Chan," he said, still smiling.

"Sorry. Chan. Please go on."

"Of course. Rescuing people from such a politically sensitive area of the world is difficult, and by definition, these missions are very, very expensive. Thus, we have to charge the families in accordance with those great risks."

Ah, the truth of the matter, thought Kane, though he was unsurprised. "In other words, it's a business for you, Chan, this *rescuing* people," he said, the word 'rescuing' intoned with obvious sarcasm.

"It's true that rescuing people, as you say, is a lucrative business. Think about it, though... what price is there on a person's life? If these people remain in Tibet, they risk constant hassle and persecution... sometimes even death. It's more than that. What's even worse than death for the Tibetan people is their lack of liberty and freedom. Did you know you can be beaten, even imprisoned and tortured, simply for waving a Tibetan flag?"

They hadn't until Lobsang told them about it. "Yes," Kane said, unable to keep the impatience from his tone.

Chan seemed undaunted and said, "Countless Tibetans over the years have *disappeared* without a trace for the innocuous act of being proud of their heritage and culture, all of which the Chinese see as a threat to the growth and expansion of what must now be labelled the Chinese Empire." Kane's eyes widened, and Chan Lee noticed. "Yes, the Chinese Empire. It can be labelled nothing less. An empire of cold, calculated and often brutal expansion under the guise of some kind of paternal right to the land. Thus, what I do is dangerous and costly, as you must realise. This may sound dramatic, but believe me, it isn't," Chan said dramatically, "but if it weren't for the few people like me who're prepared to risk everything to help, then the Tibetan people and their culture will eventually disappear entirely. Wiped from the face of the planet and erased from the history books. It is what China wants, and at this rate, it is what they will get. So, I ask you Mr. Kane, why shouldn't I get paid?"

As much as Kane despised the idea of someone making a profit from other people's misfortunes, the alternative was much worse. The truth as Kane saw it was, Chan Lee had presented a compelling argument. The bottom line, if what he was telling them was accurate, then he was literally responsible for saving the lives of many Tibetans, both young and old. And, in doing so, he was also also helping save one of the world's oldest, most peaceful cultures. Despite Kane's moral objections, he couldn't deny it was a service worth paying for.

Kane caught Ridley's gaze and felt sure she had come to the same conclusion. They looked at each other for long moments, seemingly battling their natural dislike of the man before them, but also their own consciences. If they didn't at least try to help, Kane realised, how would they live with the guilt? With a subtle nod and an almost telepathic silent agreement, they had come to a decision.

Kane stood up and looked down at Chan Lee, who now

stood himself and studied Kane with what appeared to be watchful eyes. Kane said, "Okay, how can we help?"

Over the next couple of hours and several bottles of Tiger, Mr. Lee had convinced Ridley and Kane to join him on his next "rescue" mission. He assured them they'd both be of invaluable help to the operation, either by sharing the driving burden, or offering whatever physical or medical support they could. They wouldn't need visas, he informed them, because he would arrange their border negotiation once they arrived, thanks both to his fluent Mandarin, and his healthy operational budget. He'd recruited many tourists to help him in the past, he explained, adding that every one of them had been glad to help and were rightly proud of what they'd done.

Ridley worked hard at remaining affable and keeping her misgivings to herself, at least for now. She thought it might be a good idea to meet a couple of those recruited tourists. "Chan, are any of those guys still around, the ones who went with you to Tibet? I mean, if we could meet one or two and ask a few questions, perhaps we wouldn't be so... I'll be honest and say this is making me a little nervous. We'd at least understand what we were getting into."

A shadow seemed to pass quickly over Chan Lee's eyes, but disappeared in an instant. Ridley watched him carefully as he nodded. "Yes, it's possible. I know of one kid who's still here in Little Lhasa. I'll try and locate him and arrange for you to meet. It is, as you'd know by now, a tiny town. He shouldn't be hard to find. How about... tomorrow morning?"

There was definitely something suspicious about the man. But, Ridley figured a man who worked in the smuggling business—for want of a better term—had to have at least some amount of shadiness and the ability to operate on the wrong side of the law, even if it was in the name of international and cultural philanthropy. She had met such guys before, men and women, and she'd learned there was more than one way to do what was right.

Despite her misgivings, Ridley was excited at the chance to somehow help the disabused Tibetans escape tyranny and begin new lives in the relative freedom of northern India. Freedom was something she believed all humans should be able to enjoy, and she couldn't imagine her own being taken from her. If they could speak with someone who had actually been on a trip with Chan Lee...

She could tell by the look in Kane's eye he felt the same. After last autumn's Peruvian disaster, she believed this might be present a fantastic opportunity to start mending his broken heart over those lost lives in the Andes while at the same time helping those who needed it most. And maybe, if he was lucky, perhaps—and she hoped with all her heart it might happen—Kane's nightmares would stop too.

They said a somewhat cool goodbye to Chan Lee and, after confirming the time for tomorrow's meeting, Kane and Ridley left the warm restaurant and stepped out into a clear and chilly night. It was close to ten, and there was hardly a cloud in the sky, the dark night a tapestry of twinkling stars. A little tipsy after their half-dozen Tigers each, they made their way towards their hotel.

Neither spotted Puny watching them from the darkness of a nearby doorway, nor the guilty look on his face of someone who'd just done something terrible.

Chapter Nine

The following morning greeted them with a light dusting of snow and a brisk breeze, though it felt only a little colder. The only other noticeable difference was the lack of monkeys on the pretty trail into town. *Smarter than us*, mused Kane as he huddled deeper into his jacket.

They walked their usual route, making a beeline directly to Puny's chai stand, surprised and somewhat dismayed not to find him in his normal spot. Listening to his jokes was enough to warm anyone's spirits on a chilly morning. Instead they headed straight to the coffee shop for the meeting with Chan Lee and a guy called Sam, a German tourist who had apparently helped Chan on several of his sojourns into Tibet.

They took a seat and ordered two lattes, and waited while enjoying the wintry scene outside from the comfort of the cafe. They'd scheduled the meeting for nine, but nine thirty rolled around and there was no sign of Chan Lee. They sat chatting for another fifteen minutes, and were just about to give up and search for Puny when Chan walked in, ushering alongside him a tall, skinny and somewhat dishevelled young man. After brief introductions, along with a mumbled apology by Chan for their late arrival, they all sat in the booth.

The first thing Kane noticed about Sam was how pale he was. Thin too... painfully thin. He also looked as if he hadn't showered in many days. His clothes were dirty, and without meaning to judge him, it was easy to conclude that the kid was a mess. What's more, he fidgeted in his seat, almost squirming as if he desperately didn't want to be there. Kane noticed Ridley trying hard to avert her gaze from Sam, and knew she recognised some of the kid's clear symptoms of prolonged drug abuse. It was something she had experienced herself, and though some time ago, and very much behind her, evidently it was a sobering moment.

He also noticed Sam couldn't look them in the eye, constantly glancing away as if agitated or under extreme duress. There was no doubt about it. Sam was a drug addict.

"Sam isn't feeling well this morning. Probably just the colder weather," said Chan, but he wasn't convincing. "Isn't that right, Sam?"

Sam remained silent and fidgety.

"Tell them, Sam," pushed Chan.

"Ya, Mister Lee, I am... I am sick." He looked down, his hands twitching nervously in his lap.

"So, Hiram and Alex, I believe you have some questions for Sam?" Chan smiled, but there was something hard beneath it, as though he was anxious of what they might ask or what Sam might answer.

"Yes, we do. Sam," began Kane, "we're considering helping Chan, as you did. We just wish to ask you about your experience. How was it? I mean, was it dangerous, and did you face many problems? How many people did you... erm, did you help rescue?"

Sam didn't respond immediately. Instead he looked nervously at Chan Lee as if unsure how to answer. Ridley took over from Kane.

"Listen Sam, we really want to help, but we need to make sure we're aware of what we're getting into. Could you share your experience with us?"

There was a long silence before Chan stepped in. "Oh, come on, Sam, you know how it went." His voice was soft, but Kane sensed a flinty edge to the word 'know'.

It was obvious to Kane Sam did not want to be there, and he looked so uncomfortable that he was reluctant to push him any further and doubted Ridley did either. After a long pause though, he finally answered. He still didn't make eye contact. "The first time was six months ago, perhaps seven. We drove through the mountains to Ngari, the furthest western settlement in Tibet, where most of the crossings—"

"Many Tibetans travel west from eastern cities like Lhasa and Yangbajain," said Chan, cutting him off. "Most of them want to settle here, close to their spiritual leader, His Holiness. It's a long journey, and fraught with hazards, not the least of which is the Chinese security forces. When these people finally get to us, they're relieved, and will do almost anything to cross the border." There was a hint of greed in his eyes, but Kane ignored it.

Ridley seemed to bristle at the rudeness of Chan butting in. She spoke again, directly to Sam. "And when you meet the Tibetans, *Sam*, what happens next?" she asked, fixing her gaze on Chan as if to dare him to cut in again.

Again, Sam looked at Chan, who nodded so subtly

Kane almost missed it. "We give them food and water, and... well, we..."

"What, Sam?" Ridley pressed gently. "What happens next?"

Sam froze, and it seemed as if he was fighting hard not to cry.

"We just want to help, Sam, like you did. Please, tell us what happens next?"

Sam didn't tell them, and in a sudden flurry of movement he stood up and bolted out into the cold, almost stumbling over another table in his haste.

Kane glanced at Ridley; this time there seemed more concern in her eyes than sadness. The situation didn't seem good.

"What just happened, Chan?" pushed Kane. "Why's Sam so uncomfortable? He's clearly scared of you."

"Sam isn't scared of me, Hiram. The problem with Sam is, like so many young backpackers who come to India, he's developed what you might call a serious drug habit. It's not difficult to find drugs in the foothills of the Himalayas, and of course, compared to European prices they're very cheap. Simply put, Sam has a drug problem, that's all." He held Kane's gaze, and Kane sensed the barest hint of a challenge there. "What he told you was the truth. We meet the escaping Tibetans either at the border, or, if the price is right, we're prepared to go all the way to Ngari. Then we load them in the vans and drive them south. It's a simple process in essence, but it is definitely not simple to carry out successfully without the right contacts and, shall we say, the right series of *persuasions*."

Kane was sure there was something Chan wasn't telling them, and he didn't like it. But again, it all boiled down to how much they wanted to help.

All things considered, Kane wanted to help a lot.

Chapter Ten

With the weather apparently deteriorating over the next few days, at least according to the forecast, Chan explained he couldn't fix an exact date of departure for the border, but added it would probably be within the week. He advised them to stay local, and to check in with Puny on a daily basis. They would get no more than twenty-four hours' notice before they'd need to be ready for departure, so if they were serious about going with him they would have to be ready.

"You'll need to stock up on food and other supplies for the journey, and make sure you have plenty of clothes. The further north we go, the colder it will get. There are places for us to get supplies en route, but they're limited and unreliable. It's better you bring your own." Chan looked earnestly at Kane and Ridley now, his face softening. "Listen, guys, please don't be afraid or worried about Sam. What we're doing is a good thing... a great thing... and although it's a little risky, I won't deny it, you're in good hands. I've done this many times, and... well, I've yet to fail.

And trust me... once you witness the looks of immense relief and gratitude on the faces of the people we rescue, all your trepidations will vanish and you will be very proud to have helped in something so humanitarian." He held their gazes for long moments, and Kane sensed they both wanted to believe him, to trust in what he was doing.

Finally, Chan stood. He held out his hand. "You won't regret it, and trust me, it is a great thing we do. Good day to you, Hiram, and Alex, a good day to you too. Don't forget to stay in touch with Puny." They all shook hands, and Chan Lee turned and left, paying the bill at the counter on his way out.

Kane shuffled to the opposite side of the booth so he could look directly at Ridley. "Well, what do you think?"

Ridley's face wore a range of emotions. Kane knew her expressions well, but he couldn't quite tell if it was excitement or worry, and decided it was probably both.

"Despite my reservations about Chan, mostly I'm excited," she told him. Ridley leaned in closer and lowered her voice a little. "Don't you sense something weird about Sam? I mean, he's young, early twenties and obviously has a drug issue," she muttered and looked away briefly before returning her gaze to Kane, who smiled I. understanding. "But he looked beaten up, and I don't mean physically. It looked as if he was terrified of Chan, don't you agree?"

"I'm not sure." Kane nodded. "Possibly. There's definitely something odd about the whole situation. We should find Puny, see if he can tell us anything more about Chan."

They left the coffee shop and walked to where they usually saw Puny at his chai stall, and this time he didn't disappoint.

"Hello Mister Hiram and Missus Hiram."

"You know we aren't married, right?" asked Kane.

"Yes, I know, but one day you will be, isn't it so?"

Kane glanced at Ridley, who'd narrowed her eyes. "Don't give him any ideas, Puny," she said, though they both knew that's exactly what Kane wanted.

"Hey, Missus Hiram, I have a new joke. Do you want to hear it?" He didn't wait for an answer. "A monk bought a cup of chai from me earlier, and I started to walk away. The monk said, 'Wait, where is my change?' But I told him that change must come from within, and continued walking away. He was not a happy monk."

"Is that true, Puny?"

"No, but it is funny, isn't it?" As usual, he laughed more than they did, proud of own his joke.

"That's a good one, Puny," agreed Ridley, "but not that good."

Feigning hurt feelings, the young man sniffed and crossed his arms until Kane said, "The usual, please," and Puny immediately smiled and poured two steaming cups of chai from his steel urn.

"Listen, Puny," Kane said, "Chan Lee... what can you tell us about him? I think he does good work, and helps many Tibetans out of persecution. But... well, there's just something about him I don't trust."

Puny's smile slipped a little, but he recovered quickly and tried to explain. "Mister Lee... Chan... He is a man who helps people. However, he... well, he..." Puny's gaze shifted away from Kane's, unable to look him in the eye.

"What is it, Puny?" asked Ridley. "What about Chan?"

Puny looked around as if to check nobody could listen in on their conversation. "It is nothing; I am just being silly. He is a good man who does good things for many people.

Mister Lee is responsible for many families making it safely to India."

Kane felt sure there was more to it, something unsavoury, but Puny changed the subject, and for fear of pushing too hard Kane let it slide, at least for now.

"I have many more jokes if you would like to hear them?" Puny said.

Kane needed to speak to Ridley alone, however, and said a polite goodbye. "Bye Puny, but we'll see you tomorrow."

Puny nodded, and offered a weak smile, but Kane noticed the young man's Adam's apple do a couple of backflips.

Chapter Eleven

Ridley led Kane up the hill towards Dall Lake, a small body of water surrounded by pine forests, and which was a popular place for Indian tourists to take a walk, according to Puny. Today was not the best weather for that, though, and Kane's assumption that the place would be deserted was proven correct. It felt colder now, and they kept a decent pace to stay warm. They walked in silence for a while, each likely trying to make sense of the strange situation, both with Sam, and just now with Puny.

Kane had his suspicions, but he didn't want to acknowledge it might be true. It was Ridley who probed first.

"You know, I want to believe they're only acting strangely because what they're doing is... well, technically illegal, and nobody knows who to trust. China is so powerful these days. I guess everyone's just nervous about the China Tibet situation."

Kane nodded, hoping what Ridley had said was right. Yet Kane did not fully agree with her, and it was clear

Ridley knew him well enough to sense this. "Okay, Kane, out with it. What's really going on?"

"Did you see Sam's eyes? I think we can agree the kid's on drugs." He paused, scratching at his stubble as Ridley nodded. "I wonder... what are the odds Chan is using his *rescuing* of people as a front for a drug smuggling operation? Perhaps he tricked Sam into helping with the promise of free or very drugs? The classic loss leader many dealers use."

Ridley looked stunned. Kane knew Chan had been right when he said that many tourists go to India to score cheap drugs, and the western Himalayan foothills was a notorious region for the drug trade, with borders between India, Pakistan, Nepal and Chinese Tibet. "Shit," was all she could say, and fell silent as she seemed to try processing it all.

The snow fell thicker now, and with the pine forest and clear waters of the lake before them, it portrayed an idyllic winter scene straight from a classic Christmas card. "It's really pretty here, isn't it?" she asked after several moments of apparent contemplation.

"It is." Kane pulled Ridley tight against him as they walked around the shores of the lake. They continued in silence for a few more minutes until Ridley spoke again.

"Chan seemed so sincere, and although I agree he's a little shady, doesn't that simply come with the territory? I mean, what he does is probably very dangerous, and he said himself he has to deal with corrupt Chinese security officials and border guards. I guess I just don't want to believe he's doing something much worse."

"Let's assume it's true," Kane said. "Let's assume he's a serious drug trafficker, but that he's also someone who delivers Tibetans to safety in India... away from the Chinese brutality. I mean, how do we actually feel about that? If we reported him, closed down his drug operation for example, wouldn't that then affect the suffering Tibetans, including children, who'd still be stranded under the oppressive regime? Or maybe they'd try to escape themselves but aren't as strong or brave as Lobsang, and they'd get caught and even killed in their attempts to escape without help?" He paused, and spun around to face Ridley, looking deep into her eyes. "Ask yourself, Alex... could you live with that?"

Ridley inhaled deeply and gazed out over the lake without answering. Kane knew this was a different conundrum for Ridley than the one he understood, and didn't press for an answer.

"Honestly, I don't know if I could. Obviously, smuggling drugs is terrible and I would never condone it, but... well, Chan's also doing a very good thing, helping deliver Tibetans to the sanctuary of India. It's a lesser of two evils, right? I don't think I could just ignore that."

Ridley remained silent, and she looked torn. Kane knew that as a younger woman Ridley had found herself in a battle with drugs, and by her own admission was a certified recovering addict. There had been multiple reasons why she had wandered down that destructive path, and they were genuinely heartbreaking to Kane, but he also knew that was a lifetime ago, and she hadn't touched drugs of any kind for close to twenty years.

He'd always believed that adults made their own choices most of the time, and most of the time they held themselves accountable for their own actions. Like Kane, Ridley hated when people like Chan Lee used vulnerable young people, often under duress, as mules to smuggle drugs on their behalf. It was a dirty trick, but they both knew it still happened all over the world.

Now Kane had planted that seed of thought, judging by her tormented expression, he felt sure Ridley believed he was right. Sam had fallen head first into the trap, and it appeared from his appearance and demeanour that it was a trap from which he couldn't get out.

"I agree, we can't ignore the good he does," she finally said, "but at the same time we simply cannot support him smuggling drugs into India. The potential lives that costs is massive. I... I just can't do it, Hiram. I'm sorry."

Surprised, but at the same time not, Kane led her Ridley to a bench beside the lake and sat her down. Looking into her eyes, he smiled. "Listen, Alex, I totally understand why you'd feel that way, I really do. But we have an opportunity here to help save many lives and if we're careful how we go about it, we can learn how Chan's operation works. Once we're involved, perhaps we can find a way to stop the drugs coming into the country. Why don't we try and find Sam ourselves first and get the kid some help? Then, if that goes well, perhaps he in turn can help us?"

Ridley clutched Kane's hand and nodded. "I'm eager to help any young person in Sam's situation. I know you understand that I know what it's like to feel trapped through either fear or addiction. In Sam's case it's most likely both. I want to help him. I *need* to. Perhaps we can ask Puny... he'll know how to find him."

Kane leaned in and hugged Ridley closer. "That's the spirit," he said. "It just looks like he needs someone to talk to, to support him. If he's afraid of Chan, for whatever reason, maybe we can encourage him to do something about it."

The weather was really closing in now, and snow began to settle in thick drifts on the ground and thinners ones on branches in the pine trees. It reminded Kane of his childhood, and of a time when all the world was safe and gentle and drugs and criminals were still an unknown to him. *How the world has changed,* he mused, *since those innocent days of youth.* But the deepening cold also made his thoughts turn to those many thousands of Tibetans forced to flee for their lives from their own country, traversing hundreds, even thousands of miles across the Himalayas, in weather and the bitter cold many, many times worse than they were experiencing in that moment. If Kane needed any more convincing that going to try and help those long-suffering Tibetans was the right and only thing to do, the thought of the women, their children and their elders struggling through mind-numbing cold and the harshest of terrains was more than enough. One last glance at Ridley before pulling her up by her hand was enough to feel she too was convinced.

Chapter Twelve

They left the serene lakeside and soon spotted Puny, huddled against the cold but still wearing his ever-present smile. "Hey, Puny," Ridley called out, "why aren't you inside? It's so cold I might shiver to death."

Of course, Puny responded with a joke. "Don't worry, Missus Hiram, I believe reincarnation is making a comeback." Kane thought it wasn't a bad attempt.

"Don't give up your day job Puny," he teased. "Hey, you know Sam, right, the German kid who works with Chan Lee?"

Once again, as soon as they mentioned Chan Lee's name Puny averted his eyes. As usual, he soon recovered and answered Kane's question. "I know him. We are not friends. Excuse me, Mister Hiram, why do you want to know about Sam?"

"We want to talk to him. I think there's something dodgy about Chan, and I think Sam needs help. Do you know where we can find him?"

It seemed Puny was reluctant to get involved, but it was also obvious to Kane he knew where Sam was. The young chaiwallah didn't answer, and stood in awkward silence.

"Come on, Puny," Kane pushed, "just tell us where he lives. We want to help him."

A long pause again, and several glances around, before Puny said, "Okay, but if anyone asks you did not hear it from me. Do you agree?"

"I agree."

"He lives in a very tiny apartment above the Laughing Buddha Cafe, down the Potala Road. He never leaves, except to... well, to see Mister Lee to get drugs, isn't it." Once more, Kane noticed his downcast eyes. It was almost as if he wanted to say more but was afraid, or ashamed, to do so. It wasn't missed by Kane, nor Ridley.

"What is it, my friend?" she asked. "You seem so nervous. We only wish to talk, ask him a few questions. Are you okay?"

"Missus Hiram, I am not okay, but do not worry, I will be fine. Puny is always fine."

"But you don't look fine, Puny," Kane probed. "Is it Chan Lee? Are you worried about him?"

"I told you, I am fine," Puny snapped, uncharacteristically it seemed, at least in their limited experience. He immediately apologised. "I am so sorry Mister and Misssus Hiram, so sorry. I just, well... I am just cold and tired, that is all."

"Puny, listen to me, okay?" said Kane. "We want to help. If either Sam or you are in trouble with Chan Lee, perhaps we can step in. We're certain he's up to something negative other than just helping the refugees, and we don't like it. Are you in trouble, Puny?"

"No sir, no trouble. Just, well, it is... it is nothing, sincerely. Anyway, it is time for me to go home now."

"It's not even lunch time," said Ridley. "You never leave this early."

Yet, without another word, Puny hauled his portable chai shop to his shoulder, and scampered down Temple Road. In five seconds, he was out of sight.

It was another strange interaction and did nothing to help them understand what was really going on. It appeared, at least on the outside, that Chan Lee held some form of power over the two young men. Sam, at least, was in deep trouble with drugs, probably in some kind of debt to financial Chan. That bit was likely, obvious even. What wasn't obvious was Puny's role in all of this. He seemed such a nice young man, who had said all the right things the first few times they'd met him. But now Kane wasn't so sure. Now, it seemed, he *was* involved with Chan. Kane wanted to be—in fact he really hoped to be—mistaken.

Following the Potala Road, they soon found the cosy, inviting Laughing Buddha cafe, and gladly stepped inside out of the cold. In one corner a log fire welcomed them with its warmth, and they sat as near to the blaze as possible. Served by a friendly girl behind the counter, they first ordered two lattes, then asked about Sam.

"Yes, he lives upstairs," the girl answered easily. "But he is very shy and does not leave his room often."

"Is it okay if we go up and knock on his door? We only want to speak with him."

"Of course, miss," she replied to Ridley. "It is the last one on the left."

They finished their drinks, and ordered another to take-away, as well as the biggest sandwich on the menu. They were for Sam. Kane led Ridley up the dark narrow staircase and they turned left down an even narrower corridor. Even before they reached Sam's door, the smell hit them.

"Damn," whispered Kane, "it reminds me of Evan's room at uni... damp clothes, unwashed cups and plates, and rotting food in an un-emptied bin," Kane recalled, and not fondly. There was also the unmissable aroma of hashish smoke. Ridley composed herself and then knocked.

For a full minute they waited, and got no response. Then Kane knocked, louder, and now they heard a shuffling of furniture, as if someone had moved a footstool along a wooden floor. "Sam? Is that you?"

"Who... who is it?" came the muffled, nervous reply.

"Hi, Sam. It's Hiram and Alex. We met at the—"

"Go away. I don't want to talk to you. Or anyone. Go away."

"We have coffee... and food." There was silence for many seconds, but in the end, they guessed Sam's hunger had gotten the better of him, and the door opened a crack.

"What do you want? Is Mister Lee with you?"

Ridley held out the paper bag containing the sandwich and coffee. The aroma was strong and surely tempting. "No, Mr. Lee isn't here. It's just us, coffee, food... and a couple of questions. Can we talk?"

Sam opened the door a little, his eyes darting over their shoulders as if he expected Chan Lee to be with them. When he was satisfied Chan wasn't there, and with his hunger sealing the deal, he ushered them in and locked the door behind them. He sat on the couch, and Ridley handed him the bag. A tear slipped down his cheek.

"Thank you," he said, and it was clear he meant it. They let him eat in peace for a while, watching on amazed as he devoured the food and coffee.

Eventually Kane asked him, "How long since you ate a meal, Sam?"

He looked ashamed, suddenly younger than they'd first thought, perhaps only nineteen. "It was... I ate some bread yesterday, I guess. No, the day before."

Ridley and Kane shared a subtle look of horror, as if to ask, *What is this kid into?*

"Look, Sam," said Kane gently, "we believe you're in a little trouble here and honestly, we'd like to help. You might also be able to help us. How does that sound?"

Sam's gaze flitted between them both, fear evident in his dark eyes. He was afraid. Clearly, Kane now knew, he was afraid of Chan Lee. Sam had come to India, he told them after he'd finished the sandwich, for the trip of a lifetime, his maiden backpacking adventure. He also admitted he wanted to experiment with drugs, though he hung his head in shame as he said it. It it had gone well initially.

"The first couple of months were perfect," Sam explained, as he recalled exploring city after city on his venture north from Mumbai. "I stopped in many cities in the *Golden Triangle*, like Udaipur, Jodhpur and Jaipur, and even rode camels in Rajasthan. I then came north to the Himalayas after a chance meeting with a guy in Varanasi."

Kane nodded. "I know it. It's one of the holiest cities, but where India's dirty underbelly is at its dirtiest." Sam almost smiled. Not quite.

"The French backpacker told me how available drugs were in the north, so after a couple of days together in Rishikesh, rafting and smoking a ton of weed," he said, then once more averted his gaze, "I found my way to Mcleodganj. I met Chan Lee here, and things have... been difficult ever since." Sam paused uncomfortably before continuing.

"I now realise Chan was extra generous with the supply of weed, and we become friends. At least, that's what I thought. However, somehow, all of my money was gone and I got stranded in Mcleodganj with no way of leaving and a big debt with Chan. To pay my debt, he left me with no real other choice but to help him on his journeys to and from the border to Tibet.

"Even that seemed like a great adventure to begin with. The first few times I went with Chan, drugs were never mentioned. But my... my habit began to take hold, and... well, Chan started giving me free hits of opium, so I became more reliant." Sam hung his head as it became clear the two had entwined so much he could no longer refuse.

Kane felt his heartbeat race as his anger grew, but he allowed Sam the time to tell them more. If he cut in now, he feared the poor kid might clam up.

"Not only that, but Chan ordered me to recruit other mules. I knew I was in trouble at this point, but I needed the opium to..."

Ridley stood and took a seat next to Sam, who first shifted away but then leaned into her as she placed an arm around his shoulder. "I know it's a vicious circle, Sam," she said. "It is very difficult to break alone." Kane sensed Sam was definitely at breaking point.

"I... I want to help you," he said, eyes passing between Kane and Ridley. "I... I need your help. Please." Then Sam shed a deluge of tears that had obviously been building up over months of desperation and shame.

Kane and Ridley gave him the time he needed to compose himself, and after a few minutes, when there were apparently no more tears left, Sam at last smiled. "I am sorry," he said, inhaling deeply and standing up, moving to face them both. "I know I have been very stupid. I am ready to change. What do you have in mind?"

Chapter Thirteen

Now they'd convinced themselves of Chan Lee's nefarious criminal activities, both equally steadfast in their desire to somehow help the Tibetans while simultaneously bringing down Chan's drug trafficking business, Kane knew they needed to make a plan. To make any sort of plan, however, they would need a lot more information than they currently possessed. The massive moral dilemma of inadvertently aiding and abetting Chan still loomed over them. By stopping his activities, they couldn't ignore the likelihood that many innocent Tibetans would no longer be able to flee Tibet. Kane knew they'd need to be smart.

That night they took Sam out for dinner. He needed to get out of the dingy, dark room of the Laughing Buddha Guesthouse, and he needed to eat. More than that, though, Ridley explained to Kane that Sam needed to feel he wasn't alone. They met in the late afternoon, as an absent sun at last made a welcome appearance after days of hiding behind towering, ominous clouds which luckily hadn't dumped as much snow as they'd threatened.

Sam looked better, though he was still eminently pale and weak from a serious lack of any vitamins and the effects of a difficult couple of days enduring cold turkey.

Yet, as they walked along the narrow streets of Little Lhasa, they saw him crack a smile for the first time since they'd met. Hope was a powerful thing, Kane knew, when all you've known for days and weeks, even months, was hopelessness. It was inspiring to see.

Ridley, no stranger to addiction herself, privately voiced to Kane that danger still remained and they would have to guide him carefully through the next punishing, drug-free days.

Heading back up into town, they deliberately angled towards where they hoped they'd find Puny and his chai stand. He was indeed there, and from a distance Kane knew he'd sen them coming. Puny's eyes locked on Sam, who for a moment looked anxiously around and on seemed the verge of running away.

But as they approached, Kane saw Puny notice Sam's smile, and Puny too broke into that wide, beaming grin that apparently endeared him to everyone he met. Kane also couldn't miss what seemed to be a sense of palpable relief on Puny's face.

"Mister and Missus Hiram, I am so glad to see you all on this fine day, isn't it?" He took Sam by the hand. "And you, Sam. I... I worried about you."

It was Puny who had first introduced Sam to Chan Lee, Sam had told them, though he also informed them he'd regretted it later.

Puny was a good chaiwallah, and according to himself, the very best in Little Lhasa. Despite his thriving chai business, he still made barely enough money to support himself, and there were always other avenues for a smart, pleasant guy like Puny to make additional money to survive. Sam had explained that all Chan had asked Puny to do was to steer any backpackers asking about drugs in Chan's direction. If and when a transaction took place, Puny received a small commission. Puny hated doing it, Sam said, but as Kane understood, needs sometimes outweighed morals, and never was that more prevalent than in India. Kane knew that if it wasn't Puny who guided those searching for drugs to Chan, then somebody else would.

It was simple logic. Backpackers would always find drugs, so why not make a little money from it? It didn't sit well with Puny's morality, Sam explained, but neither did the notion of his poor family at home. Both parents were too old to work, and with winter approaching, they had desperately needed that extra income. Kane had sensed the innate goodness within Puny since they'd first met, and nothing Sam had told him made him think any differently about the young chaiwallah.

"Listen, Puny, could we talk with you about Chan Lee?" Kane asked. "We know you sometimes... assist him."

Immediately, Puny's eyes flitted away, but Ridley eased his concerns.

"It's okay, Puny, there's no need to worry." She placed a hand on his shoulder. "We all know you're a talented man with a big heart, and that you only assisted Chan Lee to help feed your family. We only want to talk to you about how we can stop him bringing drugs into the country."

Puny instantly relaxed and offered a brief smile. "Well, the chai business is hardly going to make me rich today, isn't it so? I will shut up shop for the day."

Will you join us for dinner?" asked Kane with a chuckle. "You need some extra meat on your bones."

"You are right, Mister Hiram, I do need to be a little fatter, like a Christmas goose, isn't it so? But alas, I'm of the vegetarian persuasion, and thus I could only add a little vegetable to my frame, isn't it also so?"

"It is also so, Puny," said Kane. "Let's go."

Puny led them to a tiny yet popular vegetarian restaurant tucked away down a side street so narrow it seemed even India's rats hadn't discovered it. They entered through the low wooden doorway and stepped into a room that looked like someone's living room. Illuminated only by candles, the simplicity of it oozed tranquillity and seemed an appropriate place for Kane and Ridley to dig deeper into Chan's enterprise.

Puny explained what he'd learned about Chan Lee. According to the chaiwallah, who Kane imagined knew everything that went down in Little Lhasa, Chan arrived in the area a little over two years ago, and with only one genuine intention: to help the Tibetans.

"Chan is an American citizen, but his Chinese parents are still very much set in their traditional Chinese cultural ways, despite having lived in the United States for decades," Puny told them. " I hear Mister Lee was a very successfully businessman in his home town of Fran Sancisco." Kane stifled a chuckle at Puny's wonderfully flawed English. Puny didn't notice and careened on. "He imported and sold furniture from all over Asia," he declared, waving his twig-thin arms for emphasis. "But, as I understand it, he then became not happy with his life. He told me once that his parents, pro the Chairman Mao and very political, had always given him a tough time for his anti the Chairman Mao values. So, Mister Lee turned his back on his Chinese heritage and instead decided to become a very big champion for the peoples of Tibet." Puny paused to sip on some of his own chai. "It is most delicious chai in—"

"In all India!" Ridley cut in, and Puny grinned from ear to ear.

"In all Asia, Missus Kane. Mister Lee told me of how he stopped his import business, and in just a few weeks he had bought a ticket to India. One way ticket, isn't it. Mister Lee then spent many weeks and months studying the teachings of His very Holiness at the temple here in Mcleodganj where, after meeting many brave Tibetan refugees and learning more about their terrible struggles, he dedicated himself to the overall struggle of the Tibetans. He has since then successfully transported more than two hundred refugees in the last two years. He is somewhat of an unlikely hero, isn't it." Puny paused as his retelling changed into something darker.

"Mister Lee's problems started the time he was detained by two very horrible Chinese military policemen on a stretch between Chinese Tibet and India.

"Until that day he was always able to bribe the nasty security patrols with American cigarettes and many fistfuls of dollars, and they would turn their blind eyes to his missions. But they became greedy, isn't it. In Mister Lee they saw a big making money opportunity. They told him that if he did not smuggle their very bad drugs over the border into India they would shut down his operation.

"It is my humbly belief that Mister Chan Lee was a good man who had noble intentions. But like so very many before him, and many more after, he is still only man, isn't it? He had his greedy eyes turned by the chance of quick money. That is what they did him, so he should do this also, isn't it so? Money has a way of corrupting the most very genuine of souls..." Puny paused, glancing between the three of them sat listening to his tale. "I think man's weakness and greed had seen many a very good man fall. I think Chan Lee is such a man. So, the once honourable businessman from Fran Sancisco is, after all, no better than the corrupt border policemen.

"From that time, Mister Lee began using his rescue missions to bring drugs to India from Tibetan China. He made a big pile of money, isn't it. The Chinese guards were happy. Many Tibetan people still got across the border to freedom. Mister Lee is getting rich."

Kane listened to Puny's speech with interest. If it was merely money Chan wanted, then Kane probably had enough to pay him off. If he could give Chan enough money to convince him to just cease his operations for good, perhaps he just might take the bait. Yet, if Puny's tale was accurate, it sounded to Kane as though Chan had gotten himself in too deep with the Chinese security guards. If true, and if they were profiting as much as he was, why the hell would they just allow him to stop? Kane knew they wouldn't.

There had to be a better way. Kane briefly wondered if he could just pay off the Chinese guards directly himself but knew that would just weaken their position, as they would just ask for more.

Kane had money, but he would *not* reward people for their corruption. No. There needed to be something else to persuade them, something beyond money. The Chinese soldiers were notoriously stubborn and loyal to their government. It would be no easy feat to convince them. He also wondered if any of them were soldiers only because they'd been conscripted, and if they had any sympathy with the Tibetans at all. There was a chance some of the guards had humanity. Other than that, he would be relying upon the one thing that evolution had got wrong: the human tendency for power and greed.

It wasn't a great plan, but it was all they had, and money—probably endless stacks of it—was going to be their biggest weapon.

Chapter Fourteen

After moving to their favoured spot in town, the rooftop of the McClo pub, Kane ordered a round of beers and a large portion of veggie samosas for the table. The food mostly for Sam's benefit. As they all sat quietly for a few moments, savouring their beers and the view, Kane appraised them one by one, about to ask them sincerely if they were ready to embark with him on what would almost certainly be a dangerous journey.

He stood, and in his most serious tone, said, "Listen, none of you has to take this risk. Don't be ashamed to say no."

They each looked back at him earnestly. Kane was already certain what they'd say to his simple question. "Will you come with me to Tibet?"

Ridley nodded, her face determined. "I'll go with you."

"Me too. Of course," said Sam. Kane got the sense he had truly wanted to help the Tibetans with Chan Lee, and in a way, he had. It wasn't all a disaster, he'd told them, and he felt proud of what he'd achieved until the drugs became too much. "I have a lot to make up for. One hundred percent, yes!" He offered a hint of a grin, but his features were as resolute as Ridley's.

"Mister Kane, if I were not such a very important man and chai seller in our humble town, I too would go too, isn't it," said Puny, grinning. "But alas, I cannot disappoint my very thirsty customers, isn't it so?"

Kane had no doubt Puny was true to his word. He did have a business to run and a family to support. His enthusiasm was more than enough.

Kane said, "Then thank you, all of you."

"And me," came a chirpy voice from behind him. "I will come."

Kane turned, surprised to see a short, middle-aged Asian fellow wearing a black beanie. Kane didn't recognise the man, whose expression was an unlikely cross between intent and playful.

"I'm sorry... can I help you?" asked Kane, somewhat bemused.

"I no longer need any help, young man, but I think I can help you." Then the man smiled, and Kane would have recognised that mischievous grin anywhere.

"Lobsang?"

"The one and only," Lobsang replied. "I'm here, reporting for duty."

"But... what do you mean? And where are your robes? And... and how did you know what we were doing?" Kane shot a look at Puny, who, despite his customary, somewhat sheepish grin had shrunk just a little in his chair.

"Do not blame Puny, Hiram. He never could keep a secret." Kane watched as Puny slipped a little further down in his seat. "When I learned what you were planning I decided I would come along for the ride. Just don't tell His

Holiness... I do not think he would approve." The glint in his eye was disarming, though Kane sensed Lobsang was serious.

"It might be dangerous. Haven't you risked enough? I'm not sure you—"

"It will be dangerous, you can be sure of that." Lobsang gently raised his hand, cutting Kane off. "My journey down to Little Lhasa, however arduous, was a very long time ago. I am one of the lucky ones who made it out. Many are less fortunate. I want to help, so I ask you... please do not to try to talk me out of it." Lobsang smiled once more, and Kane understood that any attempts to dissuade him would be futile. "Besides," Lobsang continued, "who says monks can't have a little fun?"

With a solemn smile, Puny rose from his seat and waggled his head from side to side in wholehearted assent.

Kane stood, and raising his Kingfisher in a quiet, solemn toast, said, "Very well. To Tibet, and to liberating the persecuted."

Nods of accord were offered all around, accompanied by a clinking of glasses. Puny didn't drink alcohol but instead raised his banana lassi, apparently as proud as a soldier about to embark on a vital mission, even though he wasn't going on this one. Lobsang just stood there grinning.

It was in many ways a mission of sorts, though Kane suspected each of them had different motivations for going.

Emotionally, Kane had to help the Tibetans. He had no choice. It's just what he did.

Kane knew Ridley was much the same, but now there were secondary and tertiary motivations. Given her own past, it was clear she wanted to help Sam. And as a bonus, ruin Chan Lee.

Sam wanted to resume his help. He also sought redemption. And regarding Chan Lee... Sam wanted revenge on the man who had almost ruined his life.

Lobsang simply wanted to pay it forward.

The one thing they all shared in common, including Puny, was an obvious devotion to the Tibetan people. Those people were so persecuted by the cruel and unjust regime of their Chinese occupiers, enemies of peace and freedom, nemeses to equality and human rights, despite what they said in public and in international diplomatic forums.

Kane knew enough by now to know the world's leaders, from the U.S. President, to the British PM, were doing little or nothing to condemn the Chinese over their illegal occupation in public. Rather, they cosied up to the Chinese government, securing one trade deal after another, and privatising industries at the expense of many thousands, perhaps millions of jobs. In doing so, they were inadvertently condoning the Chinese's heinous treatment of the Tibetan people, their ancient culture and the destruction of their once beautiful lands.

Kane glanced around at their unlikely band of vigilantes. Kane himself, the archaeologist-turned-explorer-turned-expedition leader. Alex Ridley, art historian and recovering drug addict. Sam Stein, a young backpacker on his maiden voyage beyond the bubble of Germany. And Lobsang Paljor, a wise-cracking, fifty-something-year-old Buddhist monk on first-name terms with the Dalai Lama himself.

On the face of it they didn't seem to be a vigilante force to be reckoned with. Yet within their group was a collection of individuals seemingly sick of the cowardly injustices of a world in which money and power triumphed over humanity and justice, time and time again.

Kane's face glowed orange as the day's last sun dripped

over the tree-clad horizon. In his heart burned a spark of fierce determination. This was to be a journey into the unknown, including dangers both human and natural.

But Kane was a born survivor, a man who always got things done. He only hoped he would succeed this time as well.

Chapter Fifteen

It was two days into their journey and the girls had largely remained silent through fear of being beaten. Silent, except two women. One was the irksome Australian. The other had become increasingly hysterical over the past hour to the point that she couldn't stop wailing and screaming. Azim had watched on as the tall Australian had tried to warn the other, imploring her to stay quiet. Azim had already struck her several times, hence her ever-growing hysteria.

"Hey, be quiet. You know what they'll do," the tall one said.

"We... we have to do something," she yelped, "they'll kill us, we have—"

"No, we have to wait for the right moment," hissed the Australian through gritted teeth. Azim smirked.

One of his assistant couriers stood from his seat at the rear of the truck and approached the women. He raised his stick and made to strike the girl, who flinched, causing him to laugh. Azim sighed. Rather than make her quiet, as Azim knew would happen, she screamed more, all control lost and her spirit finally broken. He had seen it hundreds of times. The courier banged on the back of the driver's cab, the three solid taps a signal to the driver to pull the truck over. A few seconds later they came to a stop, and the man dragged the girl from the bench and forced her towards the back, where Azim had raised the door.

The girl struggled, flailing wildly in a desperate attempt to get free of the guard's strong grip. Azim knew that what would likely happen next would be something not a single one of those women would ever forget.

In the ensuing struggle the courier stumbled, and in an effort not to fall off the rear of the truck he pulled against the girl's weight, toppling them both back and out the door where they landed in a crumpled heap on the rocky edge of the highway. The man bellowed and jumped to his feet, itching to discipline the girl with the vicious stick. Except she didn't move.

Azim grabbed her arms and tried hauling her to her feet, yet still she didn't move, her body a dead-weight in his grip as the courier moved in to help. Azim inhaled as they laid her down again, the hint of concern on his face now turning to an expression of anger.

The girl mumbled something incoherent, finally regaining consciousness. She was dazed and confused, and had obviously suffered a concussion. That wasn't of any concern to Azim. Her appearance was all that mattered. No, Azim's issue was that she had broken her nose and, evidently, smashed an eye socket. To him that meant only one thing; now she was damaged goods.

In that state she would be useless at the market, which meant they had no further use for her. He would have to explain it to The Vulture, but his boss usually allowed for some collateral damage. Azim knew that sometimes there was a need to make an example of one of the inventory. It usually did the trick of turning the women into cowering, quivering submissive wrecks. Besides, he would blame it on the clumsy fucking courier anyway.

Without a second's pause Azim reached into his jacket, pulled out a revolver and fired two shots into the back of the girl's head.

Dead.

He glanced into the rear of the truck, as the screams of the other dozen women rose in a single deafening chorus of terror and fear. All except one. The Australian simply stared at Azim, and he sensed the murder on her mind and saw the hatred in her eyes. Azim knew she would kill him given half the chance. That was fine... that chance would never come.

"Get rid of her," barked Azim at the visibly shaken assistant, who suddenly appeared meek and afraid. "Over the edge. Now!"

"I ca—"

"Do it right now, or it will be you turning into carrion!"

The assistant nodded fearfully and grabbed the girl under her armpits and hauled her a few yards to what was the edge of a steep cliff. With a last glance back at Azim, who nodded as he joined him at the edge, the young assistant courier rolled her body over the precipice and watched on with wide eyes as it tumbled and flipped against the rock face until disappearing into a forest below. He turned and found himself face to face with Azim.

"Nobody spoils my meat," he said, then raised his gun and shot the man between the eyes. "Nobody." Less than five seconds later the young courier had joined the murdered girl over the cliff, and two minutes after that the truck was once more heading north.

Chapter Sixteen

With Puny once more acting as intermediary, Kane met with Chan Lee again the following morning. This time he went without Ridley. Instead she'd decided to spend a little time with Sam, figuring that with her experience—not experience she was proud of, she'd be quick to admit—she was in a good position to offer advice and encouragement in his battle to wean himself off the drugs.

When Kane spotted Chan tucked away in the corner booth of the coffee shop, considering what he now knew about the man it was all he could do to keep his cool. Indeed, a younger Kane might have found it difficult not to drag him outside and give him a good hiding on behalf of all the innocent and disenfranchised Tibetans he had used for his own gains. However, Kane had to remind himself that Chan had once harboured more noble ambitions, and had been half corrupted, half blackmailed by others into his new, nefarious lifestyle choices. Kane also knew violence was for the weak, those unable to employ diplomacy to make things better. The young Kane was almost such a person himself and was glad he'd changed. However, the image of giving Chan a couple of smacks round the chin cracked a hint of a wry smile across his own face.

Kane breathed deep, composed himself and approached the table.

"Hiram, thanks for meeting with me." Chan stood and offered his hand, which Kane took. "I can't tell you how glad I am you've agreed to help in this worthy endeavour. I meet so many people here in Little Lhasa who say they want to help, but when it comes right down, to it they just aren't up to it. I suppose I understand. It can be dangerous, obviously, not to mention the actual journey itself which is long, cold and fraught with its own perils. Over the years I've seen landslides, terrifying blizzards... the physical risks in this part of the world are very real. Still, if we don't try, who will?"

Kane smiled. Despite what he understood of Chan's less-than-sincere activities, he somehow sensed that beneath the façade lay a genuine passion to help the Tibetan people and defy the government that persecuted them—the government of his parents... his homeland. Still, that didn't mean Kane would not try everything in his power to eventually stop him.

"And yet I sense you are different, Hiram," Chan continued, "and Alex too. Remind me what it is you do?"

Kane spent a few minutes telling Chan about his adventure expedition business in Peru and about the terrible events of a couple of years ago.

"Wow, that's quite the story, and now you've said it, I do believe I saw something about it in the news. I guess that means I was right... you're definitely cut out for this kind of mission. I can already tell you'll be of invaluable assistance to the Tibetan plight."

Only time will tell, mused Kane.

The way Kane saw it now, maybe they could just make Chan see sense. If not in a matter of conscience, at least they might appeal to his weakness for money and simply buy his cooperation with a bribe of the wallet, if not the heart. Whichever came out on top, either Chan Lee's compassion or his greed, one way or another Kane was determined to stop the man smuggling drugs.

Few people were aware of it, but Kane was a reasonably wealthy man. Money meant nothing to him, but he had it nonetheless and had always been prepared to use it for good causes whenever he could. Kane's philanthropic nature, while certainly inherited from his family, began for him personally as a teenager. When just a boy, Kane's little brother Danny went missing. They'd been exploring an abandoned, derelict mansion known as The Old Rectory, and while they were inside, Danny had disappeared. From the terrible moment it happened, Kane had never valued anything other than family and friendship. Though he was reluctant to discuss it, he was a modest yet staunch philanthropist, helping anyone who needed it and putting all others before himself.

In every act of kindness he'd never felt alone, knowing somehow Danny was there with him. Danny was not there in body, of course, and for two decades not even in spirit, as Kane didn't believe in such nonsense. But when Danny came back into their lives a year ago after being feared dead for the previous twenty, he understood in some way, in some subconscious manner, Danny would always be with him.

Because of that innate knowledge Kane was never afraid, especially when it came to his own life. Back in the mountains of Peru those years ago, when his life was under threat from the Inca leader Yupanqui and the Catholic terrorists Angelo De La Cruz and Howie Hooper, Kane never once considered his own safety. He only cared about saving the lives of his friends and the other innocent people caught up in the drama. And, at the denouement of that deadly episode, when his life literally hung in the balance from a cliff over an Andean valley, it was his brother's face he saw as his life passed before his eyes. Seeing Danny's face in his mind's eye gave Kane the strength he needed to save not only his own life, but more importantly, the life of the young Quechuan boy hanging from his legs, mere seconds from death.

And so, it was with all this in mind that Kane decided to go with Mr. Chan Lee to the Tibetan border, and do, within reason, whatever was necessary to help bring a dozen Tibetan refugees across into the relative sanctuary of Little Lhasa. Chan laid out the plan for him.

"It seems the weather's going to be kind to us," Chan said, "and I suspect we'll be good to leave on Wednesday morning. We'll meet in the square at six a.m., load up whatever supplies we have, and head north. At this time of year, it's a two-day drive to the town of Demchok in Kashmir, a few miles shy of the border. We'll stop for a night there, and if the border patrols favour us—it's always a lottery—we'll take the old military roads as far as Ngari. In an ideal world, the package will be ready at the tiny outpost before we drive into Ngari, but it's dangerous for them to be apprehended on the roads outside town. In reality, they'll wait it out in Ngari until we collect them. Then we head back to the border as fast as the roads allow, pay our way across and drive them to freedom. It's a simple plan, Hiram, but many things can go wrong, as you might imagine."

Kane nodded, and Chan stared at him for a long moment, smoking heavily and gazing through the swirling purplish grey cloud at him. While Chan seemed to be appraising him, Kane returned the gaze in kind. Kane could see the Chinese-American taking in the scars on his face and knuckles, as well as the mostly missing pinky finger. Chan's face showed that he understood Kane had been in many dangerous adventures and was no stranger to death. Kane supposed he did just have that look about him.

Kane would be a good ally, Chan sensed, and not a man to cross. Rugged and capable, he believed as he assessed the man now, and though clearly a good man, a decent man, Chan believed Kane possessed within him the capacity for great violence.

Chan would tread carefully. When the time was right he would make his move, and if he played his cards right Hiram Kane might become a valuable asset. Chan also surmised that money was not an issue to Kane, and that there was plenty of it. Inadvertently, that notion roused Chan's sinister side, his corrupted side, and his thoughts suddenly turned to kidnappings and ransoms and all manner of heinous crimes; that other half of him, the kind half—the old half—admired men like Kane, whom he sensed was beyond corruption, incapable of betrayal. It shamed him to see his fallen self, and he soon dismissed that dangerous train of thought.

Chan's dichotomy of emotions had passed and he looked once more at Kane, whose attention had turned to the cafe's window and the clusters of tourists and locals hustling past in the cold. Chan also could not ignore the fact that, once underway on his latest mission into Tibet, destiny would somehow play its part and there was little he could do about it. Karma had a way of delivering justice. One of the few remaining parts of Chinese culture he'd grown up with that still remained was his belief in karma, both the good kind and the bad.

Chan Lee only hoped he'd done enough good in his life to be rewarded by the karma gods when they come knocking at his door.

Chapter Seventeen

"Mr. Lee... Chan... for the record, Alex and I would like to join you on this mission. We'll be at your service, and you can use us however you see fit. Within reason, of course."

"Then you are both welcome, Hiram."

"We have two requests," Kane said, more sternly now. "If the answer is 'no' we won't be joining you."

Chan's eyebrows rose a little. *Hmm.* "Okay, Hiram, what is it?"

"For the first request, the young German kid, Sam, and my friend Lobsang... They both come with us."

For a split second, Chan's eyes darkened. He'd finally got the kid just where he wanted him. Dependent. Desperate. Useful. But the lure of what Kane and Ridley could do for him was way more powerful than a single, feeble junkie like Sam might offer. He smiled, and the dark look vanished. "Of course, Sam and your friend can join us. Sam's a good kid, just a little messed up that's all."

"Then here's the second request, Chan, and there's no use trying to deny it. I know you've been supplying the kid with drugs. I also know if a kid wants drugs they will find them somewhere, either from you or someone else. Regardless, I need your word you will not supply drugs to Sam again, even if he begs. He's a nice kid, and he needs our help. Do I have your word?"

Chan Lee sighed, and after a moment's pause, he nodded. "It's true that rescuing Tibetans is not my only source of income, and it's also true I have given Sam drugs. But, and you have my word... I will not do it again." That's what Chan said. It is very far from what he actually meant. Chan stood, offering his hand to Kane.

"Do we have an understanding?" Kane asked, though Chan sensed it was rhetorical.

"Yes. Yes, we do." Chan raised his cup. "To the Tibetans. May we rescue many."

Kane responded in kind, raising his own. "To Tibetans, and to the liberation of the weak and the persecuted."

They sat again, and Chan told Kane more about the plan and exactly how exactly they would carry out the mission. "I suspect there'll be many occasions during our venture north when you're tempted to question my judgement, especially when negotiating with the Chinese security forces. But I urge you to put your trust in me. I'm a Chinese man, at least in their eyes, and I understand how they think. They will not negotiate with you, even if they know you're English and not American. They think all westerners are the same. Capitalists. Consumerists. In other words, *not* Communists. Leave all discussions with the Chinese to me and we'll have the greatest chance of success."

Kane did not look completely convinced, but Chan felt he had no choice but to agree after making his own demands. "I understand," Kane said. "None of us speaks

Chinese except you, and you're the one with experience in these... these matters. We'll trust you. We just want to help."

The two men continued their discussion for another hour, and stopped only when Ridley walked in, looking radiant, despite being bundled up against the cold.

"Miss Ridley... Alex, a pleasure," said Chan, standing. "Please have a seat."

Ridley leaned in to kiss Kane, then sat beside him.

"I'm very glad to have the both of you on board," Chan said. "And of course, young Sam and... Lobsang?" Kane nodded. "The efforts and risks are worthwhile, and the world needs brave people like you. Tibetans have been persecuted for too long, and every time guys like you help them and help spread the word about their suffering, the more chance there is of the world's politicians finally taking a stand against the Chinese government. I'm sure both of you consider the word hero over-used, but that's what you'll become to the people of Little Lhasa and all Tibet. You may also become an enemy of the state as far as China's concerned, but I assure you it'll be a price worth paying."

Kane shook his head, a wry smile narrowing his eyes which Chan noticed. Ridley slapped him on the shoulder. "My hero," she said, and Kane grimaced.

"I have one final word of warning for you all, though," added Chan, standing once more. "And you need to take it seriously."

Kane and Ridley looked up at him with intent, their smiles quickly fading.

Chan Lee looked down at them, holding their gazes long enough to make sure he had their attention. He did.

"Whatever happens up there," he said, "do not get caught!"

Chapter Eighteen

Today was the day.

They had spent the previous afternoon relaxing in Little Lhasa, rounding up a few supplies and listening to more of Sam's input about what to expect on the journey. They'd followed the long day with an early night. Kane slept little; the combination of excitement and nervous energy had kept his mind racing through the night. Ridley hadn't slept much either, so it was a weary couple who made their way slowly down the hill into the centre of Mcleodganj for their rendezvous with Chan Lee. It was still pitch black at 5:45, and though cold, they welcomed the clear skies. It boded well for their long drive north.

As promised, Puny arrived to greet them and to wish them well on their journey. Moments later, Sam and Lobsang emerged from around the corner. Of course, they couldn't depart without at least three rounds of chai each and Puny set about pouring them their first cups.

"My very good friends," he said, "today is a great day and the start of something very special, isn't it." He handed

The Shadow of Kailash

them their chai, his perpetual smile in place. "I wish I could come with you on this most excellent adventure, but alas, what would the most excellent people and tourists here in Mcleodganj drink without me?" They all chuckled in agreement.

"Not to mention your jokes, Puny," said Ridley.

"You're right, Missus Kane. Come to think of it, I have a new one for you. Ready?" As ever, he didn't wait for a reply. "A monk was driving into town up the Potala Road yesterday when suddenly a stupid dog ran out in front of his car. Sadly, the dog was killed. The dog's shocked owner ran over, and the monk said, 'I am terribly sorry, but my karma ran over your dogma'." There followed general groans of derision, but it was probably just the early hour, and Kane couldn't deny Puny was a trier.

Then his smile faded a little, and Puny turned serious. Looking about to make sure Mr. Lee wasn't nearby, he addressed his friends. "I want you all to be so, so careful. Please. I know you understand what it is Mister Lee does, but you must be careful. Deep down he is a good man who is just making a lot of mistakes. We have all done that, isn't it so?" Nods all around. "What you are all doing is a brave and very noble thing, but you must remember, you should not risk your own lives to save others. When it comes to the crunch, and very big problems happen, I am sure Mister Lee will not hesitate to leave you behind in Tibet. He has become selfish since the lure of big money corrupted him, and he is not the same man he was before. I just want you to be careful so you can come back and buy more chai." He smiled, but Kane sensed he was serious.

The roar of two loud engines fractured the peace of the morning, and they looked up to see two sturdy people carriers pulling into the square. Kane glanced at his watch. Almost 6:00. Time to go.

Puny hugged them all one by one, saving his warmest, most encompassing hug for Sam. Clearly, he was overcome with real emotion. "Sam, I am so extremely, terribly and very sorry I introduced you to Mister Lee, but I am glad you are doing better now. My heart broke when I understood what was happening to you, but I... I did not know what to do. Do you forgive me?" Tears dampened his eyes.

"I don't need to forgive you. You did nothing wrong. I asked for something, and you helped. The blame lies with me and my weakness. Now I'm going to Tibet with these good people, and I am going to do good things. You are a good man Puny, and a good friend."

They embraced again, and the affection between the two young men was clear to Kane. "You all must come back, because I have a secret I want to share with you."

"What is it?" asked Lobsang. "Can't you tell us before we leave?"

After a pause, he said, "Very well. It is my wife, Aanya." Puny beamed as wide as Kane had ever seen. "She is going to have a baby, our first child, isn't it."

"That's brilliant news, Puny,' said Ridley, flashing a smile to match Puny's own.

"So you see, you have to be extra careful on this trip, because you have to come back and meet my family, isn't it?"

And once again, Kane mused, it was so.

Chan Lee jumped from the first van, closely followed by another man who to Kane appeared to be of Korean origin. "Good morning," Chan said. "I'm happy you're all here. This is Do-Hyun Kim, my associate. He will drive the second vehicle. Hiram, perhaps you'll take a turn later. Kim and I have known each other a long time. You can trust him."

The Korean offered a hint of a smile, but didn't offer his hand, and returned to the van, organising stuff in the back. Chan continued. "Okay, who'll ride with me? Hiram and Sam? At least for the first leg of the drive, and maybe switch around later?"

All agreed with the arrangements, and just five minutes later, with their gear stowed in the truck and nothing more to do to but leave on that icy, clear Himalayan morning, the two people carriers pulled away, and before long they were snaking noisily up and over hills and down through valleys until Little Lhasa was far behind them.

Chapter Nineteen

In the back seat Sam huddled up in a thick blanket trying to get some sleep. He felt a lot better than he had just days before, when Ridley and Kane had visited him in his shabby apartment and delivered him vital food. He'd been on a steep, downward spiral in that moment, and their visit had come just in time.

Sam had almost given up on himself, and he was considering this mission a kind of second chance, a gift. He wasn't especially a religious man, though he had been raised Catholic by his super-conservative, super-wealthy parents. He'd come to India for an adventure, but also to rebel against his strict upbringing in Berlin. They were decent people, his parents, at least externally, and were well known and respected in their upper-class community and social circles. Yet they seemed to have Sam's life path all mapped out for him, and he resented them for it.

His father was an industrial lawyer, notorious for siding with large unscrupulous industries, and legally trampling over the smaller, unfortunate businesses who never stood a chance. It was a theme Sam had always hated, and there remained a long-standing coldness between him and his parents. In coming to India, he had both shocked and offended his parents, and at first it felt good. But since things had turned significantly for the worse, Sam felt guilty. He hadn't contacted his folks in more than a month, other than a brief email to say he was fine. It was a lie. He didn't want to worry them more than he already had, and letting them know he was okay was enough. When he finally went home, whenever that might be, he would explain everything and tell them he was sorry.

The sun at last crept above the Dhaudalur Ranges to the east, and a mesmerising pinkish orange glow swaddled Kane in an ethereal light as the day finally arrived. Chan finally broke the silence.

"Are you a God-fearing man, Hiram? You don't have to answer."

"It's fine, Chan, and no, I'm not. We humans are equally flawed, and no race or religion is any less flawed than another. I've seen enough shit in my time to show me that, not that I needed convincing. People who do heinous things to each other usually, sadly, go unpunished, and isn't it the case that in most or all religions, crimes are punishable?"

"Yes, I suppose that's true," replied Chan. "But don't you believe bad acts can be redeemed by good ones? I mean, a young man who, perhaps in order to feed his starving family, might steal bread. So, that bad act is really just a good one in disguise, isn't it?"

Kane smiled. That was a good point. Petty crime in many cultures, particularly in Islamic states, remained a serious offence, still punishable in some nations by having a hand cut off, or worse. Islamic law permitted such travesties but ignored the starving family. In fact, parts of India had recently come under heavy scrutiny for turning a blind eye to the rape of young girls. It broke Kane's heart. "Religion, in my humble opinion, is a series of contradictions by those in power, a collection of threats and bullying to keep the people ordered and subdued. I could say the same about many governments today. North Korea. Saudi Arabia. Cuba. China... the US." He let the point hang. Chan took the bait.

"The US? In the same bracket as North Korea? Seriously?"

"Yes, seriously. Think about it. The people of the so-called Midwest, the conservative portion of the populace, get their information about their country and the wider world from stations like Fox News, and who runs the media? Big business players like Rupert Murdoch, and wealthy families like the Bushes, the Cheneys, etcetera. People are spoon-fed lies to spread fear and subservience, and that's how they get away with it... how they've been getting away with it for decades. To be clear, it's not much better in my country."

"Wow, that was quite a speech," said Chan. "But I can't deny that I suspect you're right. In North Korea, of course, regular citizens have little or no access to the outside world. They believe Kim Jong Un and his father before him are almost like gods themselves. Luckily, each year a few fortunate citizens escape and learn about the real world, but the numbers are getting less and less every year because Chinese border guards have now been permitted to shoot on sight, with North Korean-sanctioned bribes paid for each kill. Whether or not their escaping is a good or bad thing, only the escapees themselves can answer. I read they're not getting treated that well once they make it to South Korea."

Kane knew that last part was true. He had good friends in the country, and had heard that sometimes escaping the North was just the beginning of their problems.

"I guess it must be a good thing in general," Chan continued, "considering what they left behind."

Despite what he'd learned about the man beside him, Kane was warming to Chan, and also warming to the possibility he was an inherently good man. Kane would wait to see how things panned out before making a decision, but he was starting to sense he might just be able to convince him to give up his criminal enterprise and turn over a new leaf, or rather, revert to the morally sound man he once was.

In the second vehicle Ridley and Lobsang sat beside each other in the rear seats, chatting more about the monk's unbelievable journey from Tibet to Little Lhasa. Ridley thought it was a remarkable tale of bravery and great physical endurance. That same trial had been undertaken by thousands of Tibetans over the last several decades, some successful, others not so. Those dangerous journeys would continue to be repeated, too, she knew, unless something were to drastically change within the heart of the Chinese government, something Ridley severely doubted. There were only so many refugees the likes of Chan Lee could bring to safety, and Ridley knew it was nowhere near enough.

"Well, I for one am very glad you're here," Ridley said. She leaned in, careful to stay out of view of the rearview mirror. "What do you make of him?" she whispered, flicking her eyes in the direction of the tough looking Korean up front.

"I'm not sure, Alex? Do you think he speaks English? We should be careful. And I need the loo." Lobsang grimaced.

Ridley nodded. "Erm, annyong hasseo, hello," she said, using one of the few Korean phrases she'd learned from the fluent Kane. "Excuse me, Mr. Kim, could we please make a bathroom stop? It's been three hours already, and, you know... we need to go."

The Korean's eyebrows rose for half a second at hearing Ridley's hangul, but then his harsh eyes glared at her in the mirror. "Han shi-gan. One hour. We stop." Then Kim looked away and didn't say another word.

"I guess that answers your question," whispered Ridley, causing Lobsang to grimace a little more as they settled back into the soft seats of the people carrier. Exhaling, Ridley admired the rugged vistas beyond the windows. All around them mountains angled skyward, their jagged edges piercing the vastness above. At that moment they crested a narrow ledge, which afforded them an almost three-hundred-and-sixty-degree panorama. It was spectacular, and in many ways similar to scenery Ridley had so admired in Peru when on expeditions with Kane... at least until things turned to shit and people started dying.

Chapter Twenty

A little over an hour later Chan pulled over on the deserted highway. The second van slowed to a stop behind them. "Twenty minutes," Chan said, "and we push on."

In seconds Lobsang and Sam followed Kane around the back of a large rock to relieve themselves. Over the top of the rock Kane spotted Ridley slip out of view behind some bushes, no doubt to do the same. "We know what you're doing," called Kane in a sing-song voice, somewhat childishly. He glanced over at Kim, and saw him watching Ridley's passage into the bushes, the hint of a seedy grin on his hard face. But Kane thought nothing more of it, and after finishing his business, he joined the others as they took a short stroll to stretch their legs after the long ride, and to breathe in the freshest of air within the magnificent mountains. All around—and as far as the landscape allowed him to see—stretched the snow-capped mountains of the Himalayas. Kane was in his element.

"It's so beautiful here, and I'm sure it's as beautiful in Tibet," said Ridley, glancing at Lobsang. "I just can't believe how the people are being treated. I can't imagine what it must be like, not even able to sing folk songs for fear of being beaten and tortured, and in your own country. Lobsang, I'm so very sorry," she said, clutching the monk's hand.

Lobsang smiled yet Kane didn't miss the deep sadness in his eyes. Kane said, "What the Chinese are doing, and have been doing since the fifties, is horrific, yet most of the world merely sits back and ignores it. The fact China hosted the summer Olympics in 2008, and the winter version in 2022, despite their awful human rights record, proved it. The world needs to do something, like boycotting its industry and stop selling them businesses and land. It's a travesty."

Lobsang addressed Kane and the others. "I appreciate your passion, Hiram. All of you. It is wrong, of course it is. But anger is not healthy. His Holiness says, 'The true hero is one who conquers his own anger and hatred', and he is right. We were chatting once when I was feeling down about what is going on back home. He said, 'Lobsang, do not let the behaviour of others destroy your inner peace'. Again, he was correct... the Dalai Lama is the wisest man I have ever known. It does not mean his message is easy. What I will say to you now is, try not to let your feelings cloud your judgement. We are doing what we are trying to do for good reasons. We must remain calm, and that will give us the best chance of helping those who need it."

Lobsang's serenity was infectious, and Kane felt himself calming down just by listening to him speak. He couldn't help but smile, too, and suddenly found something hilarious. "That's great Lobsang, my friend, but somehow I can't get used to seeing you in civilian clothes... you look, well... you look very funny." Kane laughed, and the others joined in, no more so than Lobsang himself, who promptly broke into a song and dance.

"Let the radiant light shine of Buddha's wish..." he sang.
"The treasure chest for all hopes and happiness,
guard all directions with happiness and love...
And may a new golden era of happiness and bliss,
spread throughout the three provinces of Tibet..."

Chan Lee wandered over, followed by Kim. Chan smiled, though Kim shook his head and walked away.

"May everyone throughout the world enjoy the glories of happiness and peace...
In the battle against negative forces,
may the auspicious sunshine of the teachings and beings of Tibet,
and the brilliance of a myriad radiant prosperities, be ever triumphant."

Once Lobsang's impromptu show was over, they gave a hearty round of applause. Lobsang, sweating somewhat from his exertions despite the chill, bowed humbly, grinning from one impressive ear to the other. However, after a few moments he once more addressed the group. "The people of Tibet will appreciate your efforts, as I already do. But remember, my friends... we have to stay calm. Our anger will help no one. And also remember this..." Lobsang's jovial features suddenly turned sincere. "His Holiness sees everything." There was a moment of silent reflection, and Kane wondered what Lobsang meant. That was, until he burst out laughing, slapping his thighs and beckoning them back to the vehicles.

Kane looked at Ridley. "Wow, quite the character, eh?" he said.

They returned to their same seats in the people carriers, resuming their original positions after Kim declined Kane's offer to drive, and were soon heading further north. They'd been driving many hours now, and the mid-morning sun was high and bright. Kane knew in a couple more hours they'd be crossing into the disputed Kashmir region, an area with a turbulent history since the partition of India by the British in 1947. During the years since, India and Pakistan had fought three bloody wars over the territory, with Al-Qaeda thought to still operate in the Pakistani administered zone. Kane wondered how many people had died in those conflicts, and how many Indian and Pakistani ghosts wandered the serene but turbulent mountains surrounding them on all sides.

Kane considered their Tibetan rescue plan; in essence, it sounded simple. The border lay just beyond the village of Demchok, where Chan would negotiate with the Chinese security guards to allow them entry. If successful, they'd drive as far as Ngari along a deserted road snaking alongside the Senge Zangbu River, a tendril of the mighty Indus. Once at Ngari township, they'd collect the twelve waiting Tibetans, and if luck favoured them, they would return via the same route back to Little Lhasa.

But Kane knew many things could go wrong, the Chinese border security the most likely obstacle. Chan warned he had occasionally come across guards who could not be bribed, no matter how much money or American cigarettes or Scotch whisky he offered them. He added that he admired them in a way, dedicated to their job and untainted by the greed of many others. But their ideology was a dangerous one. As individuals they saw themselves as simply doing what their President and his government and generals demanded. As a collective, it would soon eliminate from the planet an entire civilisation.

Thus, Kane was determined to succeed, focused now on securing the passage of as many Tibetans as possible. Of course, he wanted to do it peacefully. But despite Lobsang's message of peace and calm, Kane maintained that if things went pear-shaped, and the security forces threatened their lives with imprisonment as spies or worse, he would not go down without a fight. They would be justified, he believed, because of the atrocious treatment they continually metered out to innocent Tibetans. If the world's leaders weren't prepared to fight for justice, then Kane would.

They made a good team, Kane and Ridley, and he believed Sam Stein was a tough cookie, despite his recent struggles. Kane had seen the fire in his eyes. Kane also had a sneaky suspicion Lobsang might just have a few secrets up his robe sleeves, though he no longer wore them. That, itself, seemed a sign to Kane Lobsang might not be exactly as passive as he made out. Only time would tell.

A couple of years ago in Peru, when all the world seemed to conspire against him for those fateful ten days in the Andes, good had somehow prevailed. Since then, further dramas in Indonesia and most recently in Japan had unfolded, and it was more by luck than judgment that Kane was even still alive. Nevertheless, with these few good people around him and with the addition of an unpredictable monk, he hoped good would prevail again.

Chapter Twenty-One

Ridley jolted awake as the vehicle bounced over a deep pothole in the road. For a moment she was disoriented, but a quick glance out the windows reminded her where she was. She looked at the rear-view mirror and caught Kim's gaze, but the Korean held it for just a moment longer before looking away.

Kim then lit up what Ridley soon realised was a joint; the aromatic fragrance of opium drifting from the front of the van was unmistakable to her, and it immediately transported her back into the throes of a distant memory.

When Alexandria Ridley was just a child, her parents had died in a tragic car crash. A few years later, in her late teens and early twenties, she had gone off the rails, dabbling in all kinds of drugs as a way of coping with her anxieties and burgeoning depression. During a long, slow trip around southeast Asia, she had smoked opium.

For a two-week stretch in the village of Luang Prabang in northern Laos, Ridley smoked away her worries, and with them, she had nearly lost her life. To begin with, the constant smoking of pure opium helped a lot. She managed to claw back some measure of control and had seen the flicker of light at the end of a long and dingy tunnel. Yet, just as she began to control those emotions, the opium began to control her, and she was soon addicted. Ultimately, the addiction had occurred so swiftly that she succumbed to it totally, spending the last of her money and even trading in her return flight ticket to England. She had needed saving from herself in the jungles of Laos, and just when she needed him most, Kane had come to her rescue. He had flown out there, nursed her through her cold turkey withdrawals, and flown with her back to England.

She had never again smoked a joint after that, but then again, she had never since smelled the sickly sweet tang of pure opium; the effect on her was devastating. She hated herself for it, but there it was.

Ridley craved that joint, and it took all her willpower not to ask Kim to hand it to her. As if by some sixth sense, the surly Korean locked eyes with Ridley in his mirror, and apparently sensing her inner turmoil, he smiled and offered the joint. Ridley immediately recoiled, but then she wavered. She swallowed hard, a tear forming in the corner of her eye. Her lip trembled, and she leaned forward.

Slowly, she felt herself lifting her hand, unable to resist. Beside her, Lobsang gently but sternly placed his hand on Ridley's arm, and lowered it into her lap.

Ridley screwed her eyes shut, forcing the tears back. She opened the door's window and leaned out, inhaling outside the van rather than inhaling the residual smoke from Kim's joint. It took a minute, but finally her mind cleared and she leaned back inside the car. She turned to face Lobsang, her green eyes moist. She opened her mouth to thank him, but he stopped her with a raised hand.

"You do not need to say anything. Your gratitude is clear in your eyes," he said, and smiled.

Ridley leaned back in the seat, her left hand grasping Lobsang's. She knew it had been a close call. Her gaze drifted up to the mirror, only to be met once again by Kim's, his eyes a cruel sliver as they glared at her. She sensed something there. Disdain. And amusement. *What a prick*, Ridley thought, even more glad of Lobsang's presence, especially when Kim silently mouthed the words, *Next time*, before he looked away and took another long, slow drag of the spliff, the smoke filtering back to her. She clutched Lobsang's hand a little tighter.

Several more hours passed and the light was fading fast beyond the towering mountains. They had driven as long as they could for the day. The winding, narrow roads were hazardous enough in the daylight, let alone after dark. The convoy of two slowly entered the small village of Mood, and Chan pulled over in front of a shabby looking guesthouse.

"We'll spend the night here," he told them all as the weary group stepped from their wagons.

Ridley rushed over to Kane and hugged him tight, taking him by surprise. "Wow, Alex, to what do I owe the pleasure?"

She didn't answer. Instead she wept quietly into his broad chest. Kane glanced at her travel mate Lobsang, as if to ask what was going on, but the monk simply smiled and nodded, as if to say, 'It's okay'. Peeling herself away, she looked up into Kane's eyes and, wiping her own, said, "Just for being you." Kane was unaware of what exactly had happened and also sensed Lobsang would not tell him. If

Ridley wanted him to know, Kane knew she'd tell him herself.

The Good Mood Guesthouse—evidently the only place to stay in the hamlet of Mood—was an interesting play on words, considering its crumbling walls and dilapidated paintwork. Still, once Kane got to his room, it surprised him to find a pair of comfy looking beds and hot water, just what he, and the others, needed after almost twelve hours on bumpy roads. Chan had already advised them of a place to get a decent meal nearby, but warned them to stay close to the guesthouse.

"We'll be leaving at six in the morning," he'd said, adding, "and tomorrow will be another long and difficult day."

The four friends dropped their backpacks into the two twin rooms and wandered out into the tiny village just as the last rays of sun cast a subliminal glow on the snowy mountain peaks and ridges all around. The second the last light dipped away, they were plunged into almost pitch blackness; the only light came from a scattering of weak street lamps along the dusty road. They soon found the restaurant Chan had told them of, although calling it a restaurant was a stretch for any imagination; the one long table and two warped wooden benches hardly beckoned them in with their luxury. Nevertheless, the owner and chef of the imaginatively named *Amit's Food in Mood* restaurant was a jovial, rotund chap who took great pleasure in welcoming his surprise patrons.

"My friends, what brings you here?" he asked, his eyes beaming with delight. "Are you here for the trekking in our beautiful mountains, or for my world famous chapatis?"

Kane didn't know just how much they should tell the bubbly man and decided to humour him about trekking.

"Yes, we're going trekking in Leh," he replied, "and we're very excited about it."

"As you should be," said Amit, "because we have the world's best hiking here in Kashmir, isn't it so?"

"I think it is so," said Kane, the man's phrase reminding him of Puny back in Little Lhasa. The group soon polished off several delicious platefuls of samosas, dhal, veggies and rice, not to mention the tasty bread-like chapatis, and washed it all down with a large Kingfisher beer each. Only Lobsang declined, though Kane sensed a touch of reluctance he decided not to mention. Sam, who had barely said a word throughout the long drive, stood up from the table.

"I want to thank you," he said, looking round the table. "Hiram, Alex, I really appreciate you bringing me food at the guesthouse, and for giving me this chance at redemption." He raised his beer. "Skol! To new friends, and to helping the Tibetans. And to stopping Mr. Lee." They all responded in kind. Lobsang proffered a half-eaten samosa.

The restaurant owner, Amit, had overheard the toast, and discreetly stepped into the back room and dialled a number.

Chan Lee answered his phone and listened as Amit told him what he'd heard. Chan inhaled, the phone gripped tight in his fist as anger seethed in his bones.

Chapter Twenty-Two

In Chan Lee's room, with the door locked and the curtains pulled shut, Chan and Kim went to work. After sliding one of the beds away from the wall, and rolling back the Oriental rug it revealed, Kim grabbed a set of keys from his pocket and undid the heavy padlock. He lifted the secret trapdoor and stepped down several stairs, then pulled a chord to turn on the cellar light.

They weren't there to collect anything this time, but Chan's natural caution meant he always insisted on running through his usual checks. He followed Kim underground, and scanning the shelves that lined the walls, he smiled. Everything was in place, as he expected. However, Chan was well aware that in this business, you were never really sure who you could trust. Only three people in the world had knowledge of that secret store room; himself, his associate Kim, and Amit, owner of the nearby guesthouse and restaurant. Amit, who happily accepted the hefty payments Chan made each time he came and, more importantly for Chan, never asked questions. Amit got more money from this arrangement than if he had sold every bed, every night for a year, hence the run-down nature of the place. He simply didn't need to decorate and maintain his guesthouse, as long as Chan kept paying him his fee. Besides, Chan preferred it that way. No guests meant less chance of being found out. Still, Chan was also wise enough not to trust anyone. And that applied to Amit.

Hand-written cards labelled the shelves, the lowest of which held the drugs, with cards listing *Hashish* and *Opium*. On the middle shelf were *Grenades* and *Guns*. And on the top shelf, almost as if in pride of place, sat a dozen *Rocket Launchers*.

Chan Lee was nothing if not adaptable. He had begun his missions with noble intentions, wanting only to help smuggle Tibetan people into India... of course, while making a tidy profit. But as the difficulty of that endeavour's success grew, he had become involved in smuggling drugs. It proved far more lucrative, and in many ways, he found, far easier.

He had kept up the business of bringing Tibetans down because he needed a cover story. He also surmised if he ever got caught by any humanitarian groups he could at least argue he had been doing something noble. During those missions, he'd become entwined with one particularly ruthless Chinese security guard, who had persuaded Chan that if he wanted to make real money he would need to start smuggling drugs. Once the money started flowing into Chan's pockets, the Chinese guard sensed an opportunity, and it wasn't long before the drugs soon escalated to weapons. The guns, grenades and rocket launchers were destined for Pakistan, and into the hands of Al-Qaeda.

Morally—though his morals wore thinner with every fat payday—the idea of supplying terrorists with weapons troubled Chan. He justified the sinister endeavour by insisting on the continued transporting of the Tibetans. His inevitable bad karma, he hoped, would be cancelled out by whatever good he had accomplished.

Chan kept saying to himself, just one more mission, one more time, but each time, when the Chinese guard sensed he was having doubts, the wise arms trader doubled the payment, securing Chan's services time and again.

He would collect the weapons cache on the way back. Unbeknownst to anyone other than himself, Kim, Amit and the Chinese guard, the bottom of both vans contained secret compartments with enough room to outfit a small army.

Chan had made the trip to the Pakistan border half a dozen times now, and it was straight forward: smuggle the arms out of Chinese Tibet into India. Then send the weapons on their way, via a contact in Amritsar, to Lahore and beyond. Some would even make it as far as Kabul, Afghanistan. If Chan Lee didn't smuggle these things it would just be someone else, so why not get rich off other people's wayward religious beliefs? It was a flawed and weak-willed logic, he understood that, but then again, he remained a flawed and weak-willed man, something he could not deny.

Chan Lee's phone rang. That was unusual, as it was a private number only a handful of people had. It was Amit, the guesthouse owner.

"Mr. Lee, sir," he said, "there is something you should know about."

Chan didn't like the sound of this. "What is it, Amit?"

"In the restaurant, sir, the foreigners were talking. I think they know what you are doing. I mean, they said something about stopping Mr. Lee."

Chan gripped the phone so hard he heard the plastic crack. He fell silent for a long moment. It was inevitable that one day someone would get wise to his operations, and that it would eventually come to an end. But not yet. He wanted one more big payday.

"Mr. Lee?" Amit probed. "Sir, are you there?"

"Yes, Amit. Thank you." Chan snapped his phone shut. He had to think. Things had changed. He knew things were getting increasingly difficult. The fact the people with him on this mission seemed different, and were decent people, worried him. The young German had probably told them what he did, and though it angered him, he understood why. He'd used the boy: first seducing him with opium; then bribing him with drugs; and finally, threatening him. He never enjoyed that side of the business, but sometimes it was necessary. However, with Kane and the others... well, they were different. Older, and certainly wiser.

Maybe this is it for me? he mused. *Maybe this is a good time to bail out before I get caught, or worse, killed?* But this mission promised to be his most lucrative yet. Getting drugs into India was the easy part, and always reliable. And after the drugs, the weapons he would deliver to Lahore would secure a massive payment. But this had become a special mission for another reason. Among the Tibetans he'd be transporting down into India this time was an unnamed high-ranking Tibetan official.

Rumours had grown in Tibet and across various news outlets recently that a man named Gedhun Choekyi Nyima was, in fact, still alive. In 1995, the Dalai Lama declared young Gedhun as the 11th reincarnation of the Panchen Lama, thus becoming Tibet's second most-senior Buddhist monk after the Dalai Lama himself. The boy was allegedly kidnapped by the Chinese government as they continued to step up their sanctions and persecution of Tibetan religious leaders. The Chinese figured that if the heir apparent were missing, the already weak resistance to Chinese rule would crumble, leaving them at liberty to do whatever they wanted with Tibet. No one really knew what had become of the Panchen Lama. While some believed the Chinese had murdered him, others argued he was still alive, albeit as an incommunicado prisoner. China had never publicly said anything about the Panchen Lama's disappearance and denied all knowledge of his kidnap and current whereabouts.

Through his grapevine of contacts, Chan learned he was to smuggle a very important Tibetan official into India, and that the Chinese would pay him more than his usual rate. He didn't believe the rumours that the Panchen Lama was alive; he knew how the Chinese operated. But on the slim chance it was him—if he really was this very important figurehead to the future of Tibet and Buddhist culture and tradition—then Chan would not be the man to prevent his safe passage. Despite everything else, if anything could swing the pendulum of karma back to the good side, then that would surely be it.

Yet now, with Amit's phone call, he faced a new problem. He considered sharing this with the others, explaining how important this mission was. But they probably wouldn't believe him. After all, to them he was nothing more than a low-life criminal, despite the rescues he'd accomplished. Perhaps he could convince them it was his last drug-smuggling mission. They surely hadn't learned about the guns. Problem was, Chan didn't know how much they did know, if anything, so bringing his latest smuggling endeavour into the open was an unnecessary risk.

No. His primary objective on this mission was to bring

whomever this so-called high-ranking Tibetan was into India, snag himself one last handsome pay-off after delivering his cargo of humans, narcotics and weapons, then go away somewhere to live out his days in peace, and to try and start shedding those years of accumulated guilt.

Whatever it was Kane and the others were planning, Chan Lee would not let them stand in his way.

If he had to, he knew he would resort to violence. And with Do-Hyun Kim on his side, he knew he had a callous, dangerous and deadly ally to call upon.

Chapter Twenty-Three

Dawn shone brightly over Mood, and though Kane and his three companions hadn't slept that well due to their nervous excitement about the coming day, they all seemed to have risen in good spirits. Grabbing cups of awful but welcomingly strong coffee from the grungy reception area of the Good Mood Guesthouse, they stepped outside into a glorious morning. The low sun had already begun warming the valley, while high above, strong winds blew clouds streaming to the east, in more or less the same direction they'd be travelling. Kane gathered his crew close.

"Okay, guys," he said, "we all know why we're here, and equally, we're all aware today could be difficult, even dangerous. Make no mistake, we're dealing with a smart and experienced operator, and we all need to prepare in the event things go wrong. Anything could happen, so this is the moment for those of you who might have second thoughts. If you do, I completely understand. We can leave you here, and collect you on the way back."

He surveyed the three of them closely. First, he looked

at Lobsang, but before Kane could speak the monk waved him away with a knowing smile. Beneath his calm exterior existed a stoic determination Kane wouldn't question.

Ridley was next, and as he knew she would, she too smiled. Ridley, the bravest, most fearless woman he had ever known. Although his long-held love for her meant he was uncomfortable with her going on many of his expeditions, he knew better than to try and talk her out of this one. Kane loved Ridley for many reasons; that was just another of them.

Last to undergo Kane's scrutiny was the young German, Sam Stein. Sam had been enduring a rough time in the last few months, partly because of his own weakness and desire to rebel against his parents, which he'd explained with honesty. Sam was also fragile because Chan Lee had connived him into a form of subservience that had Sam enduring such despondency he'd even contemplated suicide, metaphorically on his knees the day Kane and Ridley had gone to see him. And yet, in the few short days since then, Sam had turned a page in the story of his life and had developed a diamond-edged determination to stop Chan Lee. Kane believed he was relishing the chance to help the Tibetans while putting Chan's corrupt business to bed. Sam nodded, no words necessary.

Kane shook both men by the hand and wished them luck, then pulled Ridley into a hug. "Be careful," he whispered. "I need a wife."

After a few moments he stepped away from Ridley and appraised them all a final time, and they greeted him with firm nods of understanding. "Good. Then let's saddle up, and ride on into Tibet."

Half an hour later Chan greeted them. They resumed

their usual seats, soon heading southeast on the thirty-mile drive to Demchok where they would take a short break.

Once more, the stunning scenery of the Indus River Valley made Kane momentarily forget how challenging the hours, perhaps days, ahead might be. He enjoyed the welcome distraction.

Once they left the main highway, the road became nothing more than a dusty, rarely-used lane, and although in reasonable condition, the ride was bumpy. The river itself raged alongside them. *If it wasn't so remote here,* Kane thought, *it would make for excellent white-water rafting.* He'd always enjoyed rafting since he first tried it on the Tully River in Queensland, though the most river-borne fun he'd ever had come on New Zealand's wild Kaituna, where he and his mother had rafted over the world's highest legally-raftable waterfall. At over seven metres in height, it wasn't for the faint-hearted, and his mother used to tease him about the fact he'd been more scared than she was. The worst part of that? It just so happened to be true. She had been a tough cookie, Kane's mum, and her death from cancer a couple of years ago had hit the family hard.

The need for home was weighing heavily now, perhaps more than ever and for reasons he couldn't quite grasp. As often happened when Kane felt anxious, he subconsciously reached for the golden Inca sun disk that hung on a leather strap around his neck. It was his lucky charm and his most prize possession. When he realised he had reached for it, he smiled inwardly.

I have a feeling I'm going to need some luck...

Chapter Twenty-Four

A little shy of two hours later they arrived in the tiny hamlet of Demchok.

Quite literally, there was nothing in Demchok other than a scattering of disused Indian Army barracks. Over the years, Demchok has been the scene of several failed incursions by Chinese troops, who were repelled by Indian forces. These days, Chan had explained earlier, both the Indian and Chinese governments still claimed the area. Both nations had long wanted to open up the region, but for differing reasons. China's reason, of course, was for trade, wanting to reestablish a modern-day silk route.

The Indians, however, had humble but no less important reasons. Mount Kailash, a mountain considered holy not only by the Buddhists, but by the followers of Hinduism and Jainism who had made pilgrimages to the mountain for thousands of years. The mountain itself remained steeped in mystery. Back in Mcleodganj Kane had read an article online about Russian conspiracy theorists who'd even speculated that the top of the mountain was actually a man-made pyramid. The wider region was indeed rife with legends of alien visitors and mysterious, magical powers, according to other articles he'd stumbled upon. Despite its relative anonymity in the western world, millions from the East still revered the mountain, which remained an important place of worship and spirituality for so many people across multiple faiths.

Today, however, the only people anywhere in sight were himself and the others. Exactly how it needed to be for Chan's operation to work, he realised with a sinking feeling.

They were literally less than five miles from one of the world's most contested borders, and Kane's heart raced. Just minutes from where they parked was a standing Chinese military force, through which they would try to bribe their passage forth. Even though Chan had done this successfully many times before, he'd explained, with Kane's recent experiences in Peru still fresh in his memory, he almost expected things to go wrong.

Yet they had no other choice... they would just have to give it a go and see how things panned out. Kane knew it was time for Chan Lee to work his magic.

The region appeared barren and deserted, but with the border to Chinese Tibet so close Kane knew they would soon see the amassed security forces. Chan was becoming more visibly nervous as the minutes ticked by, until at last, after thirty minutes of slow, steady driving they caught their first sight of the border patrols. As far as the Chinese government was concerned, the crossing was officially closed. However, in today's world everything had its price. Chan had told them just how heavy that price could be.

An imaginary line formed the border itself. Surrounded by such difficult terrain there was just one ancient, narrow road for the guards to monitor, access beyond which could only be achieved on foot. With observation posts spread at regular intervals along the border, it remained virtually impossible for anyone to cross unseen.

Chan pulled the convoy of two vehicles to a stop a hundred yards short of the checkpoint, and after visibly composing himself, Lane watched on as Chan walked alone toward the gates. In Chan's absence, Kane and his comrades stood together behind the first people carrier to watch how the meeting would unfold. Kane glanced over at Do-Hyun Kim who, as usual, seemed to be watching them like a hawk. A small knot of apprehension tightened in Kane's guts as the Korean spat on the floor and followed Chan with his eyes.

Chan approached the guards slowly, and Kane hoped he had timed his arrival correctly in order to meet with the specific guard he'd mentioned. He'd called ahead from Demchok just to be sure. That guard's name was Chang Zhu, which Chan told them meant *prosperous red*. Given the man's position as a smuggler who also worked for the Chinese Red Army, it seemed appropriate indeed. Kane saw Chan's relief at seeing Zhu, who quickly ushered him over to his small hut. Chang Zhu was in charge of that security position, thus there were no immediate superiors to worry about. According to Chan, Zhu was confident he remained immune from suspicion by other, nosy guards—those with whom he was not already in collusion.

Chan expressed no concerns about getting himself across the border. He'd done it so many times. He was only ever turned away when Zhu didn't trust one or two of the other guards. Like himself, Chan explained to Kane, Zhu understood everything had a price; since wages and working conditions were so harsh and severe, very few soldiers in the

Chinese security force were above taking a cash or whisky bribe to avert their eyes.

However, Kane sensed Chan's concern *was* himself and the other foreigners. He explained to Kane that he'd never taken more than one across before, and Sam had been enough times he'd become familiar. But now he had three others with him, and it clearly worried Chan. In order to reassure Kane, and apparently himself, Chan had explained that Chang Zhu was an older guard, close to sixty, and it taken him many years to ascend to his relatively prestigious position in control of the crossing. It was a lucrative position too, thus, prudent for him to keep things smooth. They were so remote from China's Beijing power base that nobody would ever know about his shady operation and it was also in Zhu's best interests to avoid unnecessary stops or paperwork.

As it turned out, neither Kane nor Chan need have been concerned. After just a couple of minutes of negotiations, an already slightly drunk and jovial Chang Zhu waved them through without so much as a question or a cursory glance at Chan's associates, and it had only cost Chan two-hundred dollars more than usual.

Chan signalled to Kim with a wave of an arm. Kim growled something at Kane and the others, and a minute later, with Lobsang crouching as low as possible in his seat and muttering some Buddhist prayer of thanks into the ether, they were in Tibet, and Lobsang Paljor was home.

Chapter Twenty-Five

Despite their reasons for being there, arriving in Tibet was a momentous occasion for Kane, and he had to pinch himself. Unfortunately, leaders around the world now recognised Tibet as a legal territory of China, but only so they would remain in favour with what was quickly becoming the world's number one superpower. Controlling a massive proportion of the world's trade, China dominated everything, and no leader wanted to ignore how important it was to his or her own government's economic stability and growth.

It mattered little about China's disgraceful human rights issues, not to mention its unwavering support of the notorious regime in the hermit kingdom of North Korea. With China as an ally, that country had been starving and subjugating its population for decades, in the name of power disguised as Communism.

Yet, free thinkers like Kane would never recognise Tibet and its people as Chinese. His Holiness the Dalai Lama wanted nothing more than an unrepressed homeland, with amicable ties to its neighbour: China. The continuation of Tibet's ancient traditions was paramount, and most of the liberal world agreed.

China has always been afraid of the Dalai Lama, however. His simple humanitarian beliefs and messages of love and peace for all the world inspired so many millions of people of all faiths and religious persuasions. His mere existence provided a constant, prickly thorn in China's ever-growing side.

Kane had always admired His Holiness from afar without knowing too much about the history and political turmoil he'd endured. His best friend Evan was a Dalai Lama super-fan, which is why they'd journeyed to Mcleodganj in the first place, and why they were here now. Their plans had obviously changed somewhat, but Kane knew if Evan hadn't died trying to save a young boy in Peru, he would be alongside him now, doing what he could to save Tibetans.

If everything went well from now on they would arrive at the Ngari settlement sometime before sunset. Only about fifty or so miles remained to get there, but the quality of the road had worsened and they now had to contend with potholes as deep as small bomb craters while landslides remained a genuine threat. Chan and Kim drove on with caution.

It didn't matter what time they arrived tonight, though; Chan knew they wouldn't collect their human cargo— including the mysterious dignitary—until midday tomorrow. Before dawn, Chan would be busy loading part of the hidden compartments with drugs, but after that it would be all go. *One more mission*, he thought, *only one more*. And unless he missed his guess, if it were unsuccessful there'd be no more missions anyway; not because he'd have retired, but because they would kill him. Chang Zhu wouldn't risk a mere pawn like Chan Lee implicating him, and Chan was probably right in thinking it would be his life or Zhu's. There would only be one outcome if it came to that, and Zhu held all the aces. Chan understood he would die in that God-forsaken border area, and they would never find his body.

Ridley had let her body roll with the bumps of the vehicle across the bumpy road, and had found some form of comfort in it. She'd mostly spent the long hours in the truck letting her imagination run wild over the horizons in the mountains, and occasionally conversing with Lobsang, who was currently dozing, his head propped on the jumper Ridley had loaned him.

Up in the front, Kim lit a joint, his eyes fixed on her in the rearview mirror, appraising Ridley. She knew what was coming, and stole her nerves as Kim deliberately blew his smoke into the back of the van. Yet, try as she might, once more its effects on her were immediate. Again, it transported her back to the bliss she'd experienced in Laos when she'd first discovered opium. But something had changed since yesterday. She'd had an epiphany, and Ridley knew without doubt she'd never take drugs again. At that moment she wasn't sure why she felt so certain, so convinced she could ignore the powerful, almost hypnotic lure of the drugs. But it was there. She supposed it had something to do with the fact they were in Tibet, homeland of one of the world's most loved and respected leaders, and, she believed, a place with so much innate humility and compassion.

Ridley mused that if she couldn't love herself there, then where could she?

When Kim proffered the joint over the seat, his usual sneer visible in the mirror, this time Ridley took it. For a moment, Lobsang, who had roused beside her, seemed concerned. However, the smile on the old monk's face when she casually wound down the window and flicked the joint out onto the dusty highway was priceless. They didn't need to say anything, because both understood what a significant moment it was.

She met Kim's glare in the rearview, and what was usually something between a scowl and amusement, was now something else. There was venom in those eyes, the eyes of a snake ready to strike, and Ridley wondered for a fleeting moment if she'd hadn't just made a mortal enemy of a very dangerous man.

Now into the late afternoon the sun crept towards a col between two vast mountain peaks, its golden rays setting the entire valley aglow and taking Kane's mind off the dangers ahead. With such a beautiful landscape, it was difficult to comprehend the sinister activities that had been happening here for almost eight decades. Kane tried to put himself in the shoes of the Tibetan people who had lived in these lands for thousands of years until China claimed them for itself, forcing people to flee or risk torture and death. It was reminiscent of the Spanish conquistadors in his beloved Peru all those centuries ago, and everyone knows how that turned out; an entire civilisation sent to the brink of extinction over the greed of gold and the false power of religion. Within his heart now grew a barrelling swell of anger towards the Chinese.

Though Kane was nothing if not strong-minded, and he forced himself to calm down. Instead of channelling his anger against the Chinese in a fight he couldn't win, he focussed on making this one small mission as successful as possible. If they could safely bring over the dozen Tibetans, and somehow stop Chan's smuggling enterprise, then it would be a success.

They drove on largely in silence until, just before the sun finally disappeared for the day, they arrived on the outskirts of Ngari. As he had in Mood, Chan knew of a place to stay. This time it was in the humble home of a Tibetan family, his contacts for connecting with the refugees. After parking up, Chan introduced the group to the family, and with great appreciation they accepted an invitation to eat dinner with them. After they'd finished the modest meal, the family vacated the house, willing to stay in another place to afford the travellers space to rest and plan.

Kane pulled Chan aside and asked to speak with him in private. Kim disappeared back to the vehicles while Lobsang set about regaling his Ridley and Sam with yet more tales of life in Little Lhasa.

Chan led Kane into a separate outbuilding. In the dim light, they settled on plastic chairs and began their conversation.

"Listen, Chan. I have something I consider very important to discuss, if you'll do me the honour of hearing me out?"

Chan nodded his acquiescence. "Yes, Hiram. What's on your mind?" Kane could tell Chan was both nervous and intrigued, and sat in silence while Kane spoke.

"Chan, let me start by saying that what you're doing for the Tibetans is admirable. It is, and I mean it." Chan nodded, yet Kane suspected the man sensed this conversation was about to take a more difficult course as one eye began twitching and he fidgeted in his seat. Kane continued. "But I have to admit the other aspects of your trips to Tibet sit far less comfortably with me. And the others. I'm aware everyone needs to make a living, I understand that. Using people like young Sam to smuggle drugs, knowing the harm and probable deaths those drugs will cause, well that's just terrible. I know you know this, Chan, and I sense it doesn't sit comfortably with you either. What I have to ask is simple. I'm asking you right now to stop smuggling drugs."

Chan leaned back in his chair. He wasn't surprised by Kane's request. He looked into Kane's eyes for a long moment, and saw only truth and integrity, and the intensity in those eyes shamed him. He hung his head, and his once broad shoulders slumped under the weight of his shame.

In truth, he had used vulnerable people to assist his nefarious enterprise, and he alone was getting rich from it. And yes, many people would ultimately suffer as a consequence. But what Kane and the others didn't know was just how dangerous and persuasive Mr. Chang Zhu was. Chan had wanted to stop the drug operation a long time ago, but Zhu simply wouldn't let him. Chan was in no doubt that if he defied the Chinese security man, whose reach was long and almost certainly deadly, he wouldn't survive. Besides, the amount of money Zhu was paying him, not only for the drug operation, but for the arms smuggling, proved too tempting. It just wasn't that easy to quit, however much he wanted to. With Kane at his side, perhaps the time had come.

"Hiram, I appreciate this chat. Now, I ask you to repay the compliment and listen to what I have to say."

Kane nodded. "Fair's fair."

"I have for several years been operating in and out of Tibet, though for many months now I've promised myself this was to be the very last time. I have truly meant it. Before I met you, I was planning for this to be my last money-making venture across the border. I hope you believe me."

Kane didn't answer, only offering a subtle nod.

"The security chief, Zhu, is a powerful man, and has threatened my life if I stop conducting his operations. Worse than that, though, he has told me in no uncertain terms that if I do stop, no Tibetan will ever be allowed to cross his stretch of border again. You do understand what that means for them?" He paused, and Kane nodded. "So as you can see it's not as easy as you might have thought."

Kane's expression turned pensive. He seemed to sense the truth in Chan's words. Chan continued.

"And there's one more thing, Hiram. Trust me when I say this mission is the most important for years. The Chinese have escalated their campaign of oppression and have begun targeting higher ranked spiritual leaders, so now, more than ever, the Tibetans have to resist. Believe it or not, there are those in China who sympathise with Tibet, some even with healthy political clout." He paused, as if deciding how much to say. A tiny nod, almost to himself, and he continued. "Have you heard about the Panchen Lama, the boy kidnapped in the nineties?"

Kane nodded. He had read something about that, but didn't know much. He said, "Go on, Chan."

"The Panchen Lama is Buddhism's second most important spiritual leader. Many people think he's dead, murdered when only a child in order to plunge both Tibet and Buddhism into chaos. But I've been reliably informed he is in fact alive... and has been smuggled out of the security compound where they imprisoned him for more than twenty years, and... well as unreal as it sounds, even to me, we're the ones who are finally going to take him to safety."

Kane's eyes widened in obvious shock. To Chan he seemed to be realising that if he was telling the truth, it changed everything. No words came.

"So you see, Hiram, we simply must get him out of Tibet safely, or the very future of Tibet, its culture and its people are at risk. Fail, and China might just go on and wipe the Tibetans from the face of the earth."

Chapter Twenty-Six

Kane was stunned, and took a moment to let the gravity of what Chan said sink in. *Shit. This has changed everything.*

He wasn't sure why, but he believed Chan Lee. The man looked sincere, and in his eyes, Kane saw both fear and regret. Fear of failure, likely not only for his own life, but for the lives of innocent Tibetans. The regret, Kane hoped, was because he would no longer be able to help them, and not because it meant a serious loss of income. It seemed, after all, that not only could they become allies, but they might have to.

Of course, Chan knew Kane wasn't yet aware of the stash of weapons. One way or another Chan would make good on that delivery. The guns and grenades were already over the border in India, and that could wait. He had always thought running drugs was a dirty business and was more than happy to quit that sideline. It was just a case of taking the drugs from Zhu, destroying them, and never coming back. It meant he'd no longer be able to help the Tibetans, at least not at this crossing, but he'd risked enough. It was time for someone else to step up and help.

But in Kane he sensed both a good man and a strong ally. They could handle this mission, and many Tibetans, including an important spiritual leader, would be transported to their welcoming sanctuary in Little Lhasa.

Chan was sick of the constant fear, anyway, and in that moment he decided. He would complete this venture, make a last run up to Pakistan to deliver the weapons, and finally retire from the illegal profession that had made him wealthy once and for all.

He looked at Kane, holding his gaze for long seconds before he spoke. "Hiram, thank you. You are right. What I have done is wrong. One hundred percent. And I'm tired. Tired of living in fear, tired of making money this way. I want to stop... I need to stop. But..." He paused again, and took a deep breath. "This mission is crucial. We simply must get the Panchen Lama across the border into India, and to do that, we must also transport the drugs for Chang Zhu. It's the price of any possible success. Think of it as a kind of border tax, for want of a better explanation. So I ask you... can you live with that?"

"Do I have your word we will destroy the drugs at the earliest safe location?"

Chan paused a moment longer than he meant, and said, "You have my word."

The two men stood, and shook hands, a mutual respect growing between them.

"Then I guess we need to get back to the house," Kane said. "I need to let my crew know to trust you, and tell them what's really going on. And you can trust them, Chan. I've known Ridley many years, and you won't find a more honest person. I think I can say the same for Sam, too. Perhaps you should have a word with him, apologise and promise to make it up to him somehow. Paying for his flights back to Germany would be a good start. And as for Lobsang, what with your revelation about the Panchen Lama, he'll be more invested in this than any of us."

They shared a smile, and were about to leave the room when Chan stopped Kane at the doorway.

"One more thing. My associate, Kim... you need to be very wary of him. He's tight with Chang Zhu, and he will definitely not see things the way we do. He doesn't care about the Tibetans and only cares about one thing. Money. He's a dangerous man who will stop at nothing to get the drugs over the border and get paid. Be careful Hiram, and warn the others. Never was there a man with less heart than Do-Hyun Kim."

"Thanks for the warning, Chan, and be careful yourself."

Chan would be careful. Both a shit load of money, and his life, were well and truly on the line.

Chapter Twenty-Seven

The first thing Kane saw when he found their sleeping quarters was Lobsang, badly beaten and tied to a chair. He had a swollen eye, a bloodied nose, and it looked as if it happened very recently. Even worse... there was no sign of Ridley.

"Where's Alex?" he shouted, but realised the monk was gagged. Kane ripped the cloth from his mouth. "Are you okay? Is anything broken?"

"I'm... I am okay." Lobsang choked a little, coughing blood onto his shirt. "It was Kim. He barged in and... he punched me in the jaw before I had any chance to react. He had a gun Hiram. He... he pointed it at Alex's head as he tied me to this chair. He tied Alex up too, then hit me... he hit me twice with the gun, and dragged her outside. Only ten minutes ago. I am so sorry, Hiram, I... I could do nothing."

Kane's teeth clenched and he wanted to scream, but held it in. "It's okay, it's okay. That mother fu—. Did he say anything, Lobsang? Did Kim say where he was taking Alex?" Kane said, pacing like a caged tiger.

Just at that moment Chan Lee stormed into the room, his face ashen.

"She's gone," barked Kane, "Kim's taken her."

Chan blinked several times, as if unable to believe what he'd heard. "I... I found Sam tied up in his room. I'm sorry... about Alex. I had no idea." He looked on the verge of tears, and stared at Kane, as if worried Kane wouldn't believe him.

"This isn't your fault, Chan," Kane said and wasn't sure if he meant it or not. He put those doubts to one side and said, "But we need to know where he's taken her. Has this happened before? Why would he do such a thing?"

"Yesterday, in the... in the van," said Lobsang, struggling to speak, "he offered Alex drugs... Kim did. She took it, but threw it out of the window. He said nothing, but he was very angry."

Kane nodded. It sounded like something Ridley would do, never one to be afraid of sticking up for herself. He looked at Lobsang. "Did she fight Kim?"

Lobsang smiled weakly and nodded, but the smile faded. "She did fight, yes. It happened so fast. She... had almost no time to react."

Kane knew that, one on one, not many men could handle Ridley with her fighting skills. Like Kane himself, she was a black belt in tae-kwon-do. Kane also knew she would never put an innocent life in danger to save her own, and if Lobsang was being threatened she would have complied with whatever Kim wanted until such time it was safe to act.

Chan had fallen silent, though he looked as if he was

trying to say something. But the words stuck. Kane didn't miss it.

"What, Chan? You have something to say?"

"It's... well, I heard a rumour once, but I..."

"But what, Chan? My lov... our friend is missing, and this is no time to dither. What the hell is it?"

"It was about a people-smuggling gang, a joint Indian-Chinese group operating out of Tibet and far from the eyes of the world. But I promise you, Hiram, I have never had anything to do with that. Please, you must believe me. I swear."

"I do, Chan." Kane glared at Chan, searching his eyes for the lie he suspected. He didn't see one, but he would hold his judgment for now. "You know Kim. Has he ever said anything about it?"

"No, not much. I do remember one comment, though I didn't give much thought to it at the time. He said... what were his words? Something along the lines of, many bad things happen in Tibet because the rest of the world would never see."

"Where, Chan? And why can't the world see?"

"It's more of a metaphor, really, but he said..." A pause, as if recalling the words correctly.

"What, Chan?" demanded Kane.

Chan looked directly at Kane. "He said 'the world sees nothing in the shadow of Kailash'."

Chapter Twenty-Eight

Most of the girls had faded, both mentally and physically. They'd been in the back of the truck non-stop for many days, the only respite being the sporadic bathrooms breaks on the side of deserted highways; the only sustenance, the flippant delivery of insufficient bottles of warm water and the occasional packets of rice and roti.

They were understandably frightened. They were evidently exhausted. And Azim knew they were going out of their minds, especially after witnessing the cold-blooded murder of someone just like them. No doubt each one of them feared she would be next.

That is, Azim believed, all except one. The feisty Australian was far from fading. In fact, she sat calmly, yet with a wildness in her eyes Azim found amusing, and if he were to be honest with himself, a tiny bit disconcerting. It was clear she wanted nothing more than to kill the people who'd taken her against her will and who'd already beaten her multiple times. Her will was strong, Azim had no doubt. He absentmindedly wondered what had happened in her past for her to be able to act in this manner. Whatever it was, he cared little. She was no threat to him and he turned away from her, and closed his eyes, still feeling her glowering him and wishing him dead.

The truck left the highway, and had rumbled over rough ground for an hour before juddering to an abrupt halt.

Azim barked some orders and his minions unceremoniously set about bundling the women out of the truck into the crisp, cold light of a dazzling mountain vista. It was the morning of day five of their journey and despite Azim being fed up of the uncomfortable ride, he couldn't deny the beauty of the mountains that towered above them in all directions.

He watched as the Australian, still calm, took several deep breaths. The cold air felt good to Azim and knew it must've felt like heaven to the women. He kept his eyes on her as she stretched, apparently making sure she was sharp and ready for a chance to fight back Azim knew would never present itself, not whilst he was in charge.

Azim didn't know what to make of her, but as she turned and fixed him with her icy gaze, he sensed that she believed she had gotten under his skin these last few days. *Perhaps she has*, he mused internally, but he'd never let it show. It was clear she could look out for herself. Then again, she was still just a woman, and again, she was white... and as he allowed himself to smile in her direction, Azim knew that those two simple facts combined meant she was worth absolutely nothing to the courier other than a few thousand extra rupees per day.

Chapter Twenty-Nine

"Kailash? What the hell is Kailash?" Kane blurted.

Chan answered. "It's a mountain. A holy mountain in Tibet, revered by pilgrims, including Hindus, Buddhists and the followers of Jainism. I suppose that in the proximity of such a holy place, no one would consider such odious things could happen there."

Kane glanced at Lobsang, who sat in stunned silence.

"Lobsang? You know of it?"

The monk finally nodded. "Yes. I know Kailash. I made several pilgrimages there in my younger years... it is our most holy of places, but I... I cannot believe—" Lobsang closed his eyes, unable to fathom what he was hearing. Kane turned back to Chan Lee.

"Tell me more, Chan," Kane demanded, his breaths becoming ragged, a steely glint narrowing his eyes. "What kind of people smuggling?"

Chan paused, reluctant to say more. He exhaled. "Young women, mostly, but remember, I've only heard rumours. I don't... I guess they round the girls up in the larger cities in Asia... Beijing, Mumbai, probably Hong Kong. As I said... I guess they... I guess the girls end up—" Chan couldn't finish his sentence, but Kane understood exactly what Chan wouldn't say.

Sex slaves.

Kane slumped onto the bed, the realisation of what had happened hitting him like a kidney punch. He, of course, felt responsible, though he wasn't. They'd all volunteered to travel with him into Tibet, each of them knowing there'd be risks. But those risks they had believed sat with Chan Lee, or the Chinese security, perhaps Mother Nature... Kane hadn't given the sullen, almost mute driver, Do-Hyun Kim, a second thought. Until now.

"How stupid have I been?" he said to no one. "So fucking stupid." He turned to Chan. "You even warned me!"

"Listen, Hiram," replied Chan, "I had no idea Kim was capable of anything like this. He's surly, no doubt, and I know he can be violent at the slightest provocation. But this? I just can't understand it." Chan took a seat, his head in his hands, and Kane believed he was telling the truth. Kane stood up then, his face suddenly calmer.

"Alex Ridley is tougher than any man I know. She'll be fine. In fact, I half expect her to walk back in here any minute with that low-life Kim in a headlock. She'll be okay... we just need to find her."

Chan Lee didn't look so sure. He'd admitted Kim was a dangerous man, and he'd also told Kane he only operated with him because Zhu insisted upon it. Chan's face showed that he feared the worst.

Kane sensed Chan felt responsible. All of this had stemmed from his greed, and his mistreatment of the unfortunate German kid, Sam and who knew how many other vulnerable young travellers.

Kane saw something stir within Chan Lee. Puny had said he was a placid man at heart; he was guilty only of being corrupted by greed. What man hadn't at one time or another? Kane believed that Chan was being truthful when he'd told him he planned to quit this shady lifestyle soon, ready to turn over a new leaf. Well, it seemed that leaf had well and truly turned when he stated:

"Follow me," he demanded, and the surprising, authoritative tone made Kane take notice. "We're going after Alex."

Chapter Thirty

"But what about the Tibetans?" Kane asked.

He wanted nothing more than to head straight out after Kim and Ridley, but he wouldn't simply ignore the Tibetans they were going to collect. He also knew Ridley herself would not expect anyone to help her, not with the lives of others on the line.

"I understand your concern, Hiram," replied Chan, "but we always have a two- or three-day window of opportunity when we arrange these transports. Things often hold us up for one reason or another, and we have to allow time to negotiate any number of unknown logistical problems. My best guess is that we must head to Mount Kailash, but I'm sorry... I'm not sure where it is." He turned to Lobsang, who nodded.

"I know where the holy mountain is, but I am not sure where we are now. I crossed the border a long time ago... and I walked."

Chan said, "Then maybe someone at the safe house can guide us. Let's go there... now."

Kane and the others climbed into Chan's van and sped off through the darkness to the safe house. It was risky; to travel in that area at night might alert the wrong people, namely the Chinese security. Under the circumstances though, every second counted. Kim was dangerous, and violent, but also smart, Chan warned them.

"He will assume you'd eventually go after him, so he will waste no time putting as much distance as possible between us," Chan had said.

After a relatively short drive to the modest house in Ngari, they arrived at almost seven at night. They wouldn't be expected. Chan had tried to call ahead, but phone reception in the area remained almost non-existent and he failed to find a connection. He'd earlier told Kane that twelve Tibetans in total waited for their ride to freedom, and they would be sharing just one room in that large yet simple dwelling. There would be some kind of security, though they never armed themselves with anything lethal. "Still, we'll be arriving unannounced and we need to be cautious."

Chan pulled up on the side of a small road some five-hundred yards from the house. Kane suggested it would be safer for all of them if only he and Chan approached the house on foot rather than arrive in the noisy vehicle. So that's what they did. They stuck to the dark fringes of the road and edged towards the house. There was no sign of life on the street; a good omen that their planned operation tomorrow had thus far gone unsuspected by the authorities. Obviously, the illegal trafficking of Tibetans out of what was officially China was considered an awful crime and an act of the utmost treachery, punishable by death. Chan warned there were a few members of the security forces privy to such transactions, like Chang Zhu, but added that you could never be sure who they were. Thus, Kane knew getting caught now was not an option.

They'd crept within fifty yards of the house, and Kane's pulse quickened. Twenty yards, now, when suddenly two men stepped out in front of them wielding what looked in the darkness like farmer's pitchforks.

"Stop!" they demanded, though they kept their voices low. "Who are you, and why are you here?"

Chan Lee switched on his torch to illuminate his face. "It is me, Mr. Lee. I can explain."

The two men visibly relaxed, instantly recognising the man who had helped them so often. "Okay, Mister Lee. Who is that?"

They spoke quietly, Chan explaining Kane was a friend, only there to help them. The men accepted it without hesitation, such was Chan's standing in the Tibetan community. They obviously knew nothing of his shady businesses, only that he helped Tibetans escape persecution.

"Follow us," one of them said, and Chan flicked off the torch and followed the men through a gap in the hedge and on into the dark building. Kane followed, and the door swiftly locked behind them. They ushered them into a couple of chairs, and by candlelight, they introduced them to a few of the Tibetans. Comprised of a mix of men, women and children, half of them wore the ubiquitous scarlet or orange robes of Tibetan monks. Two of the youngest among them, perhaps a brother and sister of six or seven years old, Kane guessed, ran around playfully, but when they spotted Kane's white skin they stood and stared, clearly thinking him some kind of alien. The entertaining moment soon eased the hint of tension in the room.

After the initial commotion, a hush descended over the room as a young man entered from another door. Kane thought him a serene looking fellow, though he wore a somewhat haunted look in his eyes. He approached Chan and Kane, and without any introduction, they knew his identity immediately.

"Hello. My name is Gedhun Choekyi Nyima. On behalf of my people, and on behalf of His Holiness, I thank you for all you do for us." The man bowed, held the pose for several seconds, then stood upright, and in that few seconds Kane felt as humble as he ever had. Unbelievably, Chan had been right.

Standing before him was the 11th Panchen Lama, and in all Buddhism, the highest ranking religious member still in Tibet. Here was a man who half the world assumed was dead. Although Kane didn't actually have proof of who he was—other than the Chinese guards who'd been holding him prisoner all these years, not a single person on Earth had any idea what he looked like—Kane believed with his entire being the man standing before him was the missing Panchen Lama. It was a profound moment and even Chan, despite his mistakes and flawed character, seemed just as humbled as Kane felt.

The two men bowed. It was all Kane could think to do; evidently Chan thought the same. The Panchen Lama chuckled.

"I'm not His Holiness... not yet," he said, and all those around who seemingly knew English failed to stifle their own laughter.

The rest of the group, who had been left behind in the vehicle, were summoned and now filed quietly into the room. After some polite introductions, and after Lobsang had dropped to his knees in genuine disbelief and unbridled happiness at learning his Panchen Lama was indeed alive and well, Chan apologised and asked them all to listen. He explained as succinctly as possible about how Kim had kidnapped Ridley, and because Kim was so unpredictable, they genuinely feared for Ridley's life.

Those gathered all listened with obvious horror, as the Panchen Lama himself translated for those who didn't speak English.

"We will track him east as fast as possible," Chan said, "but we're not sure from here where Mount Kailash is... did any of you arrive in Ngari from the Kailash region?"

Nobody answered. "Really, none of you knows that area?"

Kane wasn't sure he believed them, though he knew it went against Buddhist teachings to lie. "We really need someone who knows the area to come with us," he said gently. "My good friend's life might depend on it."

The Panchen Lama spoke. "I am very sorry Mr. Kane... I wish we could help more."

Just then, another young man, younger even than the Panchen Lama, very quietly stepped out from a dark corner of the room. In a voice so soft Kane could hardly hear him, he said, "I know the way... I will go with you."

Chapter Thirty-One

"I'm sorry?" asked Kane. "Did you say you would come with us?" The man—*actually, he's just an older boy*, Kane thought, *though he's very tall*—simply nodded.

The Panchen Lama approached the young man and whispered a few words in his ear. He bowed, and the two embraced. He in turn then approached Kane and Chan.

"My name is Jahm-Yang. I will take you to the holy mountain."

With solemn promises to return for the Panchen Lama and the rest of the escaping Tibetans as soon as they could, Kane, Chan, Sam and Lobsang, along with the young monk named Jahm-Yang, left the safe house and returned to the truck. Five minutes later, they'd driven cautiously away from the settlement and entered what counted as the highway. They were soon speeding east, Kane's pulse pounding in his temples as the wheels flew over the gravelly surface.

Jahm-Yang rode in the back with Lobsang and Sam. Kane was up front with Chan. No words were spoken, and Kane assumed, like hm, they all were wondering what they might find at Mount Kailash, and his own mind drifted as he fought to keep his rage in check.

Glancing at Chan, he seemed especially focused. There was an air of urgency about the Chinese-American. Of course, he would be worried about Ridley, and Kane believed his guilt was genuine. But it was more than that. Kane thought Chan Lee wanted more than just to get Ridley back safely. He assumed Chan wanted something money couldn't buy: redemption.

It was inky-black along the narrow, deserted highway, but the road here ran long and straight. Kane hoped at some point soon they would catch sight of the rear lights of Kim's vehicle in the distance. It had been less than an hour since the Korean had kidnapped Ridley, but an hour was a long time when you're the chasing party. Their only option was to drive on as fast as safely possible through the night and rely on the young monk to guide them in the morning.

What they were doing constituted genuine danger, there was no escaping it, and Kane felt reluctant to take the others along. In fact, he believed it was so dangerous he had a sudden attack of conscience and demanded a surprised Chan to pull over on the side of the highway. Kane flicked on the interior light and looked around the inside.

"I have to tell you, where we're going will be very, very dangerous. I have no doubt the men that do this kind of thing are ruthless, organised criminals, and they will have many guards, probably armed and probably willing to kill. What I'm saying is... maybe I should go on alone."

"This is my mess," Chan said, "and I'm the one who has to fix it."

Kane looked harshly at Chan Lee, whose eyes filled with what appeared to be genuine concern.

Their eyes met, and Kane nodded. "Yes, this is your

mess, and I'll deal with what you've done later. The others shouldn't have to risk their lives." Kane turned to each of them in the vehicle, though he suspected what their reactions would be. There was no need to ask. He turned back to Chan.

"We don't have to time to sit here and discuss it," Chan stated. We're coming with you."

Chan threw the van into gear and accelerated back out onto the lonely highway and on with a journey would lead them into the shadow of Kailash, and with any luck, to recover their human quarry.

They drove on, largely in silence. Kane internally appraised his allies. Without looking, he thought about the monk, and somehow sensed Lobsang's shame. He had been with Ridley when Kim had burst into the room, and he surely regretted not being able to stop him. Kane had seen Kim watching them. He was a somewhat diminutive man, but Kane sensed Kim was wiry strong, and could move fast, and he didn't doubt that within seconds it had been all over. In turn, Lobsang wasn't strong, and Kane understood violence of any kind went against the basic founding philosophy of Buddhism so important to Tibetans. There really was nothing the monk, small in stature but big in heart, could have done.

Sam had tucked himself into the corner of his seat, and sat with his eyes closed, arms huddled around himself. Kane knew from his experiences with Ridley that cold turkey could roll in like waves, quiet moments, followed by fever dreams, then calm once more. He would need more time to fully recover and feel well again.

The only one among them who appeared unmoved by the drama seemed to be the new recruit, Jahm-Yang. Kane secretly stole a glance at him in the rearview mirror. He remained aloof as they drove, a distance likely borne from both shyness, Kane guessed, and also out of respect. The kid didn't really know what had transpired, other than the fact a woman had been taken. Kane felt guilty using him like this, but he had volunteered, and Kane knew there was zero no room for sentiment... Ridley was out there, and her life was almost certainly in danger.

Kane himself remained silent too, focusing his energy on Ridley's safe recovery. Only a few people in the world knew how he felt about Ridley. It wasn't only his friend and travel buddy Kim had kidnapped, but the only love of Kane's life. For many years Kane had had to contend with the fact Ridley wasn't the marrying type, and though she loved him in her own way, they had never become a genuine couple. It's not that she didn't love Kane. He knew she did. But she didn't seem able to open up to him the way Kane wanted. Unable, or unwilling? He wasn't sure. At very best, they were an on again-off again duo. While forever leaving Kane unfulfilled in love, he understood it was better than not having her around at all.

The reason they had travelled to India in the first place was to honour their friend Evan Craft. During those traumatic days in the Peruvian Andes, both Kane and Ridley, along with Evan, John O'nians and A J Waters, had nearly died. It had undoubtedly brought Kane and Ridley closer than they'd ever been. Kane had hoped that a rejuvenating trip to peaceful, spiritual India was exactly what they needed. He'd even assured Ridley he would not leave that beautiful country without sliding an engagement ring on her finger. She'd laughed and immediately agreed to go with him. However, due to other unforeseen circumstances, this trip had been delayed around eighteen months, and though when first planned Kane had believed he would at last get what he had for so long desired, he also feared that maybe he had missed his chance.

Now, she was gone.

Kane's anger was building up inside as every mile passed, and every minute took them onwards into dangers both known and unknown. Kane knew one thing for sure; he would do whatever it took to get his love back regardless of their status now or in the future.

Chapter Thirty-Two

Some twenty-five miles ahead of them, Do-Hyun Kim pushed the people carrier to its limits, the tyres screaming across that dusty, gravelled surface, the vibrations juddering his bones. He'd removed the bulbs from the rear lights to disguise the van from behind, and he knew the highway to Kailash so well he didn't need his headlights on at all. Not that they would encounter anything or anyone on such a deserted stretch of road. Besides, the sky was clear, and the road was visible beneath nothing more than a sliver of moon and a vast swathe of stars.

Tightly bound and gagged in the passenger seat beside him sat the Ridley woman. He hadn't covered her eyes though, and she stared at Kim with such hatred and intensity, it began to get under his skin. Because he had beaten and held a gun to the monk's head, she had offered little resistance when he'd tied her up. Kim knew a dangerous individual when he saw one, however. He would not take this one lightly, even though she was just a woman. The bitch's eyes continued glaring at him so intensely, it was as if she believed he might be the last thing she ever saw alive. Kim smiled, because he suspected it might just be true.

After another fifteen minutes her vitriol-fuelled stare so perturbed him that he pulled over and slapped her hard around the head. She didn't cry out, only stared back even more intently, if that were possible. He whacked her hard again, twice, this time opening a nasty gash above her left eye. Kim couldn't believe it.

Is that... are you smiling? The crazy bitch is fucking smiling, he realised. *Okay, I will wipe that smile from your face.*

He pulled the gun from between his legs and, carefully pressing it against her forehead, he slid the gag from her mouth. The cold grin that greeted him both shocked him and made his guts flutter. He would make it stop.

"Do you understand what they will do with you, once I sell you to them? No? Well, they are not good men. If you think I am cruel, think again. They are animals, these Chinese businessmen. You will become a slave of the worst kind." He paused, waiting for a reaction. Nothing, just coldness in those ice-blue eyes. He slapped her with an open hand, and then again for good measure. Again, nothing, not even a wince. She was a tough cookie, no doubt about it. He was just about to smash her with the butt of his pistol when she spoke.

"You know, Kim, you're pathetic. I've known children who hit harder than you. How about we fight, just you and me? Untie me, we step outside, and we fight. I'm not going to run away, am I? Come on... not scared of a woman, are you?"

There was nothing Kim wanted more, other than the red-blooded obvious, than to beat the will out of the bitch in front of him. However, damaged goods always fetched a smaller price at the market in Kailash. There could be no visible cuts or bruises. There was something else, though he would never admit it to anyone. He could barely admit it to himself, but Kim was a little afraid of her. There was something in her eyes that warned him he'd be better off just putting her to sleep rather than letting her talk him into something stupid. It was wise. She was obviously in good physical shape, and was an inch or two taller than him. Given fair chance, he assumed they were more or less a physical match. Kim re-gagged his prisoner, this time covering her glaring, smiling eyes with a scarf.

Kim drove on, but Ridley's head still faced him. He felt certain she was mentally staring at him. *Damn!* Do-Hyun Kim felt unnerved.

For reasons unbeknown to her, and despite her predicament, Ridley felt at ease. She sensed the cowardly prick was weary of her, and knew full well that, given even half a chance, she could kick his arse. She also felt she'd just been close to goading him into it. Ridley was nothing if not patient. She would bide her time.

She would remain on her guard and stay focused, conserving her energy as best she could. With these thoughts in mind, she finally turned away from the bastard, letting her eyes close beneath the scarf. Kane was coming, she knew that. He would do everything in his power to come to her aid.

But until then, she focused on only one, irrefutable fact: before this day was up, she, Alexandria Ridley, knew she would make Kim pay, and revenge would be hers.

Chapter Thirty-Three

"Where exactly are you from, Jahm-Yang?" asked Sam. "I mean, I know Tibet, but what is the village called?"

The three of them—Sam, Lobsang and Jahm-Yang—had been engaging in a little easy conversation. Jahm-Yang knew that his knowledge of the area might prove crucial in tracking down Kim and the woman whose name he'd learned was Ridley; he sensed the others trying to make him comfortable. He took a while to answer, but finally he did.

"My village is tiny. There are just three families. I have left behind my mother, and my two younger sisters," he muttered, as tears came unbidden into the young man's eyes. He was sad he'd left his family behind, but that only constituted half the truth. He owed his sadness to the shame he felt over his disappointment about missing his chance to leave, and it tore at his insides. His strict Buddhist training demanded complete disregard to self, yet there he was again, being selfish. He finally managed to compose himself, wiping a couple of stray tears from his eyes with his crimson robe sleeve. Sam gave him a moment then asked another question.

"How about your father, Jahm-Yang?"

There followed a long pause as a hint of anger rose in his chest. Finally, he said, "The Chinese security forces killed my father. They murdered him."

"Why?" asked Sam. "What did he do?"

"Nothing. They have banned us from displaying any national pride. My father walked home from the fields one afternoon, singing a song to himself, when two guards leaning on the barn out of sight surprised him and lashed at him with batons. He protested, of course. They beat him anyway, and continued to beat him until he—"

"It's okay, you don't need to say any more," said Sam.

Jahm-Yang sighed. "We learned this from a family friend, who witnessed it from too far away to do anything. They killed him for nothing... for singing a song. They left us to care for ourselves for a long time. Life in Tibet is getting harder and harder, and their rules are barbaric." He knew his anger was understandable. They had murdered his father, on his own property, just for singing a song.

Jahm-Yang could see that his story had affected them, and he wished he had more self-control. Sam looked at him with sadness in his eyes.

Lobsang, who hadn't said a word, leaned over and placed his hand on Jahm-Yang arm. He suspected the older monk had heard this kind of story too many times.

Jahm-Yang described his village and its location just a few miles from the foot of the mountain. It wasn't far from a small lake called Luowanggua Cuo, where the cattle grazed and watered, and the place where they'd struck down his father.

They halted for a short break on the verge of the highway. Sam relayed what he'd learned from the novice to Kane and Chan. Chan needed more information, and spoke gently to the monk. "Have you ever heard of any kind of trafficking activity in the area, or of a facility where this kind of thing might happen?"

The young man looked thoughtful for a minute. "No, I have not heard of that before, but it is true there could be a place where it happens. There are cave systems all over the eastern face of Kailash. I know there is a Chinese military camp somewhere that way. But I am not sure where."

The others—Kane, Sam, Lobsang and Chan—looked pointedly at one another, and Chan assumed they were all thinking the same thing. *It's there, but he's never seen it because it's in the shadow of Kailash.*

That proved all the motivation Chan needed, and at least they had a rough direction in which to look. Chan knew it meant leaving the main road; due to the terrain, they would probably need to leave the vehicle altogether. If they had to pursue Kim on foot, then that is what they would do.

They'd been speeding along the highway for several hours now and had covered more than half the distance to Kailash. It was early hours of the morning, and the clear, starry sky illuminated the road well. But Chan was tired, and although Kane offered to take the wheel Chan insisted it was better they stopped for a few hours. There was no way they could go off-road into the mountains in the dark, he said. They should wait until first light.

"No! It's better we go in the dark," Kane stated, which will make it more difficult for any guards to spot us approaching."

Kane had made a strong point, but Chan insisted. "Hiram, we don't know for sure if such a place even exists. It's simply too risky to wander blindly into the mountains. Surely you must agree?" Chan sympathised with him, understanding Kane's desperation to go after Ridley. Yet Chan knew he was right. It was dangerous. If they wound up lost, they themselves might perish. He pushed his point. "Imagine if we go off-road, if we get lost... we'd have no chance of finding your friend then. We must wait until morning. At first light, with Jahm-Yang's help we can make some discreet enquiries and go in cautiously on foot."

Chan watched as Kane hung his head, understanding Chan had spoken the truth. Chan understood he just wanted to go after Ridley. He at last acquiesced, and they all tried to get some rest in the uncomfortable van, if just for a few hours.

Sleep eluded Kane, his nerves completely on edge. Even though Chan had a point, it just wasn't in Kane's nature to wait. Kane had lost people before, his younger brother and best friend among them, and a horrible knot formed and twisted in the pit of his stomach from an inherent fear it was happening again. He wasn't sure he could take losing someone else he loved. It would be too many times.

First his great grandfather, Patrick Kane, himself an adventurer and the trusted assistant to legendary explorer and pioneer Hiram Bingham. Patrick had inspired both his grandfather's and his own love of travel and adventure, and the day he died was a dark day for all of them. Even worse than that was the day his younger brother Danny went missing, never to be seen again and presumed dead. Kane had carried the weight of that guilt around always, and understood it would forever haunt his dreams. Finally, there was the loss of Evan Craft.

He would not allow anything like that to happen to Ridley.

As the starry and moonlit sky illuminated the wide river valley on all sides, he sat on the bonnet of the van, itching to close the gap on Kim and to prevent what would be another unbearable tragedy. Kane was only forty-one, yet had already witnessed too much death and suffering for one man. He was sick of it.

He could not let it happen again.

He *would* not let it happen again.

Kane stood, willing the sun to rise. He wanted to approach the mountain of Kailash before the sun reached its zenith, and cast its malevolent shadow over the world.

In those three hours until the sun at last, reluctantly it seemed to Kane, appeared over the eastern horizon, he had to do battle with his own demons. Refusing to sleep, he instead went toe to toe with all the negativity from his past. The first nemesis he always faced was the guilt he felt about his brother Danny. Deep down he knew he wasn't to blame, but when all was dark and he was alone, those old emotions came back at him with a vengeance.

They were just kids, Hiram ten and Danny seven, when Danny went missing from the Old Rectory mansion near where they lived. They had never seen him since, a fact Kane's estranged father pinned on him like a painful scar the very day it happened. That also plagued Kane's conscience; the fact he and his father barely ever spoke. His mother had died in recent years too. All the events combined meant Kane's immediate family was fractured, at best. Those, and many other things haunted Kane's waking and sleeping hours, and it was all he could do to keep focused on the task ahead. Simply, save his friend and love, Alexandria Ridley, from whatever sinister fate Do-Hyun Kim had planned for her.

Chapter Thirty-Four

As the sun delivered its welcome first rays across the western Himalayas, Kim shoved Ridley through two low wooden doors into a tiny adobe dwelling. The shack butted directly up against a granite cliff face that towered hundreds of yards above them, angling away and out of sight.

Ridley's whole body felt stiff from being strapped in one position for the long ride east from Ngari. She couldn't see anything, due to the scarf over her eyes, but she soon smelled what was obviously an open wood fire. The sudden warmth of it made her realise how cold she was. Her blood circulation had been hampered due to the tight restraints around her wrists, arms, waist and legs. Now, as the blood flowed freely, she suffered painful pins and needles throughout her extremities. *At least I'm alive.* Ridley understood it could so easily be different. Trying to compose herself, she took a few slow, deep breaths and waited to see what would happen next.

To her surprise, the scarf covering her head was unceremoniously and without warning yanked off. Kim ushered her into a nearby plastic seat. Even more surprising was the fact she sat alongside three other women, all Caucasian, all probably in their early twenties. The women looked frightened and exhausted, but otherwise unharmed.

What is this place? she wondered, though deep down she believed she knew. The three other women were pretty, extremely, and for just a split second Ridley, at thirty-eight, felt flattered she was there with them in what was almost certainly a human trafficking operation. They were all probably destined for some filthy sex trade market. Glancing around the space she saw several men, Chinese, she guessed, and she surmised the girls' final destination was probably Beijing or Shanghai, perhaps Hong Kong.

She tried to look at those other girls, get their attention. However, all three looked only at their own feet, no doubt too scared to look up.

Ridley thought quickly. She guessed all four of them had arrived recently, and would be kept there throughout the day until it fell dark. They would then be transported further east, perhaps to a remote airstrip where they would then be flown to those cities. If that were true, she had approximately ten hours to free herself and the girls, and to kick the shit out of Kim and the other traffickers.

Of course, she expected Kane and the others to burst in through the door at any minute, but she couldn't count on it. Ridley was nothing if not resourceful, and was always confident in her own ability to make the best of things. She would give it a couple of hours, then try to make contact with the other girls. If Kane hadn't arrived by early afternoon, she would make all hell break loose in that small building where, for now, she and three other kidnapped women were prisoners awaiting a fate she didn't want to dwell upon and which she would allow to happen only over her dead body.

Chapter Thirty-Five

Kane and the others had awoken, now stretching the cold and cramps from their limbs. That is, except Jahm-Yang, who Kane spotted sitting cross-legged on a rock, eyes closed and facing east as if looking at some unseen place beyond the others' vision. The young novice was gazing at Mount Kailash, praying to the Lord Buddha, Kane assumed. He looked the personification of calm, yet inside Kane imagined his heart roiled in turmoil.

At Kane's urging they were soon once more flying east along the highway towards an unknown destiny. Five men rode in that van, yet Kane suspected all five were experiencing a range of differing emotions. The one thread that bound them together was the knowledge that humans did bad things to other humans. It was a simple fact, and if Charles Darwin were alive today he'd say it gave undeniable and irrefutable evidence of his so-called theory of evolution, which had in fact ceased being a theory a century and a half ago. Kane mused at how humans had seemingly become so smart and so independent they no longer cared for each other. In individual cases, humans still cared, he knew, but en masse the race of humans continued destroying each other all over the planet in what could only be described as evolution gone crazy. Darwin of course wasn't alive, but Kane, a man who held the long-deceased evolutionist in great esteem, knew he would surely be turning in his grave at what humanity had devolved into.

It was a little after seven, and the mountain shadows slowly shortened as the sun eased from behind its nightly hiding place. Chan, with Jahm-Yang's guidance, speculated they had about two hours left to drive until they reached the novice's home village, from where they would begin the search for some kind of hideout or structure at the foot of Kailash.

Kane stared straight ahead, willing the miles and the minutes to pass. He tried to imagine what they might find. Certainly, Kim couldn't be operating alone. Okay, so he'd snatched a woman, which a physically powerful man of zero morals could likely handle. But what next? There must be an ulterior motive. Money? Trade? Revenge? It could be any of those things, or most likely a combination thereof. Kane believed there had to be an operation in place, some way in which Kim could profit from kidnapping Ridley. Kane expected they would find other girls, wherever it was they were destined. The thought of what that might mean both chilled him and set a fire in his belly.

Human trafficking in Asia had become horrendously common, though to Kane's knowledge it remained more prevalent in southeast Asian countries, such as Thailand and Cambodia. Though certain it happened, he hadn't heard about it too often in eastern Asia, in countries like Korea, Japan and China. Then again there were thousands of wealthy Chinese businessmen these days, and he felt sure many of them had a taste for white-skinned western women.

Women like Ridley.

His jaw clenched and unclenched as the anger slowly grew, his teeth grinding as he focused on what he would do to Kim when he got his hands on him. That was, if Ridley hadn't dealt with him first. The one thing that kept him from going crazy in that moment was his absolute certainty that Ridley, given even just a glimmer of a chance, would kick the living shit out of Kim. After she'd done that, she'd make him swallow his own balls. She had always been a tough cookie, tougher than any man he'd ever met. Tougher even than himself. When cornered, she was a dangerous creature. Kane pitied any man on the receiving end of her wrath.

Two hours later, they slowed to a halt on a remote, dusty lane just south of the highway known as G219. Nothing more than a narrow, pot-holed strip of rock and dirt, it was the road that led to Jahm-Yang's hamlet and the lake he'd mentioned earlier. It was also the road that had led him to Ngari from where he'd hoped to gain his freedom. Seeing the area he had so recently fled brought upon him a fresh swelling of emotion and guilt. He was a young man, and yet young men here and Tibetans in general had witnessed so much suffering at the bloodied hands of the Chinese. It was once a normal thing to do, seeking a better life in new lands; now it was a means of survival. In the lucky ones who escaped, it became a constant source of guilt. Jahm-Yang was one of the lucky ones.

That is, if he ever made it clear of Chinese-occupied Tibet. It looked unlikely now, in light of the events of the last sixteen or so hours. In a way it was a good thing. He had never been that comfortable leaving his family behind, especially since his father had been killed. His mother had almost had to beg him to leave. She sat him down a few months previous and gave him a solemn lecture about his duty to his family.

"My son," she began in their native language, "you are a brave boy. I know why you want to stay, and I admire your courage. Your father would have been very proud of you, as would be all Tibetans if they knew of your sacrifice. But we are just a small, simple family. There are bigger and more important things than us. Tibet itself. You must leave, and you must fulfil your destiny to follow in our enlightened leader's footsteps. Young men like you are the only threat to China. Once you are gone, they will leave your sisters and I alone. Then one day, you will return, along with all the other brave young Tibetans. You will return to a free Tibet, a land prised from tyranny and restored to its former self at last. Tibet will be free, but it will only be free if brave young men like you continue to leave and continue learning about our spiritual nature and our peaceful, wonderful culture. Go, my son, and never look back. One day you won't need to, and we will embrace you all upon our return."

It had been an impassioned speech, and deep down, Jahm-Yang knew what his mother had said was true. In order to maintain Tibetan culture and tradition, young people simply had to leave. Because, those who didn't were being murdered one by one. Now he was back there, just a few days after leaving, and Jahm-Yang had changed. He no longer wished to leave, and he no longer wanted to feel selfish. He was back, and he would make things right. The world's press had revelled in the disturbing reports of Tibetan people self-immolating in protest about the Chinese occupation. It was wrong that it took such atrocious acts to make the world take notice. If that is what it took to highlight the atrocious occupation, then it was a just cause. And he, Jahm-Yang, was mentally preparing himself for such a glorious end. If nothing else, he would at least be free of the awful, crushing guilt he had been bearing these last five days, during his selfish and cowardly passage to India.

Chapter Thirty-Six

Chan spent a couple of minutes in quiet conversation with Jahm-Yang before calling them all together. To Kane, he looked energised and focused, as if he knew things were about to get dangerous. "Please, all of you listen, just for a moment. I know you must think the worst of me. I have done bad things in the recent past, and they undo all the noble things I originally set out to do. However, I ask for your understanding from now on. Jahm-Yang will show us into his village, where he will speak with some older members of his community. He says if there is such a place as that which we're looking for, then someone will know about it. If they do not, then it doesn't exist. We will meet his mother, and in his home we will take breakfast. Then we will find what we have come to find. I ask now for your trust. In return, I will do whatever it takes to right the many wrongs I have done against the people of Tibet."

It was a short and, Kane considered, a heartfelt speech, and having witnessed it Kane believed in Chan Lee's sincerity, and that he truly carried a burden of guilt. It seemed to

Kane that underneath the façade was an emotional man; a man determined to do the right thing. He understood that concept well. For many years Kane had been trying to make the world a better place. It was a determination that developed from a deep well of his own guilt, whether justified or not. In Chan's case it was certainly justified, but Kane sensed a kindred spirit among their unlikely rescue team that filled him with renewed confidence.

They left the vehicle partially hidden behind a seemingly derelict barn, and walked the last few hundred yards into the village alongside a slow-flowing stream. It couldn't have been more remote or idyllic. Kane soon warmed to the idea of such a pastoral, peaceful existence. In doing so he knew he was consciously blocking out the many atrocities that had happened there at the hands of the brutal Chinese regime, and subsequently, within him stirred a little hatred. But just for those placid few moments, while walking into the novice monk's village, he revelled in the silent solitude, fully aware he needed to make the most of it before the world got a little crazier.

Just a few minutes later, two young girls came running towards them from a nearby field, crying, "Cho, cho. Cho, cho." *Brother. Brother,* Kane guessed. They embraced Jahm-Yang, who seemed humbled, and brought tears to his eyes. They seemed delighted to see their big brother again so soon. They pulled him along, each girl clutching one of his hands, towards a tiny, humble adobe building not far down the lane, so Kane and the others followed along behind them.

"Amala," they cried. *Mother?* Before they reached the building a tiny lady, dressed in the native Tibetan clothes so familiar to anyone who has ever seen an episode of National Geographic, came limping out of the wooden doors. She looked towards the random group of family and foreigners rushing towards her. Kane smiled as within an instant she recognised her son, and stood there as if witnessing an apparition.

"Jahm-Yang, gnu net?"

"Rey, Amala. Yes, Mother, it is me," he answered, translating for his guests.

The prematurely-aged woman shed immediate tears of obvious joy and hugged her tall son before quickly barking a series of stern words at him. He turned to his new friends, and shrugged good-naturally in a manner that said, to the men from different places, 'Women, right?' None of them laughed, but Kane wanted to. It was the first light-hearted moment for too many hours.

Within twenty minutes all five of them were seated around a central fireplace and tucking into a traditional Tibetan breakfast of freshly made bread and some kind of noodle soup. They washed it down with the super-sweet tea favoured in Tibet, though Kane did his best to drink as little as possible, certain it was half full of the dreaded yak's milk. Lobsang noticed this and grinned at Kane, who felt certain the cheeky monk would blow his ruse and was relieved he didn't. Each man thanked their host with smiles and deep bows.

During the cooking, Jahm-Yang explained the situation to his mother, and she looked at the group gravely, clearly concerned. Through her son, she explained that she herself didn't know about any kind of place they might be looking for, but her old neighbour, Tenzin Choedrak, had lived and worked these lands for seventy out of his eighty-three years. If he didn't know about it, then it could not be there. She instructed the assembled group to wait around the fire, poured them all another round of yak's milk tea, and slipped out of the tiny house, dragging Jahm-Yang with her.

Not ten minutes later, she returned with the old man and led the group out into the open where he sat on an old log. With a stick, he slowly and carefully marked out a crude map in the dirt. The map showed the main highway they'd travelled east upon, and the lake that sparkled beneath the rising sun behind them. To the north side of the highway was an image of the thing that had dominated all their thoughts for the last dozen hours. There was no doubting its identity. Even in the simple stick drawing, Mount Kailash loomed menacingly over everything else.

It was strange, though, mused Kane. The mountain had been revered by millions of people for many thousands of years, according to Chan and backed up by Lobsang, and was only ever seen as a source of hope and spirituality and good for all. Yet now, in lieu of what might be happening unseen in the ancient folds of its foothills, Kane thought it it loomed rather than glowed. Looking up at it, craning his neck as he noticed it for the first time, it glowered at them, menacing rather than welcoming. The malevolence of the shady, corrupted people working at its base had infected the once holy mountain with the worst of humanity, diseasing the sanctity of it and changing the world forever.

The old man had, apparently, given very precise instructions to a location only an hour back from the highway. Jahm-Yang translated, and explained to the group that they'd find a small adobe building that from the outside looked like nothing at all, perhaps a shelter for a yak herder. However, inside, he said, lay a vast network of tunnels and caves that had long been occupied by the Chinese forces. He had no idea what they were used for nowadays, if anything, Jahm-yang explained, though Tenzin was adamant about what they would find if they followed his instructions.

When asked about how he knew of such a place, he replied with a glint in his eye, saying, "I wasn't always such an old man. I was a wide-eyed, adventurous kid too, once upon a time." It was a fun story, yet it ignited a fresh round of pain in Kane's heart, reminding him of the last time he and his brother ever went exploring together. They entered an old mansion, and one of them was never seen again. Thirty years later, the pain remained as raw as ever.

He didn't share it, but Kane felt an unholy chill creep through his soul, knowing as he thought he did that the ignoble actions of a few corrupt, callous men lie somewhere within a few miles of their position.

It was a holy mountain, but Kane was prepared if necessary to do very unholy things once he got there. He was not religious, but as he gazed up at the looming slopes of mighty Mount Kailash towering above them, he couldn't help but utter a silent prayer to any god he knew wasn't listening for a peaceful and death-free outcome to whatever happened in the next few hours.

Chapter Thirty-Seven

Kane had no idea who or what they would face if they actually found some kind of installation, and he knew they must all prepare for every conceivable outcome. The most likely of which Kane figured would be facing off against a gang of armed and dangerous men, whether military or otherwise.

Kane had often been told he was a natural-born leader, albeit a compliment he accepted reluctantly. It was true that in the real world he had led numerous expeditions all over the world. Mountains were his preferred playground, too, and Chan had willingly deferred to the more experienced man. It's not that Kane wanted power of any kind, but he had to admit he was good at what he did. Lives so often depended on the decisions he made, and he made them with safety always the first priority. On his last expedition official in Peru, lives had been lost and he would always feel responsible for that. Yet those young Quechuan boys did not die because of decisions Kane made. In fact, the opposite was true. Through his quick thinking and what others told him was bravery, he had saved more of them than could have been expected.

More recently, during trips in Bali and Japan, he had found himself in nefarious situations in which more lives had been lost. His was almost among them.

Kane was no stranger to death.

Here again he somehow found himself inadvertently charge of another group of men, some experienced in the mountains, others not so, but who were all willing to do the right thing. They would apparently follow Kane and take orders from him if necessary. Even the young monk Jahm-Yang, who still wore only his crimson robes, seemed transformed somehow, as if facing his own personal vendetta. His piety would never change, Kane suspected, but it seemed as if he'd decided he had to do something about the men who for so long now had been terrorising what had once been the most tranquil and peaceful place imaginable. He had actually mentioned as much to Kane in a quiet conversation on one of their short breaks on the road. If what they were heading to do would cost him his place by the Dalai Lama's side, he'd explained, so be it, but he was on a mission to do right. If, in some way, he got to exact some form of revenge on the men who had killed his father, then he would do so. Kane had questioned the young monk, knowing it went strictly against Buddhist teachings, but Jahm-Yang had told him in no uncertain terms that he was just a man, and men were fallible and always would be. Kane had to agree.

They numbered five initially, but when word spread that a woman had been kidnapped, possibly being held nearby, two local youths volunteered to join them. Kane was reluctant and firmly told them no. He already had enough people to worry about. But when one lad said he knew exactly the place they were searching for, Kane thought of Ridley and the reason they were going there, and relented, reluctantly agreeing they should come.

He split their number into two groups. In the first group would be himself, Chan Lee, Jahm-Yang and the older of the two new lads, Sonam, the boy who claimed he knew the way. In the other group, led by Lobsang, would be Sam and the younger brother, Noman.

The off-road trail, according to the old man's instructions and confirmed by the Sonam, snaked about a mile north of the highway, and followed a small stream with a rocky path to its eastern bank. Across the stream was an old sheep and yak path that, while manageable by humans, was a little more treacherous, though it offered greater stealth. Kane would lead the first group up the eastern flank, with Lobsang's group following the animal path and hanging back a little.

They didn't have any weapons; Kane hoped beyond hope they wouldn't need any. What they did have were heavy, solid sticks that the new guys had grabbed from their nearby homes; these cudgels were what they used to shepherd their modest herd of yaks. They'd give someone a nasty bruise if connecting with bony heads. Kane gathered them around.

"We have only one objective, and that is to get our friend Alex back," he said, as Lobsang translated for the village boys. "We can't be sure she's even up there. However, in my gut I believe she is. So we'll try to surprise whoever's holding her and rescue her without violence. This man Kim, and the guys who are likely holding her, are almost certainly armed and dangerous. You must be careful." He looked at each of them, holding their gazes for a second or two each. "But, if things get messy... do what you need to do. They are criminals, and they are doing bad things to good people. To your people," he said, looking at each the Tibetans again one by one, then glancing at Sam and Chan.

In all their eyes he saw they were ready. His gaze lingered on Chan, who was ultimately responsible for them being there in the first place. Yet, he also saw a new man standing before him; he was not the slimy criminal he'd first met in Little Lhasa, but a brave man seemingly desperate to atone for his many mistakes, his heart now in the right place. Kane trusted him not to let them down. Sam, the young German who'd hardly said a word since they'd met him, also seemed resolute to make this right. Kane discreetly felt Sam believed he owed himself and Ridley for what they'd done for him. To them it was nothing more than to show him a little kindness; to him they just might have saved his life. He now had a chance to help save hers, while perhaps restoring a little pride to his beaten-up soul.

As for Jahm-Yang, the timid novice, well, he too seemed transformed. He exuded a calm persona, but in his eyes, Kane sensed a fire had been lit. His face was now set with hard determination. With his six feet of height and the shoulders of a farmer, he looked more like a warrior monk than a mere novice. Kane didn't want this to be about revenge, yet he'd needed Jahm-Yang to get to this point, and if his motives were now a little selfish, then Kane could deal with it. After all, the Chinese, who were almost certainly involved in this, had killed his father and made the lives of the local Tibetans one of constant and long-suffered fear. They deserved punishment for their actions. It looked for all the world that Jahm-Yang was a man preparing to do it.

As for the new lads, in their late teens, Kane guessed, well, if he was being honest, they looked like two kids who wanted an adventure, more out of boredom than any righteousness. There seemed to be little in the way of entertainment around here, and although their intentions were apparently noble, Kane believed they were mainly in it for the fun. They wouldn't have met too many foreigners either except for the invading Chinese, so it represented a rare opportunity to see some action, and they didn't want to miss out.

He did notice them acting a little wide-eyed and fidgety, almost over-eager to get going. Kane hadn't much experience with drugs himself—he'd never done anything other than smoke the odd joint when a lot younger—but if he wasn't mistaken these boys looked to be high on drugs right now. Of course, they weren't. He doubted a couple of young farm hands would even have access to them. They were so remote here that they might have never left the tiny hamlet before. *No*, he reassessed... *probably just bored out of their minds and excited for some action.*

Now Kane was certain they were all ready. With a last check of his own readiness and a silent prayer—or whatever it was when you didn't believe in such things—to his grand- and great-grandfathers, and to his brother Danny, he took a deep breath, then led them away from the tiny village and deep into the shadow of Kailash.

Sonam waited until the others moved away, let himself fall behind them by a few yards, then ducked behind a clump of bushes. He pulled a mobile phone from his pocket and made a quick call.

Less than thirty seconds later he fell into stride at the back of the group, and ignored the curious look his brother gave him.

The Chinese guard took the ringing mobile phone from his pocket and checked the caller ID. He threw his cigarette onto the ground and stamped it out, then answered and listened to the speaker for a few seconds. He inhaled and without saying anything, ended the call and lit another cigarette. He then placed a call of his own.

"Tell the boss at the market to prepare the guards," he said in his native Mandarin. "We're going to have company."

Chapter Thirty-Eight

Ridley hadn't seen a guard for more than two hours, but had heard them close by. They had pulled her blindfold back down over her eyes, and she remained gagged. However, she wasn't especially uncomfortable and they hadn't hurt her. Yet. From what she could make out, it was only herself and the three other women in the room.

She'd heard several people coming and going, all speaking in what sounded some dialect of Chinese, though she didn't know which. She also figured there must be a second doorway that didn't lead back outside, but which led further into whatever structure they now held them in. From the acoustics, she believed she was surrounded by stone walls, almost like a cave, and surmised they were probably underground. Even though she wore a blindfold, she sensed darkness, felt it closing in.

Ridley guessed the time to be around mid-morning, maybe ten, and she still had a few hours to wait before she felt she had to make her move. What that move might be, she hadn't yet worked out. But it was coming. They had her strapped to the chair with what she felt were old-style bungee cables, the kind her dad used to strap suitcases to the roof. It caused her mind to wander a little, a welcome distraction, if only for a few minutes.

When they went on road trips to the south coast of England, they would drive down from their home in the village of Hebden Bridge in Yorkshire during the school summer holidays, where they would spend a week at one campsite or another. Those were carefree holidays, spent mostly on beaches and swimming in the sea, or walking in the woods and building dens.

Yet it was the road trip itself that Ridley remembered most fondly. In those days the family car was an old Austin Allegro estate, as ugly as any car ever built though as comfy as a bed for a young kid. They would fold the back seats forward and the young Alexandria was free to spread out in her sleeping bag, almost as if she had her very own double bed. They drove down in the middle of the night in order to arrive early the next day and make the most of her father's one week holiday from the university. Thus, they flew through the darkness of night and Ridley remembered lying in the back of the car and looking out the windows as the stars flashed by in her very own private space show. She didn't have many memories of her parents, as they died in an accident when she was just eleven years old. However, the memories she did carry with her were good ones; she knew they had given her as perfect and happy a childhood as any kid could have dreamed of. Exotic, too, having spent half of those formative years in her father's native Egypt, in Alexandria, after which she had been named.

Her lips curled in a wry smile, stifled as it was by the gag and blindfold, thinking about her most recent road trip, bound and gagged at the hands of a hostile lunatic. Ridley knew that in years to come, the only memories she would have of him were the ones when she kicked his arse all over this damn cave.

The only other noises she heard were the distant, restricted cries of the other girls being held. Ridley was tough, and unafraid of anything. The others, however, were probably not like her, and were understandably terrified of what might happen to them. She had to help. Ridley was a resourceful woman; she had the skills necessary to not only survive this ordeal, but to make whoever was behind it pay for what they were doing.

Wriggling her hands around behind her, she felt the bungee cords stretch out. That was their purpose, of course, though she sensed these to be past their best. They would eventually give way altogether. She just needed to get one hand free. The rest would be easy. She still expected Kane and whatever cavalry he might have been able to muster to arrive at any moment, but she was a fiercely independent woman who would never rely on anyone, no matter how much she trusted them... how much she loved them.

Kane. He deserved better than her, she knew that. She had in one way or another been stringing him along ever since they'd met some twenty years ago, but as yet, had not been able to bring herself to go all in with him as he wanted to with her. She knew why. At least she thought she did.

Perhaps after this is over I could...

Ridley stopped herself, annoyed she'd let her mind drift to things that right now were not important. Two hours. That's how long she would wait for him. In the meantime, she would get her hands free in preparation while keeping them hidden behind her. It didn't seem that risky. She could clearly make out the men in the next room. In the echoing, cave-like structure she would hear their heavy boots approaching the interior door, which meant she'd always have a few seconds' grace in which to conceal her escape efforts.

Just as she'd thought this, she heard what she believed to be the thudding footfalls of two men approaching that door. Seconds later she heard the hinges protest and the men's gruff voices sounded in the room. Suddenly someone ripped off her blindfold. Standing before her was Kim with another man, a big, ugly military-type with a fat, yet hardened face, cheeks red from exertion or alcohol, likely both. Both men stared at her as if she were nothing more than a slab of beef, and they looked hungry. They then ripped off the hoods of the other three women, who shrieked in obvious fear yet kept their heads bowed.

Ridley looked at the women, desperately trying to get their attention, yet not one of them looked up. She saw their faces well enough, though, and her worst fears now seemed to be true. She didn't really believe it herself, but Ridley knew people considered her pretty, sexy even. She had always been popular with the men, a fact about which Kane constantly teased her. *There's just no accounting for taste*, she often told him and now mused internally. If it were true, added to the fact that the three girls nearby were undeniably beautiful young women, she understood for certain now exactly what this was: a market, where the only goods on sale were the women themselves.

The large Chinese soldier continued leering at them for long, uncomfortable moments. Ridley could only imagine the scene playing out in his depraved mind. She mentally shuddered, while keeping her composure.

"Look at me!" he suddenly barked in English, making all the other girls jump, and their tears fall anew. "You will look at me, or I will introduce you to my friend." He smiled, a thin, wicked smile, and slowly raised the knife he'd been holding by his side. He stepped forward, and lifted the young woman on end's head. She started crying, though Ridley sensed she fought desperately to hold in the tears. Then her nose started to run, and the girl, for that's the age Ridley believed she was, was now on the verge of hysterics. "You are very pretty... for a white girl. Don't you want to stay pretty?" He spoke in a quiet, calm voice, though Ridley sensed an unmistakable trace of disdain within it. "Those eyes," he said, "would you not like to keep them?"

The poor girl, whose blonde hair and bright blue eyes suggested a Scandinavian origin, burst into torrents of tears, which set off the same in the other two.

Only Ridley remained in control, resisting the burgeoning urge to rip off her bindings and then rip off the heads of the cowardly men in front of her. *Patience*, she said in her mind and exhaled slowly through gritted teeth. She understood she shouldn't antagonise the men, and guessed that if she played along with the situation and stayed compliant, within reason, they would probably not harm her further.

She could do that. She would play their game.

For now.

Until she wouldn't play it anymore.

It took another ten minutes, but eventually the other women calmed down and did as they were told. Once the tears stopped flowing, a guard ordered them to sit still and keep their heads up. After another minute, the outer door opened, and bright mountain light flooded the room, temporarily blinding the girls. Four men traipsed in, followed by an icy blast of frigid Himalayan air, and sat down on a row of seats opposite the girls. Ridley realised without question she had been right.

They were for sale, and these bastard men were the shoppers.

Chapter Thirty-Nine

The Chinese man ushered Kim into the inner area beyond the door behind Ridley. A minute later he returned with two others, one man and a mean-looking woman. Ridley guessed these were the sellers, the owners of the goods sat before them that Kim and others delivered. The new men started questioning the Chinese man and woman, though she could only speculate on what they were saying. Ridley guessed them all to be of Chinese origin, probably high-ranking military types though dressed in civilian clothes. Maybe the woman wasn't military. She obviously held power though, and it seemed a fair amount of respect among the others, too.

Ridley also didn't believe these would be straight cash transactions. Rather, she guessed they were about to be bartered for goods of another kind. Ridley's best guess was based on the strategic route between the Chinese cities to the east, and the fact China was now actively selling weapons and arms to Islamic groups to the west. This deal was probably an arms trade, pure and simple.

Women for weapons.

The notion sickened her. On one hand, the women would surely be forced into prostitution or sexual slavery in someplace like Hong Kong or Shanghai. On the other hand, the weapons exchanged for the girls would find their way into Islamic terrorist cells in Syria and Pakistan.

This was huge. They—meaning herself, Kane and the others—had a chance not only to bring down a horrible drugs ring, but also a human trafficking operation and an illegal terrorist arms trade. *So much for a relaxing, spiritual break in north India.* Despite herself, Ridley almost cracked up laughing. She had always wanted an adventurous life; since she met Kane she'd had enough adventures to last many lifetimes. Do-Hyun Kim didn't miss her smile.

"You think this is funny?" he asked in his thick, accented English. His eyes formed the narrowest of scowls. "I assure you, it is not."

Ridley stopped smiling, externally at least. She didn't think the situation was funny at all. The man made her skin crawl. Though she wasn't afraid for herself, she was concerned for the others girls' safety and she had to bite her tongue, aching as it was to fire a volley of ripe verbal abuse his way.

"No, Mr. Kim. This isn't funny. We're just scared, that's all." Ridley hung her head to feign her subservience.

"Good," replied Kim. "You should be afraid."

After a few more minutes, and some heated discussion between the seven men and one woman in the room, they hauled the girls to their feet and marched them through the inner doors into a bigger, more spacious cave. Once her eyes adjusted, it amazed Ridley to see the cave stretching far out before her. There seemed to be many other caves adjoining it on all sides. It appeared to be a complex network, and she was as impressed as she was surprised.

In contrast to the sprawling Tibetan Himalayas, to Ridley this cave system still seemed small and remote enough that it would be easy to keep hidden from the rest of the world. All sorts of shady transactions could, and probably always had, taken place within these ancient walls.

The women were marched another fifty yards into the growing darkness, and then split up; Ridley was paired with the Scandinavian. Each pair was then shoved into two smaller caves on opposite sides of a wide tunnel. Their captors forced the women to sit, and then had their blindfolds unceremoniously shoved back on. It didn't seem to matter that there was nothing to see; Ridley understood the blindfolds were merely a tool to keep them in fear and to prevent them from communicating with each other. The men stuffed the gags back in too. Then the traffickers left them alone. Heavy doors swung closed with a metallic clunk, shrouding the women in complete darkness.

Ridley only heard two noises: the sound of her own thumping heart and the soft whimpering of the other girl, obviously beside herself with fear. Ridley knew she had to talk to her. After a few minutes of relentless stretching, where her yoga and tae-kwon-do skills came in more than useful, Ridley had managed to free one of her hands from the weakened bungee cord. Her second hand soon followed, and she relished the immediate relief it gave to her swollen wrists. Listening intently, she tried to figure out if there were any footsteps nearby. Satisfied there were not, she slowly lifted her blindfold.

The darkness was absolute, so she waited a few minutes until her eyes had adjusted somewhat to the stygian darkness of the cave. Finally, her pupils dilated enough to take in their surroundings. They were sat on a natural rock seat against a cave wall; the floor was also rock. The cave room was small, barely six feet square, with a slightly higher ceiling under which most adults could comfortably stand up. The sturdy-looking wood and metal doors were the only manmade thing in the room, other than a naked light bulb hanging above. It was off.

She looked at the girl beside her. The whimpering had abated somewhat; now Ridley heard her sniffling gently, as if after a long cry.

It was time to make contact.

Chapter Forty

Beyond the cave structure, Kane and his group had made steady progress along the stream's edge. If it weren't for the fact they were trying to locate a kidnapped woman—probably many women—the scene couldn't have been more beautiful. The stream trickled merrily under the ever-present force of gravity, where it would eventually run into the Senge Zangbu, part of the Indus Valley River system. All around them wild flowers clung to rocks and lined their path. In every direction, towering mountains loomed large, and directly above them, stretching out of their line of sight, Mount Kailash shrouded them in perpetual shadow. Due to its position, the sun rarely penetrated the narrow valley they now traversed, and Kim's words were ringing true to Kane:

"... never be seen in the shadow of Kailash."

It was an enigmatic sentence. Now Kane fully understood why it had sounded so ominous. Yet he would not be dissuaded. They'd been walking close to an hour, and according to the young Tibetan, Sonam, in ten more minutes they would reach the entrance to the caves.

Kane stopped for a moment, looking across the narrow open space to the other side. He couldn't see Lobsang at first; however, a moment later his new friend briefly showed himself with a wave of a scarf. They'd agreed it was best if the other group remained out of sight, only occasionally letting Kane know they were close by. Once at the cave, they would scan the scene. If the stream were easily navigable, then they would remain across the other side until needed; hopefully that moment wouldn't arrive. If it were more difficult, they would come across the stream before they entered the caves and form into one group.

Kane pushed on, slower now, and trying to keep as quiet as possible. He had no idea if there would be guards or not; he hoped the latter. It was so remote here it was doubtful they ever needed guards. The Chinese in Tibet were arrogant. Kane hoped it would be their undoing; he didn't just mean now. He meant it in the bigger picture of their occupation of Tibet.

They were simply doing whatever they wanted, despite the fact the world's news cameras were there, recording acts of violence against innocent Tibetans, and even more often, against protesting monks. Eventually, Kane thought, the world's leaders had to do something. The best thing to do would be to block trade with China unless they pulled out of Tibet. Everyone knew that, yet it was China's unbridled arrogance that prevented other nations from doing so. *One day*, Kane thought, *the world will finally get behind His Holiness, and demand the Tibetans once more be set free.* The Dalai Lama could then safely return to the Potala Palace in Lhasa, where Tibetan rulers had governed peacefully for hundreds of years. Right now that seemed as if it would never happen, not in Kane's lifetime... not even in the lives of the young Tibetans with him now. His heart went out to the hundreds of thousands of suffering Tibetans, both here in their homeland and abroad, where they'd had to flee for their lives.

Once this was all over, Kane swore he would do what he could to raise more awareness for the people of this magical and once blissful land. For now, he refocused all his energy and attention on the task at hand: the emancipation of Alexandria Ridley.

Chapter Forty-One

At his desk within the security room in the cave complex of Mount Kailash, the Chinese guard hung up the phone and turned his attention to the bank of monitors on the wall, focusing on one in particular. The view was of outside the only entrance into the system, provided by a discreet camera hidden high up above the small door and attached to the rockface. Using the mouse on his desk, he clicked to the controls of that camera and zoomed in. As he'd just been told, there outside and approaching the entrance were a group of men and a child.

"Good boy, Sonam," me muttered. "Good boy."

There it was. A tiny, barely visible wooden door, just as the old man had told them it would be, and just as the young Tibetan farmer had confirmed. Kane wasn't sure why, but it surprised him. He hadn't doubted the old man, nor the kid; rather, it was the opposite. Kane doubted Tibetans even knew how to lie, especially the Buddhists among them, which was, by default, all of them. No, it was far simpler than that.

Kane realised he was in denial.

He just didn't want to accept that people might be capable of taking other people against their will. His people. It was naïve, of course. People had been doing terrible things to one another for many thousands of years, and they probably always would. Yet, Kane refused to believe most people were bad. Instead, he put his faith in the innate goodness of humans, even though his recent experiences, both here, in Bali, Japan and in Peru, among other places, had done their best—and worst—to convince him otherwise.

Whatever Kane did or didn't believe mattered little right now. The fact was, some cold-hearted scumbag had kidnapped the love of his life and was likely holding her captive somewhere inside that mountain.

He looked around at the three men with him: Chan Lee, Jahm-Yang and Sonam. They looked determined, ready to face whatever came their way. Kane had no better plan than to just throw open the door and charge in. He was about to signal them towards it when he heard the screeching of ancient, overused hinges, then watched in horror as the door began creaking open. Before he realised what was happening, Chan grabbed the others and pulled them over a low bank to the stream's edge. In three seconds, the four men were out of sight of the door just as two men emerged from it. From their position below the bank, with a few bushes and a patch of tall grass in front of them, Kane felt sure they'd remain unseen. That was good, because each of the big Chinese security men had a gun holstered at his waist on one side and a baton clipped on the other.

Kane's team all held their breaths and waited in silence;

the only sounds were the gentle gurgling of the stream and the guards' conversation. Kane understood nothing they said, and doubted any of the Tibetans could either. Chan spoke decent Chinese, he'd explained earlier, but had added he was rusty. But when the taller of the two guards said 'English girl', Kane understood that and his growing anger ratcheted up at least three notches. Still, the two men had guns, and he willed himself into stillness and silence.

The guards surprised them by turning away from the door in the opposite direction, but to where, Kane couldn't know. How long they'd be gone was also something he daren't second guess. What he did know was that, however many guys waited through that door, it was now two fewer.

Kane had nothing more to think about or wait for. This was it. It was time to go in.

Looking at the girl next to her, Ridley saw she wasn't gagged. Small mercy. "Hello," Ridley said, barely above a whisper. "My name is Alex. Can you hear me?"

The girl didn't say a word, but flinched, showing Ridley she had.

"Do you speak English? Nod if you do."

The girl gave a gentle nod.

"Good. That's good. My name is Alex, what's yours?"

After a long pause, the girl answered. "Linn... hello." A definite waver in her voice revealed her terror. It was understandable.

"Hi Linn. Where are you from? May I guess... Norway?"

"Yes, Norway. My town is near Oslo. Are you English?"

"Yes, I'm English. More or less. Listen, Linn... how're

you doing? I mean, I know you're scared, and I'm scared too," Ridley lied.

"I am so scared, Alex. What are they going to do with us?" Her voice went up a notch as the panic returned. Ridley had to pacify her quickly.

"It's okay, Linn. I'm going to take off your blindfold. Don't worry, we're safe for the moment."

The girl's breathing slowed again, and her shoulders relaxed, if only a little. "That's good, Linn. Okay, I'm moving to you now. It's dark. Ready?"

She nodded. Ridley stood, and gently raised Linn's blindfold. Her eyes were still screwed tight shut, as if not daring to open them. Slowly, the eyelids peeled away from her eyes and she blinked several times.

"There, you see? It's only me and you. You're safe for now."

"Thank you. Where are we?"

"We're in some kind of cave system, I think. This is the situation, and I'm afraid it's not good. I think... I think we are going to be sold or traded to some terrible people. I believe they're Chinese. Probably a trade, and my guess is for weapons. Do you know the other two girls?"

Linn slowly shook her head. "I don't, but I heard them whispering together. They are from France, or maybe Belgium, but they spoke French. Maybe sisters?"

"Okay, that's good. They won't be as scared together." Ridley considered something sinister too; that two young French sisters would be very desirable to some ruthless, callous purchasers, and that this could all end so badly for all of them. "Okay, listen carefully Linn. I have friends who will come looking for me... I expect they will be here soon. In case they are not, however, we need to escape by ourselves. I have my hands free, and I'll untie you. First, I'll try to get out of this room and survey the situation, while you stay here. If the guards come back, pretend you're still tied up."

"No, don't leave me, please."

"Sshh, it's okay, Linn. Please, we need to whisper or they'll hear us."

Linn swallowed hard, and tears slid down her puffy cheeks. Ridley moved quickly to untie her so she might wipe her own eyes. In a few seconds, Linn nodded she was okay.

"Okay, I need to scan outside, work out where we are and check where the guards are. I'll only be gone a few minutes. If it's safe I'll come and get you. Then we'll go to the sisters and untie them." Ridley placed her hands calmly on Linn's shoulders and met her gaze. "Why don't we get the hell out of this shit hole?" Ridley smiled, and Linn stared at her in what seemed to be awe.

"What are you, military or something?" she asked, a tiny smile creeping onto her lips.

"Ha. No, not military, but I am a badass bitch when I need to be, and I fully intend to kick the arse of the slime ball who took me all over this damned mountain! You just watch me."

The look in Linn's eyes at that moment suggested she fully believed Ridley would.

"Okay, put your hands back behind you, and keep them there. I will put the blindfold back on, okay?"

Linn took a deep breath and nodded her assent.

"At least if I'm caught, it will look like it's only me, okay?" Again, Linn nodded.

Ridley moved to the door, and with her head hard up against it, she listened. Nothing. "It's clear outside. Stay calm, okay, and I'll be back soon. How old are you, Linn?"

"Nineteen."

Ridley swallowed down her rage and exhaled through her nose. "Nineteen, huh? Well stay brave, kiddo, and we'll be out of here in no time."

Chapter Forty-Two

"Okay, on my signal," said Kane. With his hand extended so all could see, he silently counted down from five. Four... Three... Two...

He never got to One. Jahm-Yang ran to the door, yanked it open and a second later had disappeared inside.

"Shit!" blurted Kane, and leapt up and raced after the novice monk, no idea what he'd find beyond the door.

He needn't have worried. They'd entered a small cave room, and found nobody inside; only a few empty seats lined up along the left side stone wall, with a long wooden bench on the opposite side. At the back of the room was another door, though it was closed and locked from the outside. Kane exhaled through gritted teeth, anger and frustration notching up another level. He turned to confer with Chan about what to do, when a horrific noise froze him solid.

Evidently, Jahm-Yang was on a mission. Before Kane could react, he had grabbed a loose rock from the floor and smashed the padlock off with one hefty strike. The echo chilled Kane to his core, and he fully expected a swarm of well-armed Chinese security to burst through at them, shooting first and asking questions later. Once more, Kane was surprised. *No one was there. Is that it? Only two guards... and they've left?* He didn't believe it, and he looked at Chan, whose face wore an angry expression.

Chan grabbed the young monk by his robes and wheeled him around to face him. "Listen here... you may have a death wish, but if you get us all killed how can we help anyone?"

The young novice merely glared at him, and for a moment it looked as if the monk might strike him. He didn't, but with strong arms he eased Chan away from him, who breathed deeply, seemingly trying to compose himself. He stepped back, nodded, and, as if to say 'okay', then spread his hands in the universal gesture of 'calm down', and smiled.

Kane watched on as the monk nodded and closed his eyes for a few seconds, as if trying himself to keep calm, then offered the hint of a smile too. The other young Tibetan, Sonam, was the calmest of them all; in fact, he almost seemed to be having fun. He didn't speak any English or, it seemed, Chinese, Kane thought he appeared to understand all that was happening. Sonam pointed through the door, as if to confirm it was the correct way, and smiled. *The kid really does know these caves*, mused Kane, unease starting to prickle his senses.

Chapter Forty-Three

Ridley stepped out into the dimly lit stone passage way and made just three quiet steps to her right when a sudden loud bang echoed throughout the cave system. It took only a second for her to reach a conclusion: *Kane!* At least she hoped it was Kane, and if it wasn't... then, *What the hell was it?* All fell quiet again. She knew if there were still guards around they'd have heard that bang and would soon come running to investigate.

Rather than turn around, it only inspired her to push on further, edging along the passage she believed was taking her deeper into the cave complex. She hoped to find a room full of guards with a door. And a lock. She would turn the key, lock the guards inside, and all the girls would live happily ever after. She dismissed thoughts of starting a little fire in the room first, immediately admonishing herself for being as fucked up as they were.

"Come on Alex," she whispered into the gloom, "you're not like them," though sometimes she questioned that.

Crossing the widening passage, she edged towards

where she guessed the sisters were being held. She paused at the closed door to listen and heard only the now familiar sound of a young woman sobbing. *Just one?* Ridley swiftly opened the door and stepped into the room. There was only one girl. After Ridley had closed the door behind her, the girl tried to scream and strained against her bonds, clearly expecting Ridley to be one of the bad guys, her obvious fear making her desperate.

"It's okay," Ridley whispered, "I'm not one of the men. My name's Alex. I am here to help you." The girl stopped struggling as fiercely and fell quiet. "Please listen. I will remove your gag and blindfold. Please don't scream. Nod if you agree."

The girl nodded quickly, and Ridley stepped forward to remove the gag. The girl sucked in some deep breaths as Ridley removed the blindfold. Beneath the mask Ridley saw another young woman of around twenty, clearly traumatised but pleased to see a friendly face. "Comment-t'apelle tu?" Ridley asked in her passable French. *What's your name?*

"Madeleine," the girl replied, tears streaming from wide green eyes. "Mon souer?" she said. *My sister?*

"I don't know," replied Ridley, "but I will find her." She stepped back to appraise the girl. She was young, and very pretty. They were all pretty. Ridley was just about to ask her a couple more questions when a look of sheer terror infiltrated Madeleine's delicate features. As Ridley turned to see who or what was there, someone struck her with a blunt instrument and all the world went black.

Chapter Forty-Four

"What the fu...?" Kane blurted.

They all heard the agonised screams coming from deep within the cave complex. Somehow, it seemed even louder than Jahm-Yang's rock smashing the lock. *Well, anyone alive in these caves heard that,* Kane thought, as the screams echoed loudly enough to wake the ghosts from a thousand years past. With a quick look at the others, he said, "Let's go!" his anger now complemented with a healthy dose of fear.

They surged into the cave system, relying on a string of naked bulbs to light their way. *This place is vast,* Kane mused as they moved inside, fully expecting them to be attacked any moment. Still no one came. They moved on, deeper into the darkness. *There have to be guards here, but where are they?* They paused at a point when the main passage opened wider, perhaps fifteen feet across, unsure how to proceed. Kane was certain now that Ridley was here. Though that scream was not hers, he felt sure. That meant at least one other girl was here, probably more. *There might be dozens being held against their will.* But where?

Chan suggested they split up as the passages arced out in several directions. Kane would go with the young farmer; Chan would stay with Jahm-Yang. They wished each other luck, then moved off quietly in their new directions.

Still hidden across the stream, Lobsang fidgeted with impatience. Only ten minutes had passed since Kane led the others inside, yet the aged monk didn't imagine the inside to be very big and he wondered what had happened. *Ten more minutes*, he thought, *then we go in.*

Sam too seemed restless. Lobsang sensed his urgency, and admired his conviction to help. He put a gentle hand on Sam's shoulder and smiled, appealing for just a little more patience, certain their time would come.

As for the young Tibetan kid, Noman, to Lobsang he looked as if he were on a picnic, and as he leaned back against a rock, a long blade of grass wedged into the corner of his mouth, he couldn't have appeared more relaxed. Under the circumstances, Lobsang thought Noman was enjoying himself a little too much.

Kim quickly subdued the screaming girl and turned his attentions to the stricken Ridley. "Thought you could beat me, did you? Stupid bitch," he growled, and spat on the floor. He would make her pay for that. First, he had other business to attend to. He dragged Ridley's prone form to a corner of the cave room and slid open a barely visible door built into the sheer rock wall. It was so discreet, if one didn't know of it a person might never find it, especially in the dim light. Kim ducked and stepped into what could only be described as a walk-in arsenal.

Wall-to-wall sat weapons of every kind, including heavy duty, military grade stuff. Beneath one of the shelves was a deep recess. Kim stepped out again, then dragged Ridley's body into the recess. Satisfied she was still unconscious, he turned to leave. As an afterthought, he spun back around and kicked her hard in the stomach, just for good measure. Muttering to himself about stupid fucking women, he locked the sliding door behind him and checked the bindings of the remaining sister. Confirming she was secure and silenced, he turned off the light and locked that door behind him too. Kim entered the passage way, removed his boots and moved stealthily back into the main cave, now more than ever ready for action.

Edging towards the cave Kim spotted a shadowy movement, and realised it was three of the Chinese security guys ducking behind a natural rock wall. Good. Like him, he assumed they wanted to keep the element of surprise, and allow the foreigners to make their way right to the main chamber. That central chamber was the most open area of the entire complex. In its centre was a natural well, a bottomless shaft into which glacier water ran from deep within Kailash. If anyone were to fall into that crevasse, Kim knew his or her inevitable death would be slow and icy. There could be no escape. It seemed to Kim as if he'd come to the same conclusion as the guards. By offering no resistance, eventually the invaders would find themselves at the main chamber, first tricked, and now trapped. Kim grinned. They would never see the light of day again.

After a conversation with Kim, who'd told them what he knew of Kane and the others—that they were not dangerous, but could cause them some problems—the head of the

Chinese security team decided to be proactive. Their assets were too valuable to risk anything happening to them. It was not only his lucrative job on the line, but likely his neck.

Thus, before the intruders had even made it as far as the first cave, he'd ordered the guards to swiftly and efficiently round up the assets, who were soon being ushered at gunpoint into the rear of the main chamber, where they could be more effectively monitored.

Seventeen girls huddled there in total, all traumatised and weak from lack of sleep and food. Some of them had been held there for more than a week. It was a vast operation, and the trade in both girls and guns was very lucrative for both sides. In collaboration with The Vulture, the Indian supplier based out of Mumbai, they'd been operating out of the Kailash Caves for several years and had now become the biggest supplier of girls to the Chinese sex industry anywhere in Asia.

It was a insanely successful business. China massproduced weapons which were highly prized by many Islamist militant groups all over Asia and Africa. These customers found supply from other sources had become more difficult and increasingly risky. Just as in almost all other industries, China had the ability to make the weapons easily and cheaply. What they needed were girls. White girls. Lots of them.

India had long been a destination for travellers, many of whom were seeking a spirituality lacking in their own countries. And, every year hundreds and thousands of solo, Caucasian women, often travelling alone, went to northern India in search of enlightenment, thus becoming easy pickings for men like Do-Hyun Kim.

Over the last three years alone, Kim, and others like him, had, via The Vulture's operation, supplied over three hundred women to the Chinese operators. In return, many millions of dollars' worth of weapons had made their way across Tibet into India, Pakistan, and many Muslim strongholds, arming groups such as Al-Qaeda, Al-Shabab and Boko-Haram.

Chinese men were getting rich. Islamic terrorists were getting powerful. And western girls were getting ruined and killed in ever-growing numbers.

Kane and Sonam had made it more than two hundred yards into the cave and hadn't heard any more screams. Kane dared not guess if that was good or bad. It might have meant that whoever had screamed was no longer scared or in pain. *Or worse, it might mean she's...* Kane halted that train of thought.

Sonam hadn't said a word. Kane knew the Tibetan kid didn't speak English, but he hadn't tried to communicate in any way at all, which Kane thought a little odd. They came upon a fork in the passageway. Kane paused and held still, listening and hoping for some kind of sign or hint as to which way to go. Nothing. Kane wasn't a spiritual man, though he couldn't deny a little superstition on occasion. As a boy and as a younger man, he played a lot of sport, often captaining the teams he represented. His coaches told him it was because of his natural leadership qualities. When it came to the coin toss before a football or rugby match, Kane always called tails. He didn't know why or how the superstition started, but he always called tails and he'd almost never lost. For some reason unknown to him Kane considered 'tails' signified left, the 'head' of a coin indicating right. With nothing else to go on now, he drew a coin from his pocket and flipped it, knowing before it landed what it would be. Tails. And it was. Left.

He'd taken only two steps into the left-hand passage when Sonam suddenly grabbed his sleeve and shook his head. He pointed right. Kane had no idea why or how the kid knew to go right, but since he had no better guide than the flick of a coin and what was essentially a ridiculous superstition, he agreed.

"Okay, right," he whispered. The kid grinned. *How does he know?* Kane wondered, and his unease grew just a little more as he followed Sonam into the ever darkening tunnel.

Hazy images of dappled sunlight filtering through jungle leaves flitted through Ridley's mind... southeast Asia... the sweet tang of opium... the smoke curling from the joint into the trees... her hand reached for it...

In her bed, the weight of the quilt crushed her as if made of bricks. *Why can't I move?* She opened her eyes, but saw only blackness. Then a wave of nausea, brought on by a crushing headache, threatened to overwhelm her. *Am I hung over? Probably.* She tried to sit up but couldn't. *What the hell? Where am I?* And then it slowly returned in dull flashes, images of a cave and ropes and a girl and... and a scream.

She sat up suddenly, her head smashing against something unforgiving. "What the... Damn it!" She laid back down, trying to recall. *Ah...* Now she remembered. She was in a... a cave. In Tibet? She'd been talking to a blonde girl. French. A sister? Yes, Madeleine.

Kim!

Ridley raged against her bindings, a rage that had been growing steadily—dangerously—since the moment they'd met Chan Lee.

That rage is what freed her hands now from their shoddily-tied restraints. It was rage that kicked the door out from her temporary prison, regardless of who or what waited behind it. She immediately dropped into the fighting stance of the tae-kwon-do expert she was. Yet no one waited there. Ridley felt almost disappointed. *Probably best though.* She felt stiff and sick from her injuries, and needed time before she was ready to fight. However, time was one thing she doubted she had.

Looking around, she gasped upon seeing the wall-to-wall cache of deadly weapons. An understanding settled over her and she found herself nodding and inhaling, then exhaling through her teeth. The trade would be the girls for weapons, just as she surmised.

"Well," she muttered through gritted teeth, "this girl isn't being traded for anything or by anyone." Her heart already belonged to someone. Kane. That was all she'd allow. Stealing herself for whatever lay ahead, Ridley kicked her way out of the wooden door and made off into the complex, eyes narrow and adrenalin heightening her senses further with every purposeful stride.

Alexandria Ridley was mad.

Time was up. Lobsang could wait any longer, and sensed Sam felt the same. Their anxiety of the unknown had become too much to bear. Even Noman now seemed more keen to venture into the caves. Lobsang thought it looked almost as if he knew what to expect. He was still smiling, and the monk couldn't shake the notion it was at least a little strange, if not altogether disconcerting. The kid appeared too relaxed, as if aware there'd be nothing to fear inside. Lobsang shook his head, and slowly eased himself out of their hiding place. After a quick stretch and a look around to check they weren't being watched, he led them across the stream. Within a few minutes they were into the caves. Lobsang didn't know what they would find, but as the seconds and minutes passed, and no guards of any kind had shown themselves, he began to fear the worst.

Still the kid smiled.

Chapter Forty-Five

If it were somehow possible to look down upon the scene from above, it would have looked like the inner workings of a termite mound. Inside that mound were a series of tunnels and chambers. Within those dark spaces ran both individuals and groups of termites, all homing in on one main area, as if some invisible siren were leading them. In a way, there was, but for each of them the siren took a different form.

For some it was the lure of protecting their assets... it was the place where they would deal with the enemy entering their midst.

For others it was the quarry they sought, the knowledge that the girl or girls they had come to emancipate were hidden somewhere there.

For others it had become a mission of revenge; it was as if the termite Queen had stolen a rival's treasure, and these invading termites had come to put it right.

There existed an unseen gravity, a mysterious tidal force pulling all the players of the drama in the same direction.

The only difference among them all was that those players on the stage already knew what would happen; the latecomers to the drama, the unsuspecting lead characters, did not.

It mattered little to the Chinese guards that they operated in Tibet, a country they had invaded and occupied for seventy years. The Chinese felt they were the rightful owners of that land, and the Tibetans were the illegal invaders. They would make sure it stayed that way, whatever it took.

There would be inevitable deaths this day, and they would not be Chinese.

Chapter Forty-Six

Upwards of forty smaller caves made up the subterranean complex within mighty Mount Kailash. The Chinese had converted many of those lesser grottoes into a kind of barracks for the security forces, although this action was one hundred percent unofficial, as was the entire operation. The government was aware of certain activities in the region, but it didn't fully know what occurred here and turned a collective blind eye to the unauthorised operations. Only one thing remained important to China along this section of the border, as with the rest of its 1,500-mile length: as long as the imaginary boundaries to India and Nepal to the south were secure along Chinese Tibet's length, then the Chinese government remained content to continue turning a thousand conveniently blind eyes the other way.

The Chinese border guards situated the barracks sections in the deepest reaches of the tunnels, beyond the main chamber and its central well. Only one way existed to get into that claustrophobic labyrinth of smaller caves; the narrow passage beyond the main hall. At any given moment they stationed as many as one hundred guards back there. It served as the operational base for the illegal trading of drugs, women and weapons, which lay strictly outside governmental control. Thus, none of the security on duty today were officially employed by the Chinese military.

Those caverns stretched so deep into the mountain that there would be little chance of any of the guards or higher-ranking members of the military knowing anything of the drama unfolding in the outer caves. Most slept or drank, while some gambled. The more superior ranked of them might be enjoying an unwilling girl or two.

Including the seventeen girls rounded up in the main chamber, the three newcomers, and Ridley, some twenty-six women were being held against their will in the Kailash caves. Some of them had been so abused that they had given up any thoughts of freedom, and sat waiting, even begging, for death.

Kane now rushed along the passage, hoping Sonam knew what he was doing. He had little choice at this stage but to trust him, and followed him wordlessly; there was still no sign of any resistance ahead. That now worried Kane. They'd traversed at least several hundred yards into the complex. With no help, he doubted he would ever find his way back out. *Where is everyone?* It just didn't make sense. He now wished the group hadn't separated.

Then out of the darkness, more screams, straight ahead, perhaps a hundred yards. He pulled Soman to a stop and put his finger to his lips, silencing them both. He strained his eyes and ears into the gloom, but saw nothing other than the gentle flicker of what might have been candlelight. He heard even less. Of equal concern to him at that moment was the smiling boy behind him. *What the hell is going on?*

He set off again and they pushed on for another minute until a morbid thought suddenly crossed Kane's mind. *Surely not?* He finally turned to question the young Tibetan. To his utter amazement Kane found himself staring down the barrel of a gun.

Lobsang hustled them along the passageway until they heard a horrific scream that stopped them in their tracks. They turned to face each other, eyes wide with alarm. Without even realising, they'd traversed almost quarter of a mile into the complex. Yet they had still seen no one. *Weird*, the monk thought.

He and Sam looked at each other, then he glanced at Noman. Lobsang could not comprehend what he saw. The Tibetan kid, no more than seventeen or eighteen-years-old, stood pointing a gun at him. At last the odd smile had gone, replaced by a steely eyed look that demonstrated without any shadow of a doubt that this was no longer a joke.

Before Lobsang could stop him, Sam erupted, launching himself at the kid. Sam wasn't quick enough and Noman got a shot away. The bullet thudded into Sam's shoulder, the resulting puff of blood splattering onto Lobsang's exposed face and hands as Sam dropped to his knees. Somehow it wasn't a fatal wound, and from the ground Sam glared up at Noman. Lobsang saw hatred burning in his eyes.

The monk stood there, too stunned to move. His initial thought was that it had been both brave and incredibly stupid of Sam, who was lucky he hadn't been killed. They both were. However, Noman had a gun, which meant he had control. Helping Sam to his feet, and turning to

Noman, sadness filled his heart. This kid was Tibetan, like him, and yet... and yet...

He's working with the Chinese? There existed no situation conceivable to the peaceful, ageing monk that might have led to this most unlikely of events, after everything the Chinese had done in their country... and most probably had done to Noman's family.

In that moment Lobsang realised something else. Noman's brother Sonam probably worked with the Chinese too. Kane and Chan Lee were likely in the same situation. Lobsang closed his eyes for a second and muttered a quick prayer for guidance... until Noman barked a command at him to turn and walk on. Lobsang now glared at the boy. It wasn't lost on the monk that Noman could not meet his eyes, which were quickly averted while shoving Lobsang forward.

With little choice but to obey, for fear of what might happen to Sam, he allowed Noman to lead the two of them along the passage.

Lobsang had been under threat of death from adult soldiers and a mighty government most of his life.

This young kid didn't frighten him one little bit.

Now only Chan Lee and Jahm-Yang—and, though none of them knew it, Ridley—remained free. The others were all restrained or held at gunpoint. Neither group knew the status of the other. For now, each of them had to assume he or she was operating alone. So, as they descended deeper into the darkening passages beneath Kailash, lured by unseen and unknown forces, edging slowly nearer to the main chamber, not one of them could have guessed at what might happen next.

Unknowingly, each group approached that central chamber from opposing sides, Ridley from the east, Chan and the novice monk from the west. At that same moment, guards were shoving Kane the last few yards into the main area, while simultaneously from another tunnel emerged Sam and Lobsang. The two Tibetan brothers acknowledged each other with a nod as they came into view, satisfied with their work.

None of the foreigners could believe their eyes. An enormous, cathedral-esque chamber sprawled out before them, its vault-like ceiling so far above as to be almost invisible. In the centre of that vast space gaped a wide, seemingly bottomless pit. Beyond that pit and chained to the stone wall, like animals, slumped a line of young women, many of whom seemed barely conscious, most likely drugged and thoroughly subservient. Next to the girls stood a dozen heavily-armed guards, apparently relaxed, and leaning on the cave walls smoking, as if it were just another day at the office.

Kane shook his head as he surveyed his new surroundings. Things were far worse than he had imagined. He scanned the line and counted close to twenty girls. He did not see Ridley. He then noticed a narrow passageway behind the guards, so narrow that only one person at a time could move along it. *Just how deep is this cave system?* he wondered, as it brought to mind a diving trip he'd once made in Mexico's Yucatan region, and the many miles it descended into the earth. Except the Yucatan cave system was world famous, and this place, as far as Kane knew, remained completely unknown. Unknown, that was, to everyone except the Chinese criminals standing before them.

The other thing Kane noticed beyond any doubt was that they were all in deep shit, deeper even than the caves in which they stood. He had led them here to rescue Ridley and any other girls they found. Now it seemed Kane himself needed rescuing. He glanced over at Lobsang and Sam, and his heart sank. The innocent monk had only wanted to help, and the young German had been trying to put things right. Sam was clearly injured, too, his sleeve drenched darkly in blood. Kane spotted blood spatters on the monk's face. He searched Lobsang's eyes for a sign, something to suggest they still had some control over the situation. He saw nothing of the sort. The Tibetan kids had fooled them all. Just kids. *Damn, we're getting too old for this shit.*

It wasn't funny. Not funny at all.

The only comfort for Kane now was that he'd seen no sign of Ridley. If she had somehow escaped from Do-Hyun Kim, the chances of which were high, then it was left to her to come and save the day.

Then we do have a chance, he mused, and he almost smiled.

Chapter Forty-Seven

Ridley was running now, closing in on the scream she'd heard, anger blinding her to her own dangers. Then she stopped suddenly and turned. Walking back a few yards, she spotted some scarcely visible steps carved into the bedrock. On a hunch, she took them; the only light was the soft flicker of a sconce-mounted candle every few steps. She didn't know what she'd find, yet Ridley had a feeling this would give her some kind of advantage over the dirty motherfuckers running this shit show.

After climbing almost thirty steps along the narrow stairway Ridley realised she was right, as she stepped out onto what she could only describe as a gallery overlooking a natural amphitheatre. It immediately reminded her of the scene from The Temple of Doom, where the brainwashed Thugee Cult chanted Kali-Ma before they sacrificed the female star, and Indiana Jones came to the rescue, with a little help from Short-Round. It was almost comical, almost... except this wasn't a movie, and it certainly wasn't funny.

This was real life.

Then she spotted Kane and her heart dropped like a stone into her stomach.

Down below, surrounded by a crowd of armed men in military uniforms, stood Kane. They flanked him, and it was immediately obvious that he was under strict guard. Ridley dropped into a crouch and edged nearer to the edge. Kane didn't appear to be injured at least. She soon spotted the monk, Lobsang and Sam as her eyes darted about. Then she saw something that took her anger up another several notches. Standing right behind Kane was... a child... perhaps in his mid-teens. He had a gun pointed directly into Kane's back. Glancing about, she saw another kid with a gun. *This is absolute madness...*

"Think, Alex," she muttered, inhaling and exhaling slowly in an effort to calm herself.

What the hell am I supposed to do? There were so many guards, and Ridley was unarmed. Or was she? Ridley cursed her stupidity. She had just escaped from a room with hundreds, if not thousands, of weapons inside. While she had been there, she had immediately dismissed thoughts of grabbing a weapon. She shared a hatred of guns with Kane, an aversion that had made her leave without securing a weapon. Though those weapons were likely destined for the hands of terrorists, her core principle remained the same: no matter how bad things become, no weapons. *But...*

Ridley felt torn. The man she loved and many innocent people were being held at gunpoint by dangerous criminals who she now felt certain would kill people if necessary. *What if I just grab a gun*, she thought, *but don't load it... Only for appearances...* Even the notion of that went against their personal ethics. Yet, this was a desperate situation, and though her heart resisted, her mind kicked in to gear and she knew what she had to do.

Ridley raced back to the stairwell, retraced her steps, and sprinted off towards the weapons cache.

As she flew around the next corner she ran directly into someone, sending him flying into the stone wall. She yelled, ready to fight and dropping into a defensive stance, but in a second they each recognised the other and Ridley breathed deeply, helping Chan up.

"You came to find me?" she asked, a lump forming in her throat.

"Yes. We all came."

"I know. Thank you." Ridley inhaled, then said, "They have Hiram. I saw them being guarded by a load of armed soldier types. Lobsang and Sam too."

This was evidently news to Chan, and he closed his eyes, his shoulders drooping.

"There are a load of women as well," she explained. "They didn't look in a good way. We have to help them, Chan. Now!"

Ridley then saw another man, very young, dressed in the familiar robes of a Tibetan monk.

Composing himself and dusting himself down, Chan made a quick introduction to Jahm-Yang.

"I want to help," he said, and Ridley took his hand to thank him.

"Do you have a plan?" Chan asked Ridley.

"I found a way to get above the main central chamber where Hiram and the others, and the women, are being held. I spotted about twenty guards. I also found a huge number of weapons—"

"No guns!" the young monk cut her off, and with surprising authority. "It does not matter how bad these men are, we cannot become them." Ridley knew the young monk had referred to the laws of Buddhism. "The true hero is the—"

"... is the one who conquers his own anger and hatred," finished Chan, quoting The Dalai Lama.

Ridley understood. She explained that she wanted to take just one gun, unloaded, in order to gain any slight advantage she could, but with no intention of firing it.

Jahm-Yang looked at Ridley, and she sensed he was trying to appraise her honesty. After a few moments, he nodded, and apparently trusted her word she did not intend to fire a weapon.

"You have my word. There are kids down there too. Local kids, I think... with guns."

Chan and the monk looked at each other then, as if her words had triggered something. Jahm-Yang's eyes screwed shut, as if he was suddenly in pain. Chan asked Ridley to describe the lads and what they were wearing, and as she tried to, Chan began nodding, and looked as if he'd been given awful news.

"It appears as if our guys were double crossed by the young Tibetans," he explained. "They came with us from Jahm-Yang's village to help us locate this place. Do you know them, Jahm-Yang?" he asked, turning to the monk.

Jahm-Yang didn't open his eyes, but nodded slowly, and his broad shoulders slumped. "Yes, I know them. They are farmer's sons, like me. Most of the men from the villages have been killed by the Chinese, so there is no one to keep an eye on the younger men. The brothers lost their father about six months ago. In their need to provide for their mother and elders, they must have been coerced into helping the Chinese. It is not their fault."

Jahm-Yang was clearly distraught by what had

happened to those young men, but then a strange expression morphed onto his face. He opened his eyes and said:

"They offered me money to help them too. I told them I would rather die, and they beat me. But only my body... they will never beat my mind."

Ridley noticed the young monk's gaze drifting, as if an idea was forming in his mind... She spoke up, returning the novice from his thoughts. "At the back of the main chamber, beyond a large kind of well in the centre, I saw an entrance to what might be a tunnel. My guess is that it leads into another section of caves. Perhaps that's where the guards sleep, maybe even live. It might be the only way in or out. The tunnel is so narrow it looks as if people can only move through one by one. What if we... I mean, if we somehow tricked the guards to go back through into that section, and somehow manoeuvre our guys back out. Maybe we could trap them inside. It's not much of a plan. It's all I've got."

Both Chan Lee and Jahm-Yang appeared to be thinking hard about the plan. It wasn't great, but at least it was something to work towards. Jahm-Yang spoke again, turning to Chan.

"Mr. Lee, once this is over, are you going to keep your word and help the others back in Ngari over into India?"

Chan smiled. "If I make it out of this godforsaken cave alive, I promise to honour my pledge. Yes, I will take your people to safety."

The young monk nodded. "Good. And thank you. Would there be room for two more?"

"Who?" asked Chan, though Ridley thought she knew. "There is not enough room in the transport."

Jahm-Yang ignored that comment. "If I can speak to them, promise them a passage to India, I think they will help us. They were good kids. Honest. It is just life that has changed them, desperation caused by hunger and despair. They will listen to me. There will be enough room," he said, his gaze fixing onto Chan's. "I am certain!"

Ridley had no idea how the monk could be so certain of anything under such desperate circumstances. And the question remained... just how the hell where they going to get to Kane and the others with so many armed guards surrounding them.

Chapter Forty-Eight

Kane's mind raced in multiple directions as he subtly took in his surroundings while remaining as still as possible. It took all of his self-control and will power, learned over two decades of martial art's training, not to lash out at the nearest guard. He had to do something to help the poor women lined up like cattle in front of him. Something. Anything!

But what? He'd counted at least twenty armed men spread out before him, and those were just the ones he could see. He hadn't forgotten that little shit Sonam, either, and knew he was close behind him along with who knows how many more fuckers with guns.

He had no idea of Ridley's status, nor her safety or whereabouts. His fear and anxiety were through the roof and he had to force himself to inhale a few deep breaths. And how about Chan and Jahm-Yang? Had they also been betrayed by the brother?

Kane hated not being able to do anything. Helplessness was not something he was used to. His mind took him back to the day his brother went missing. He was just a kid himself, and nothing he could have done would have changed what had happened. On top of that feeling of helplessness was the fact he had no idea what might happen to them now.

It remained quiet there in that main chamber; the guards were hardly speaking and if anything, most appeared bored. The only sounds were the pained, dismal whimperings of the clearly terrified girls. People seemed to be just... waiting. *Waiting for what, though?* Kane wondered. Whatever it was, for many of them there that cave it would not be good.

Although Sam had been shot, the injury didn't seem that bad. He appeared to be in no immediate danger of dying from the wound. Lobsang had met Kane's gaze a few times and nodded, stoicism written into his weathered features. Kane figured that at least for now, they were safe. He had to remain on the ball; at some point he hoped an opportunity would present itself, and they needed to be ready. If it didn't present itself, he would have to make it happen himself.

Kane looked around, cautiously, so as not to raise suspicion, for some sign of Ridley and the others. Without moving much, he glanced at the few passages that led into the main chamber, and he looked among the guards. No sign of her. Something caught his eye... High above to the left, almost overlooking them, was a deep recess into the cave wall he could easily have missed. *Was that movement?* Kane thought he might have seen a shadow pass from view out of sight. *A guard? Alex?* Something in his mind told him it was her.

In the lull, Kane discreetly edged his way closer to

Lobsang, which somehow went unnoticed by the guards. Sam now did the same. Sonam and Noman, the two Tibetan kids, had noticed, the only non-friendlies to have seen the movement. They didn't seem to care. Kane wondered why.

Noman glanced at his older brother, eyes wide, as if looking for instruction. Sonam simply shrugged and nodded, but didn't do anything else. He'd seen the tall foreigner move towards the old monk. He didn't care. All he wanted now was to get paid. He didn't care for the Chinese in any way. In fact, the brothers retained a deep hatred for them. Times had been so hard in the valley, especially since their father had been killed; they had been desperate. The only way to make any money was to assist the Chinese. They hated to do it, but Sonam knew they had little choice.

The Chinese had taken almost all their livestock and most of their family's land, claiming it under the imposed restriction laws. They'd been left with almost no way to sustain their family. Several months ago, they'd been approached by a couple of the Chinese security men. The brothers, reluctant at first, but urged on by their mother's failing health and spirit, were soon sucked in by fistfuls of cash and a seemingly never-ending supply of opium, which they smoked until it ran out, only to be replaced the next time the Chinese needed some chore or other from them. Though their mother had given her blessing, Sonam was aware she didn't know exactly what the Chinese expected of her sons. It was expedient; either help the Chinese, or starve, and she'd told her boys that she would not watch them starve, in this life or the next.

Now Sonam found himself deep in the Kailash Caves,

his self-given duty done, his conscience strained and the bravado-inducing effects of the opium they had both been smoking that morning completely worn off. Now Sonam wanted nothing more than to get their money and get out of there.

Chan Lee was considering a new plan, though it seemed nothing less than suicide for all of them. Yet he saw no other way. Since it was Ridley who Kim had taken, she was obviously the main prize. Neither the Chinese nor the Korean would want to miss out on that potentially huge windfall. Chan was banking on that consideration when suggesting his plan. He took a deep breath, unsure whether to even say it at all. But when he looked upon the resolve and strength in Ridley's eyes, he knew she had what it took, both mentally and physically, to make it work.

"Alex, you're a valuable asset to both sides in this market. The wealthy Chinese would find you, erm... well, very lucrative, I'm sorry to say, and make no mistake, they *will* chase you down. My idea is that Jahm-Yang and I will enter the main chamber, making some kind of distraction, though not enough to get ourselves shot. Jahm-Yang will do his best to speak with the brothers, and hope they have the knowledge of what is beyond that passageway at the rear of the chamber. Meanwhile, you will sneak around to the rear too, and somehow make it through the tunnel into the back. Once the guards see you, they'll naturally follow you, since you're one hundred times more valuable to them than any of the rest of us men put together. Once they're all into the tunnel, the rest of us will try to make some kind of barricade. I only hope you somehow find a way out, ideally with the help of the brothers. Like I said... it's not much of a plan, and well it's... it's obviously a perilous idea." Chan hung his head, as if certain the idea was stupid and would fail even before it started. To his surprise, Ridley nodded.

"Actually, it's a good idea. I believe there is another way out of these caves. There's no way the Chinese guards— disgusting cowardly criminals that they are—would be stupid enough to back themselves into a corner like that. I'll just have to hope I can find it, with or without the boys' help."

So it was decided. Ridley told them she felt confident she could somehow scramble around the rock face after descending from the gallery unseen, finally dropping close enough to the back tunnel that she could enter it before the guards had a chance to react. It appeared to be the only viable way to make the plan possible. She assured Chan she would try, and he knew it to be true. Chan watched as she scanned the shelves of weapons and settle on a mid-sized revolver. She turned to Chan and shrugged.

"I won't be firing it anyway so this is as good as any." She turned to Jahm-Yang and nodded. It was returned.

With that, Ridley was gone.

Chan fixed his eyes on Jahm-Yang. He sensed in him that same determination and bravery he'd seen in Ridley's eyes. The monk looked back at him, his stern, bright eyes exuding confidence. The young man was ready. Chan only wished he were as brave as the other two.

He led them out of the weapons room and they walked at pace in the direction Ridley had told them, knowing that within just a few minutes they would emerge at the opening to the main chamber. All they needed to do was make enough fuss to cause a disturbance among the crowd of guards and captives, enough so Jahm-Yang could locate the brothers and get close enough to talk to them. Once again,

Chan thought his plan seemed nothing short of suicide as doubts and fear swirled through his mind. The guards would surely be edgy enough, probably even trigger-happy. They had a lot to lose, but they were probably stoned or drunk or both, and that might make them reckless.

They walked on, and sure enough, the dark passageway gently widened, the darkness gradually receding as the passage at last opened into the central cavern. They edged into the shadows, remaining silent for now, desperately scanning the chamber for Kane and the others. Chan soon spotted Sam and Lobsang, and there between them, his head a good six inches above all the others, stood Kane. Chan immediately felt better. Something about seeing Kane bred a sudden confidence in Chan he'd rarely experienced, and like Ridley, Chan somehow knew he was a formidable ally to have alongside him in a crisis. He hadn't yet seen the brothers, but in that instant he guessed Jahm-Yang had, because the monk surged off to the left in a direct line, barging people aside as he went.

This is it, thought Chan. "Hiram!" he shouted, "Hiram!"

Chapter Forty-Nine

Kane spun on his heels after hearing his name yelled, and immediately saw Chan making his way through the scattered guards towards him. Chan saw the disbelief in Kane's eyes. Who could blame him? He must be wondering if Chan had lost his mind. Then Chan saw realisation dawn on Kane's face. He obviously thought Chan had a plan. And he did. And it worked.

The sudden shouting and commotion caused a stir among the gathered guards, and they swarmed towards Chan, their weapons drawn. Chan made it to Kane before the guards arrived, and as they got close he raised his arms in a dismissive gesture. If Chan knew one thing about Chinese people, himself the son of Chinese parents, it was that they hated not being in control. The fact that they hadn't known Chan's whereabouts clearly enraged the guards. Although he was now surrendering, they knew they needed to punish him, to make an example of him to the others. The first guard who arrived at Chan Lee slammed the butt of his rifle into his forehead with sickening power, crumpling the man where he stood.

Kane flinched, but knew better than to react. At least not yet.

In the melee, he spotted that Jahm-Yang had arrived too and approached the two brothers, who now stood together. Kane watched as they lazily held their guns out, but he sensed no real threat and they seemed to be listening to the monk.

Kane's adrenalin surged, his fists clenched so tightly the knuckles blanched white. He stood poised for action, certain it was coming, his breaths deep to control his flexing muscles. Kane was a highly skilled hand-to-hand fighter, and if these bastards didn't have guns, he knew he could handle several of the sloppy guards. He looked up from the stricken Chan, then back down again. Then his eyes shot back up, and he blinked, because he couldn't believe what he was seeing. Just three feet above the entrance to the rear tunnel, and out of sight of all the guards, Ridley, the love of his life, was scrambling down the wall like a human spider. As she looked up, she caught his eye, paused for the briefest of moments, then dropped out of view.

The stealthy, shadowy figure of Alexandria Ridley descended the rockface from high above, believing that the flickering lamps in the arena below made it almost impossible to see her as she scaled at an angle towards the rear tunnel. "Ten more yards," she whispered, her teeth gritted in concentration. She glanced down and her heart leapt as she saw Kane looking her way, unsure if she could see him. She inhaled and nodded, then focused on the rockface. *Five more yards.*

Ridley dropped to her feet with all the grace of the martial arts expert she was and backed discreetly into a natural niche in the rockface beside the mouth of the tunnel. She stood unseen for a moment and analysed the situation. No one had noticed, except perhaps Kane. Then she spun and looked into the darkness of the tunnel behind her, took a long, deep breath and, holding the gun aloft so everyone could see it, Ridley yelled at the top of her voice: "Hey, arseholes. I'm here. Catch me if you can."

Chapter Fifty

Kane faltered and inadvertently staggered a couple of steps backwards. *How the hell did you do that? Why the hell did you do that?*

Kane was torn, somewhere between amusement, admiration and outright horror about the amazing climb down. His next thought was that Ridley had surely entered a death trap. In his situation, guarded closely by armed and possibly unhinged security guards and with his comrades all up the same shitty creek minus their paddles, he was in no position to do anything.

Surely Ridley had a plan, because, although as brave as any human he had ever known, she did not have a death wish. *Or does she?* He realised had actually no idea what Ridley had been through since Kim abducted her. For all he knew she now harboured a dangerous vendetta. Ridley was a passivist, but experiences changed people, sometimes for the better, often not. *Perhaps Kim had...*

Kane didn't allow himself to continue along that dangerous channel of thought. Hesitating while he tried to formulate a plan, he looked around, and saw Jahm-Yang now in a heated discussion with the two corrupted brothers. *What are they talking about?* He caught Chan's eye too. The look he received seemed to be telling him something, as if a plan existed which he didn't yet know. He had begun to trust Chan, and he would trust him now. He just needed to get closer so they might communicate.

Just then, the tall novice monk looked around, nodded deliberately at Chan and, shifting his gaze, he nodded at Kane. It seemed to be a signal, but Kane realised, unless he knew whatever plan they'd forged between them was, he would be of no use to them at all.

He had just started moving in Chan's direction...

Then all hell broke loose.

Someone had raised the alarm about Ridley's entrance to the back tunnel, and every single guard suddenly surged in that direction, skirting around the sheer edges of the immense well and streaming single-file through the tunnel entrance and out of sight.

Now the guards' focus had shifted elsewhere, Kane quickly huddled the others together. "What the hell's going on, Chan?" demanded Kane. "What's through that tunnel?"

Jahm-Yang answered. "Sonam told me. I trust him." The young brothers looked so ashamed in that moment that it was difficult to understand why they'd betrayed Kane and the others. *For money? Drugs?* Kane didn't know. He did know that life often forced humans into difficult choices, though he doubted how much choice these impoverished, disenfranchised kids really had. Jahm-Yang continued. "Sonam said there are many guards back there, perhaps forty, but that some of them are new and probably do not know the tunnels as well as he does."

"Is there a way out?" Kane demanded again, a little more forcefully than he meant. "I am sorry. Please ask him if there is a way out beyond the tunnel."

The novice quickly asked the kid in their native Tibetan, and he smiled shyly and nodded at Kane. He seemed keen now to do the right thing. Left with little choice, Kane had to trust him. Again, though he was well aware how that had turned out last time. After a quick discussion with Chan, Lobsang and Sam, now pale, and beginning to falter through a loss of blood, they decided the eldest brother would go with Kane after Ridley, because he was the only one who knew the alternative exit. The others would stay this side in case she came out followed by all the guards. They would need to be ready, although Kane insisted they use no weapons. They were certainly prepared to fight.

Only seconds later, Sonam was sprinting off through the tunnel, closely followed by Kane.

In Kane's absence, Chan assumed a little control. He positioned them around the near edge of the deep well, knowing they had little chance of being able to do much, except maybe throw a few rocks and punches. It was futile against guards with guns, but he owed them, and he would do all he could. Jahm-Yang seemed especially focused. He stood muttering to himself, his head rocking back and forth, almost like some kind of personal mantra. Chan sensed he was struggling internally with something, but he'd done a good job getting the young brothers back on-side. Whatever it was tormenting him, Chan had to believe it was grounded within good intentions. As for Noman and Sam, well they seemed ready for just about anything, despite Sam's injury slowing him down.

Chan Lee glanced across at Sam and felt nothing but shame for the way he had treated him. He was a young man, vulnerable, and like so many other youngsters, Sam had made some ill-advised decisions. Yet Chan had capitalised on the lad's weakness. Chan knew that whatever he did or said to make it up to him, asking forgiveness of any kind was probably beyond his reach. He would try anyway. With all that was happening, though, now wasn't the time.

Ridley raced in what amounted to an almost blind run through the dark tunnels, expecting the guards to attack at any moment. She was focused, and her mission was simple; find Kim, kick the shit out of him and make sure he never hurt another woman again. Then she had to try her best to get back out of the tunnels to Kane and the others before the guards killed her. In her heart of hearts, she doubted she'd succeed. Yet, if she somehow helped take down this nefarious enterprise, at least she wouldn't have died for nothing. Like everything else she did in her life, Ridley would do her utmost. She was a survivor, and she wanted to survive this so she could help rid the world of scumbags like Do-Hyun Kim.

All around her she could hear the confused shouts and barked commands of the Chinese guards, though she hadn't yet seen any. That was good; it meant they probably hadn't seen her.

Kim, you scumbag, where are you? And then she stopped. The chances of just randomly running into Kim in this labyrinthine maze of tunnels was slim at best. In what must have seemed to anyone who might have witnessed it like nothing less than a suicidal tendency, Ridley stopped in the next wide crossroads of tunnels, and at the top of her voice, shouted, "Kim... Kim, where are you, you disgusting fucking pig? Where are you?" Then she waited.

Ridley still had the gun; now, however, she feared that if the guards or Kim approached and saw it they may decide to take no chances and shoot her dead. That was not acceptable to Ridley, because she wanted a fair crack at Kim. Therefore, she quickly hid the gun behind a rock and resumed her position in the open, her arms out at her sides so all could see she had no weapon.

She also knew that any man who underestimated her in hand-to-hand combat would get a nasty shock. She only hoped the gutless pig Kim would give her that chance.

Then they came...

One by one the guards found the source of the unknown female voice, and streamed into the crossroads to surround Ridley. What at first were angry faces and raised guns, soon became looks of cautious bewilderment, then outright amusement. Ridley scanned the growing crowd, looking each of them in the eye. Most of them seemed so young. *It's just a woman*, they seemed to be saying to each other; a few even chuckled. They lowered their weapons, unsure what to do. Ridley sensed they no longer worried about the surprising intruder to their inner sanctum.

They circled her at a distance, like curious kids at one of those human statues on bustling city streets, half expecting a sudden movement. Ridley just watched them, certain now that sooner or later her nemesis Kim would arrive. And, knowing Kim to be a weak-willed machismo type—a man who would have no qualms and would, in fact, take great pleasure in beating up a woman in front of these young guards, of that she was certain—she could easily entice him into a fight.

No sooner had that heartwarming thought entered her

mind, the ever-growing crowd of guards parted, and a grinning Do-Hyun Kim entered the scene.

Ridley fixed her own narrowed eyes on Kim, and watched as his smile soon faded, replaced by a look of pure and unadulterated hatred.

Chapter Fifty-One

Kane and Sonam raced on. *How has it come to this? Again?* Kane focused entirely on the task of finding Ridley. He knew that if he let his mind dwell on the fact he'd somehow found himself in yet another deadly confrontation with some of the world's low-lives, then the devastation he felt at once more being embroiled in such a nefarious situation would get the better of him. He shut off his own feelings and concentrated on trailing close behind the boy.

They passed tunnel entrance after tunnel entrance on their left and right. Sonam ignored them all, apparently zoning in on a specific destination. Kane hoped the kid knew what he was doing. It wasn't long before he heard the muted yells of the guards in pursuit behind them along the rock-hewn corridor. Sonam accelerated.

Where is you Alex? Then, and as if in slow motion, Sonam skidded to a juddering stop before tumbling under his own inertia and coming to rest at the feet of several guards, all of who levelled guns at his head. Kane arrested his momentum to stop a yard or two short of Sonam, but the same fate awaited him as a range of guns took aim at his face. *Shit*, Kane seethed through gritted teeth.

They hauled Kane up and though he tried shrugging off their grips they were too many, and he and the boy were manhandled together through a gap in the guards, then forced in front of a huddled mass of bodies. Not for the first time in recent minutes, Kane could not believe what he was seeing.

Do-Hyun Kim and Ridley were circling each other like two enraged tigers about to engage in mortal combat. Kane strained forward, desperate to get at Kim, but a guard promptly smashed him across the skull with a heavy rifle butt. Kane wasn't knocked out, but he wobbled on unsteady legs.

As his head cleared Kane scanned the guards. There seemed to be great amusement and anticipation among them, as if they fully expected to see Ridley receive a good hiding—or worse—at the cruel hands of Kim.

Neither of the combatants saw him, each fighter focused solely on the other. Still they circled. Kane knew fighting. He'd sparred with Ridley hundreds of times over the years. She was taking her time, patiently waiting to see her opponent's first move. Kane watched Kim's facial expressions, and judging by his raised eyebrows and wide eyes, it soon became clear he understood Ridley knew how to fight. Her frame was strong, and her feet agile.

Kim eyed the bitch who thought she could beat him. He thought it was hilarious. *You're just a woman*, he mused as they circled each other, slowly moving crab-like in an anticlockwise direction. He was toying with her, though he would remain cautious. *I'll let you have a little fun, then at just the right moment, I'll give the crown what they want. And what I want. I will take you out.*

Kim knew the prize of his inevitable victory would be worth more to him than the ten thousand dollars he'd receive if he sold her at the market as originally planned. It was only money, Kim knew, and there would be plenty more girls.

There were always more girls.

Chapter Fifty-Two

From the corner of her eye Ridley spotted Kane. She was a highly trained martial arts expert, but what she did next went against all her innate instincts and years of hard-core training. Ridley paused. It was only a split second, but in that moment she dropped her guard, and inexplicably looked at Kane. The hint of a smile parted her lips and she—

Big mistake. Kim was opportunistic—it's how he ran his business—and even though he didn't need to take advantage of the mistake to win, if the dumb fucking woman was stupid enough to let her guard down, then he would not waste the opportunity.

He slammed her with a solid right cross, and since she wasn't looking, the cowardly punch almost did for her. She rocked back, dropping to one knee as blood sprayed from a deep gash on her cheek.

Kane bellowed in horrified rage, but was kept in place by a dozen trained rifles.

Kim stepped back, a little surprised she hadn't gone

down completely. He'd thrown weaker punches that had taken down bigger men than this woman. No matter. The next one would tag her real good. Kim stepped forward, but before he could launch the next attack Ridley's survival instincts kicked in. She fell to her side and rolled out of reach, immediately springing back up to her feet. She shook her head, clearing her blurred vision, and breathed two long, deep breaths. Next Ridley stole a more cautious glance at Kane. He stared back at her, wide eyes pleading with her to back down or run like the wind, or to...

Or to what? Ridley was a born fighter, and Kane knew that's exactly what she'd do. He'd always known it. She would fight. Finally, she looked back at Do-Hyun Kim, a deep well of hatred now burning in her eyes. And, surprising everyone in the room, not least Kim himself, Ridley smiled.

There could be nothing more infuriating to a man who thought he was tough than to be mocked by someone weaker and inferior to himself. That the someone else was a mere woman proved to be more than Kim could stand. He launched himself full-tilt at Ridley, expecting nothing less than landing a punch that would end the contest; maybe even end her life.

That's what he expected.

That is not what happened.

Ridley dodged the big man's wild swing with ease. As his momentum carried him a few paces away, she spun and turned to face him. This time he growled something in Korean and wound up his big right fist before literally launching himself at her, his feet leaving the ground a few inches... as it turned out, it was the same distance by which he missed Ridley's jaw.

This time his momentum was such that he spun wildly

and lost his balance, ending up on his backside and eliciting a round of chuckles from the guards. They weren't colleagues as such, more a combination of allies, each needing the other to complete their trades of drugs, weapons and girls. Against all the odds, a woman had shamed Kim and made him look an idiot in front of them, younger men than he, and men who expected the tough Korean, a nation China looked down upon, to dispatch the woman in a second.

Kim rose to his feet and inhaled. He spat on the rock floor and stared at Ridley, clenching and unclenching his knuckles. He glanced around at the guards; some appeared sheepish. Others grinned. He didn't care. Not any more. The girl was his. He would kill that bitch and wipe the smirks off all their faces.

Kane realised Kim was tiring of Ridley's games, glaring at her with eyes of fire. The Korean growled and spat on the floor, then reached into his waist band and pulled out a knife.

Oh fuck. His gaze shot to Ridley and he saw a flicker of worry pass across her face. She'd had many years of weapons training, though to his knowledge she had never before faced a real knife in a real life or death situation. *If she's not careful this'll be all over in seconds.*

Again, they paced, Kim now at least affording Ridley a little respect. It seemed to Kane, though, as if his impatience to get this over with might get the better of him as he swung savagely at her, slashing from right to left in sweeping arcs, then back again, missing, but not by much. Kane saw Ridley was sweating and breathing hard. It was warm in the tunnels, and along with the constant moving and the cloying press of thirty or more guards in the airless confines of the subterranean space, she was clearly slowing down.

Ridley was dodging the blade comfortably, but as she tired and as Kim's rage grew, Kane knew it was only a matter of time until he sliced her, maybe fatally. He started to move to get to Kim, but he'd made it half a step before being sucker-punched with a rifle butt to the back of his knee that sent him sprawling.

From his position on one knee, Kane watched as Kim swung left and right, then swung again. This time it was a decoy and he quickly adjusted the angle, coming at her from below, like a vicious boxing upper cut. Ridley clearly wasn't expecting that. Kane winced as the blade sliced her shirt up the middle, cutting deep enough to open the skin on her chest and continuing up to leave a deep gash in her chin. It was so dangerously close to being a fatal, neck-slicing blow that she actually put her hand to her throat and Kane stared in horror, expecting the worst. Fortuitously, the lucky escape only instilled in her a new urgency, and Kane knew the Korean gangster would surely now pay.

Evidently gaining in confidence, and with a sense of imminent victory palpable in the arena, Kim began gloating, smiling at the boisterous crowd and raising his hands in the air in a victory salute. He simply didn't see the flying knee coming his way. Too late he reacted, and Ridley's right knee connected with his jaw with a nausea-inducing crunch.

"Go on!!" Kane roared as Kim tipped backwards like a felled tree. It wasn't quite a knockout blow though, and he recovered quickly. Ridley was now on him, and she followed the knee with a roundhouse kick to his left temple, staggering the solid man like a drunk. *Damn he's tough*, Kane thought, as Ridley unleashed two more roundhouse kicks that connected expertly, the first crushing his nose, the second fracturing his jaw.

Kim dropped to one knee, the blade clattering to the floor. He was down, and he was almost out. Ridley looked down at him, sweat flowing from her brow. She exhaled and wiped her eyes. Kane sensed she was debating whether she should finish him, take him out once and for all, or merely incapacitate him, perhaps destroy a cruciate ligament. She paused, a silence suddenly descending across the cave as all the guards stood in what could only have been shock. They had obviously thought Kim was toying with the woman, certain that at any given moment he would take her down. Now, to Kane, and likely the guards, it looked for all the world as if she were about to kill him.

Ridley could have grabbed the knife and slit his throat before any of them could react, with not a damn thing Kim himself could do about it. She stepped forward one yard nearer, leaving about three feet between them, just enough that she was out of reach.

"Alex!" Kane called out, but she was oblivious now. "Ridley!"

With rifles digging into his back, Kane was powerless to do anything and he watched on as Ridley smiled at Kim and Kim smiled back at her, his teeth smeared with his own blood and his nose a pulpy mess.

Ridley took a step back and was about to launch into a full kick when Kim pulled a gun and Kane bellowed as he fired at her chest from what was now almost point-blank range. Kane turned his head away and vomited on the ground.

The bullet ripped right through the flesh of Ridley's arm and continued on, ricocheting off the cave wall and embedding in one unfortunate guards' neck. Kane heard a scream. It was not Ridley. He glanced up in time to see the fire in her eyes as she crouched, and wound up her right foot for what would surely be a killing blow against a now defenceless Kim, who now had only seconds to live.

Kane used the power in his legs to force himself up and off the ground and, ignoring the possibility of getting cut down by a hail of bullets, he launched himself at Ridley just at the moment she left the ground to destroy what was left of Kim's face and end his life.

The two soul mates collided and crashed to the unforgiving stone floor. Kane was quickest to react and he locked his two strong arms around her and, without a word, hauled her away through the passage at full speed, Sonam alongside, and the guards in chaos as the defeated, raging Kim fired bullet after bullet in the fleeing pair's direction.

He fired twelve bullets in total and seven of the guards were hit, three mortally. The rest of their comrades responded. Ignoring the departing girl, they turned their attention on the fallen Korean.

Chapter Fifty-Three

"Get off me... get off me right now... I'll kill him," she screamed, "I'll fucking kill him."

Kane had no doubt in that moment Ridley would do exactly that, but he also knew if they ever made it out of there alive she would look back later and regret it, no matter the injustices he'd exacted upon her. Kane glanced over his shoulder. The Chinese guards seemed to be taking care of Kim's mortality themselves.

Despite the bedlam behind them, Kane was certain the Chinese guards did not want to lose their prized asset and at another glance over his shoulder he saw vast numbers of them begin to give chase.

"Okay, I'm good. Thanks!" Ridley yelled, shrugging out of Kane's clutches as they ran in what was essentially a fox hunt; a pack of bloodthirsty hounds chasing them down a rabbit warren deep within Mount Kailash.

Due to the mad dash down the tunnel and pumping adrenalin, neither of them had noticed Ridley had lost a lot of blood. Kim had inflicted pretty a serious wound down her midriff, and the blood was seeping down through her waist band and soaking her combat trousers. Kane had been more focused on getting Ridley away from trouble. He had no idea what the situation would be back in the main chamber. He only hoped that Chan, Sam and the others had managed to somehow get the girls to a safe spot while the guards were absent.

At last they rounded a long sweeping curve in the stony passage and entered the final stretch to the main cavern. It did seem as if it was the only way in or out, and now that was a good thing. They only needed to exit the tunnel, and somehow barricade the opening for long enough to get everyone, including all the abducted girls, out of the Kailash caves and away from danger.

Finally they emerged, far ahead of the pursuing guards. Kane scanned the scene, delighted to see no guards here. Chan, Lobsang and one of the women were busy shepherding the stricken girls towards the exit; some were clearly too weak to rush, and it was a slow process, but it seemed at least as if they could all walk. The one woman helping in the evacuation caught Kane's eye. She was a tall, striking young woman who, unlike the rest of the captives—who all appeared afraid and mentally broken—seemed perfectly healthy, both physically and mentally.

"Hey," Ridley called out, getting the woman's attention having also spotted her. "Are you okay?" The girl trotted over.

"Yeah, I'm fine. I only want a chance to smack those shit heads who brought me here... but I guess they're far away from here by now... chicken shits!"

Ridley smiled, despite her painful injury. "My name's Alex. What say we get out of here; one day you might get that chance."

The girl smiled back. "I'm Kayla... and you've got yourself a deal."

"Okay, we have to move!" Kane shouted, and they headed out.

Ridley and Kayla mingled among the terrified girls to offer soothing words of encouragement and physical support, with Kane and Chan bringing up the rear. Last in line, though, came the young novice monk, Jahm-Yang, muttering inaudibly to himself.

Suddenly Jahm-Yang grabbed Kane by the arm, forcibly stopping him. He looked into Kane's green-brown eyes and stared for a long moment. He said, "Thank you for helping my people. May you be at peace and at ease in all you do and all that's done for you." Jahm-Yang turned away, made a swift loop of the well and, inexplicably to Kane, he sat down at the entrance to the tunnel. Of course the entrance was by default the exit, since it provided the sole way in or out, and a horrendous thought entered unbidden into Kane's mind when he saw the young man sitting calmly on the floor, effectively blocking the exit.

At that moment Kane heard the growing rumble of dozens of Chinese guards approaching the end of the tunnel, their yells and the thunder of their boots thudding against stone echoing in the vaulted acoustics above. Kane assumed they were desperate to recover not only their lost asset of Ridley, but wanted to prevent anyone trying to rescue the other girls.

Kane knew that it they all managed to escape the caves and expose the heinous enterprise to the world's media, their shameful operations would be shut down forever.

The noise ascended as the echoing thunder of footsteps grew. Just when it seemed they would burst out of the tunnel, Jahm-Yang looked around at Kane, then grabbed one of the flaming paraffin lamps from the wall. Kane felt as if a cannonball had landed in his guts and he winced at as the novice monk closed his eyes, and tipped the contents of the glass lamp over his chest. An instant later, the crimson robe he wore so humbly erupted into a roaring inferno, blocking the entire exit of the tunnel and causing the on-rushing guards to skid to a stop before being engulfed by the blaze of the flaming monk's human barricade.

Kane screamed "Nooooo! and all the fleeing girls froze where they stood, screaming too as the flames twisted in devilish forms, licking the ceiling of the cave and scorching the rock face where Ridley had made her brave entry just thirty minutes before. Despite what must have been excruciating agony, Jahm-Yang didn't move, his eyes closed, as if in meditation and with a look of peace on his handsome face.

Beyond the blaze the guards backed up as their comrades bundled into the back of them, one after another of their bodies piling up like a multi-vehicle car wreck.

The flames began to spread down the tunnel, where years of oil lamp residue whoomphed into deadly flames, turning the stony corridor into one of unimaginable pain and death for the dozens of desperate guards.

Kane had been as transfixed by the macabre tableau as the others, but he suddenly snapped out of it. He had witnessed enough innocent deaths in recent years, and he would not stand by and watch Jahm-Yang sacrifice himself. Without another thought, Kane sprinted over to the monk's burning form and, ripping off his own overshirt, he frantically padded at the robes, screaming at the others to come and help. Chan raced over and joined in. Upon seeing Jahm-Yang was still alive, Chan hauled the monk's inert body away from the tunnel. Kane knew it wouldn't be long before the guards somehow found a way to get through the flames and attack them once more. There was only one thing for it...

He cast a glance Ridley's way, then back into the tunnel, then back at Ridley. "Get them out of here... get them all out. Go now, Alex!"

It was almost as if she'd had a sixth sense about what Kane was going to do next. She stared into his eyes, imploring him not to do it. She shook her head, tears beginning to fall as she finally understood his intentions.

Tears formed in Kane's own eyes as he mouthed the words "I love you," and turned toward the tunnel and launched himself into the fiery fray.

Chapter Fifty-Four

Lobsang had been watching events unfold. Although he wanted to stop the madness, wanted to stop Jahm-Yang from sacrificing himself for the others, he'd refrained because he also knew it would be sending another powerful message to the Chinese... one that would be heard around the world if the rest of them made it out alive. It was a difficult, heart-breaking choice to stand back and watch, but one the wise monk felt it would be more beneficial for the greater good of the Tibetans in the long run.

All that changed when Kane threw himself into the fire. He knew the death of an innocent foreigner wouldn't change a single thing. First of all, the Chinese would never allow that news to leave these mountains. They would simply kill everyone, and with that, the story would die too. The Chinese were just too powerful. Of course, Kane was in Tibet illegally and breaking several international laws.

Lobsang could stand by no longer.

He sprinted after Kane, leaping over Jahm-Yang's smouldering robes and launching himself into the fray after

Kane, grabbing his arms and pulling with all his strength to clutch him back from the inferno. After battling for a few seconds, he used his momentum to fall back and bring Kane with him, the two men tumbling over each other.

"Get out of here," the monk yelled. "Go now and take every one with you. Take the girls, take Jahm-Yang and go now before it is too late."

"No Lobsang, it has to be me—"

"No!" Lobsang stated with unwavering authority. "You have done enough... you have to leave here and tell our story... get those girls and those kids out of here. Do it now!" Lobsang spoke with such stoic determination that Kane backed down. "Go, now!"

Kane turned to look at the procession of young women with Ridley. "Remember the mission. Get those poor women and the others to safety." Kane finally nodded his agreement and turned to thank him.

Lobsang was gone, and the last thing Kane saw before being pulled away by Chan and Sam was the monk disappearing over the piled up corpses to be engulfed in the inferno from which he would never return.

He's gone!" Chan shouted at Kane as he strained to go after the monk. "There's nothing you can do for him now," Chan yelled, clutching Kane's t-shirt. "We have to go. The guards will get through soon or find another way; they won't let us leave here alive. Let's go. Now!"

Kane relaxed his shoulders and stopped struggling. Chan was right, as had been Lobsang. With one last look back at the raging wall of fire blocking the tunnel exit, he turned to catch Ridley's eye and in saw etched onto her face the pain he felt at the latest tragic loss of life. They shared that moment for long seconds. Then, as if they each knew what the other was thinking, they set about helping the others along the stony trail with Chan and Sam, who assisted the terribly, almost mortally burned Jahm-Yang as they hustled down through the rocky passages and into the final stretch. At last, they burst out of the cave and into the dark shadows of Mount Kailash.

Chapter Fifty-Five

They'd left behind them utter carnage. In their desperation, guards who'd been caught in the tunnel, unaware of the alternative route out and within seconds of being consumed by fire and smoke, had at last battled past Lobsang's fiery barricade. They dove over their fallen comrades, blinded by smoke and suffocating, only to then plummet to their deaths in the pit in the main chamber, their screams lost to the depths. The seventy-foot fall ended abruptly onto a sheer rock surface dotted with massive protruding stalagmites, which became a final macabre resting place for several of the smashed or skewered guards.

Still more died in the tunnel, perishing where they fell. Most were unable to move forward or back due to the bottleneck nature of the passage and therefore burned or choked to death. It was the very definition of chaos. For twenty-six men, the vast majority of those corrupted guards and criminals, it was all over.

Amidst the deadly carnage, Lobsang Paljor's body lay in ruin. He had martyred himself, not in the name of the

Buddha, but for all Tibet and for Tibetans all across the world. In sacrificing his life to help save the lives of innocent people, Lobsang had known he was breaking the sacred Buddhist cycle of reincarnation. He would not be reborn. Fortunately, if it were this chaotic, brutal and selfish world on the brink of social collapse into which he would return, then Lobsang would not have changed his mind.

In the final seconds before he died, after images of his lost family flitted through his mind, alongside the smiling face of his mentor and spiritual guru, The Dalai Lama... his friend... Lobsang smiled too. Jahm-Yang was a young man, a novice. Now he would get the chance to continue his Buddhist studies, and not just anywhere, but under the wise guidance of His Holiness, just as Lobsang himself had once done.

Then he was gone.

Chapter Fifty-Six

Kane expected them to be chased down and shot. In his darkest of hearts, he thought they'd be dead before they made it out of the cave complex. By some miracle, perhaps, or by the unquestionable bravery of two men, Jahm-Yang and Lobsang Paljor, they'd made it out into the open, unhindered. They were safe. At least for now. A small bubble of hope began to take shape in his mind.

Chan Lee had been clear about how dangerous this criminal organisation was. He remained so certain they'd be followed away from Kailash and hunted down until all were caught and dead, that Kane did not let them slow for a moment. He urged them on, insisting the danger wasn't over yet. Most of the malnourished girls stumbled along on weak, unsteady legs, having been chained down for so long. Ridley and the courageous Kayla helped many a girl to her feet after a fall.

Despite their weariness and fear, and in some cases injuries, Kane understood that the collective desire of the girls and the others to escape pushed them to the edge of their mental and physical limits. Thus, they somehow made it down to the highway and into the relative safety of the tiny village in just twenty-five minutes. Once there, though, the reality of their situation hit home to Kane. *Just how will we get all these people to real safety?*

They all found a spot to take a welcome seat now they were out of the cold shadows of the mountain, each allowing him or herself a moment to recover their composure. The sun shone, though it was approaching dusk and already getting chilly. And in the cold light of that day Kane understood they remained nowhere near to being truly safe yet. Not even close.

The girl Kane knew as Kayla and another of the girls did what they could to assist Jahm-Yang who, although not audibly complaining, Kane realised must have been in excruciating pain. The fire had burned most of his upper body and there were terrible blisters and other burns across his legs and face. The poor kid was suffering in silence; it was obvious he wouldn't last the night without the right emergency treatment.

Sam's life was not in danger due to his injury, but he too needed significant medical care to stave off infection in his wound.

Ridley's situation seemed more precarious. She'd lost an awful lot of blood, though it had slowed, and she still bled from her chest wound. Kane couldn't take his eyes off the wound to her chin, And he still seethed internally at what Kim had done to her. Two inches lower and it would have meant her death… it was only her skilful dodge that had saved her. It would heal in time. There would be a scar, and it would be a constant reminder of Do-Hyun Kim. Kane knew how these things worked. Scars were both physical and mental. He could sense Alex thinking of Kim even now.

As they rested quietly, she wondered aloud to Kane whether Kim could have by some miracle made it out alive. Kane thought he understood where she was coming from. Although Ridley didn't say as much out loud, he sensed her annoyance at not knowing for certain one way or another. If he had somehow made it out, Kane knew, Ridley would always worry he was going to hurt more girls and young women.

"I don't think so, Alex. I don't think Kim is ever leaving that mountain." Kane hoped it was true. The way Ridley closed her eyes and turned away from him suggested she didn't really believe him.

Chapter Fifty-Seven

The most obvious problem the rescue team faced was the sheer number of people now in their party. With the rescued girls, they numbered over twenty. They had no idea of the location of Do-Hyun Kim's vehicle; Chan's could hold fourteen at a push. Aside from the two brothers, they knew no one in the tiny village other than the boy's mum and the old man. They also didn't know who they could trust and Kane didn't want to risk getting betrayed again.

One fact remained: they had to get as far away from Kailash as possible.

But how? They had just one van. The only other wheels Kane had seen were a couple of broken down tractors that likely hadn't seen action in months, perhaps even years, and several unused bicycles, most of which had flat tyres. They were in trouble, Kane knew it, and with no obvious solution in sight, his heart sank.

"Can I chat with you for a moment?" Kane asked Chan, leading him by the arm. He needed to speak to someone, but didn't want to burden Ridley. Once away from the group, Kane unloaded his concerns on Chan. "We aren't safe here. You and I both know that. We can't trust anyone, and there's no transport. We can't walk out of here and Sam and Alex... and all these women... well, they need help and we have to go. Now. Basically, Chan, I'm all out of ideas."

Chan shook his head, unable to add anything useful. "I'm so sorry, Hiram, I can't tell you anything you don't already know. And I'm sorry... you know... for everything."

Chan's head dropped and Kane sensed genuine emotion in the man. But unleashing his anger on Chan about his part in all of this would not help them now, so he inhaled and let it slide.

Kane looked around and for a few moments despair threatened to get the better of him. He paced back and forth a bit, nervous energy expelled through his movement.

Then Sonam came running over, and Kane saw a definite glint in his eye. Kane had seen that glint before and he was wary, but Sonam had bravely led him to Ridley, so he would trust the boy now. He grabbed Kane's sleeve and beckoned him to follow.

Sonam led Kane to the quirky old fellow who'd scratched the map into the dirt what had seemed a lifetime ago but was just that very morning. He sat in an old bamboo chair enjoying the last remnants of warmth from the sun behind his tiny adobe home. He smiled at them as they approached, and did not seem at all surprised to see Kane. Sonam seemed to have understand Kane's dilemma. Over the next few seconds, using a few precise sentences and hand gestures, Sonam relayed their predicament to the old man. The withered old farmer smiled again, his toothless grin suggesting his age to be at least eighty years old. He muttered a few things to the boy whilst looking pointedly at Kane.

Then, a moment later the old man stood, and Sonam's smile flashed as wide as the Indus river valley, causing Kane's hopes to rise.

The lean, sprightly old timer led them across the dusty farm track towards a giant clump of overgrown shrubs and bushes. It wasn't until they got closer that Kane noticed those bushes hid a low-roofed barn that, unless you knew of it, you would never spot. The skinny, ancient farmer seemed to have a spring in his stride as they approached; Kane's curiosity piqued even further.

Digging deep into a pocket in his tattered trousers, the man pulled out a key and went to work on the rusted padlock. It held firm, unwilling to yield having been unused for a long time. At last it gave way, and with a look around him, as if about to reveal an important secret, the old farmer swung open the protesting, warped wooden doors with a flourish. What Kane saw was the last thing he'd expected.

To his amazement, there in that dilapidated barn sat a compact old military bus, short in length, and with about thirty seats. It was covered in what Kane guessed to be a decade's worth of dust and debris, and had several flat tyres. Otherwise it appeared in solid condition. Whether it could be started or not was another question.

Is he giving this to us? Kane knew asking in English was futile, so he placed a hand on the old man's arm, tilted his head and pointed his other hand at himself. The farmer's eyes smiled the answer, and a nod confirmed it. Pulling another set of keys from a cloth bag he had draped over his scrawny shoulder, he handed them to Kane, who quickly tried the bus door. It opened with a creak. Jumping into the drivers' seat, Kane tried the ignition. Nothing. Not even a flicker of life, and Kane's heart sank once more. The old man nodded and offered Kane a knowing smile. He raised his hand and rolled it in a forward motion as if to say 'again'; Kane did. A low grumble and grind deep within the old bus followed, then silence. The old man tipped his head again, and again Kane tried. This time it roared to life; it was the most beautiful sound Kane had ever heard.

With no time to waste Kane sprinted off to inform Chan and the others of their good fortune, but found a crowd gathered around Jahm-Yang. The poor guy was murmuring something none of them understood and his body had started convulsing from the pain. It looked to Kane as if he might finally succumb to his horrific injuries. Kane knew the novice's mother lived nearby and sent Noman racing off to find her.

Despite his concern for the heroic monk, Kane focused his attention on getting the bus ready to move, and that meant fixing the tyres. He figured Sonam to be a farm hand and was surprised to find him hard at work changing the wheels with the old farmer. The fact there were enough spares was surprising enough, but the speed with which Sonam worked provided evidence of his mechanical skills.

With the bus in the capable hands of Sonam and the old man, Kane returned to find Jahm-Yang's mother and two young sisters knelt by his side; the mother seemed serene, her eyes soft, despite the agony her son quite clearly suffered. She held one of his hands in hers and rested her forehead against his arm. They spoke in hushed tones, the Tibetan words alien to Kane. The light in both their eyes spoke of love and pride, and of the inevitable to come. The two young girls wiped away tears of confusion as each one of them clung to their brother's feet.

"Give them some space," said Chan Lee softly, and the others backed away.

"No, Mr. Kane," rasped Jahm-Yang, his voice a breathy whisper. "Please... come here."

Kane shot a glance at Ridley, who nodded and smiled, then winced at her own pain. Kayla came and took each sister by a hand and led them and the others away as Kane approached the novice monk and took a knee beside him.

"I... I am sorry, Mister Kane."

"Sorry? For what? You are a hero, Jahm-Yang, a hero—"

"No, I am weak. I wanted revenge. I wan—"

Jahm-Yang's voice failed him, and his mother looked at Kane, a curious mix of sadness and pride beneath the flow of tears.

Kane understood that in Buddhism, reincarnation was a crucial pillar of the belief system. In trying to self-immolate, the novice would have broken that cycle and entered the realm of the one-life mortal. Since he hadn't died that way, he would still find his way to enlightenment. Kane was lost for words. This young man, dying before him, had given his life to save people he had never known and now never would. There were no words Kane could give to offer comfort and to prevent the inevitable. Kane's already fragile heart fractured just a little more.

"Thank you, Mister Kane. Thank you for help—" The words fell away as another convulsion wracked Jahm-Yang's ruined body.

Kane's eyes closed for a moment, fighting off tears. Then he grabbed the brave monk's hand and looked him in the eye. "No, Jahm-Yang, thank you. From the bottom of my heart and on behalf of all those people over there, we thank you. The world will know of your courage and bravery, and the world will know what you have given to make it a better and safer place for the rest of us. Lobsang would be proud of you. His Holiness will be proud of you."

The young monk's eyes closed. Kane wasn't sure if Jahm-Yang had understood or even heard what he'd said. But, it was true, and Kane only hoped that he would at last find peace after so many years of struggle and suffering.

Jahm-Yang's mother looked up into Kane's eyes, tears blurring her own. Despite her suffering she smiled, and it was one of the bravest things Kane had ever seen. In that smile Kane also sensed a message. She was telling him he wasn't to blame, and she was also instructing him to go and finish the job they had come for: to get the innocent victims of the Chinese brutality to safety. Kane knew she was right.

He had to leave. They could do nothing for the brave novice, who had fallen perfectly still. He had breathed his last breath in this life. As Kane walked away, his heart as heavy as he had ever known, he only hoped Jahm-Yang's next life was one of peace and harmony.

Chapter Fifty-Eight

Kane's thoughts of the fallen hero quickly faded as he spotted Sam and several of the woman leaning over a pale, stricken Ridley who was now leaning back against a tree, her usually radiant skin as pallid as he'd ever seen.

"Alex!" he yelled. "Is she... is she okay?"

"Take it easy, Hiram," said Kayla. "She's okay, but she's lost a lot of blood and is very weak. I've done a little first aid before... if we just had a basic kit with needles and thread I could... well I could probably patch it up well enough until we got to a hospital."

Kane sent Sam off with the sisters to rustle up some boiled water and towels, then sprinted back to the military bus, hoping his hunch was right. To his surprise, it was, and he raced back to the cluster of concerned people whom surrounded Ridley, First Aid kit in hand.

Kane and Kayla gently lifted Ridley into a standing position, and led her with care to Jahm-Yang's mother's house. One of the Tibetan boys ran off to fetch the mother, and despite what she was going through, sitting with her recently deceased son, Kane believed she'd help. Five minutes later and they had lain Ridley out on a makeshift hospital bed, and Jahm-Yang's mother had returned with a pot of boiling water and towels, and an unopened bottle of vodka, willingly contributed by the old farmer. After first using the boiling water to sterilise the needle, then cleaning the wound with a combination of the water, towels and alcohol, to which Ridley aimed a colourful burst of expletives in the direction of the brooding mountain, Kayla set about stitching up Ridley's chest wound.

Clutching her hand, Kane stood amazed as Ridley locked eyes with him throughout the entire process, unflinching as Kayla threaded that needle in and out of her torn skin a total of thirty-six times. Just ten minutes later, as Kane and Kayla cautiously raised Ridley up into a sitting position, Ridley grabbed the bottle from the table and took two long swigs; in that moment Kane knew she was going to be okay.

"Thank you, Kayla," Kane said as he hugged her tight.

"Yes, thanks," added Ridley, and downed another few swigs. "And get off my man." She winked, sensing a real friendship in the making.

"Handing me that bottle is the only thanks I'll need," Kayla said, and winked back as she took a single long swig herself. "Right, let's get outta here."

Sonam and the nimble-fingered old farmer had changed all the ruined tyres, filled the bus with a stash of fuel hidden in the barn, and had even given the windshield a swift rinse. Amazingly, the ancient bus was ready to roll out and take the unlikely mix of escapees to safety. They first needed to return to Ngari to pick up the waiting Tibetans, including the Panchen Lama.

Chan made it clear that they couldn't delay another

second, certain that any minute now the Chinese guards would be there in the village with death on their minds and fingers on their triggers. "We have to leave now!" he barked, and more or less dragged them all onto the bus.

He eased the old military transport out of the barn and swung it onto the dusty lane. Kane was last aboard as he had gone to pay his final respects and thanks to Jahm-Yang's mother, who had handed him a small cloth pouch. She smiled as he accepted it, and his heart ached as he saw the pain hidden behind those brave eyes. She ushered him away, and Kane reluctantly turned and left. As he jogged to the waiting bus, he turned back to wave goodbye. Jahm-Yang's mother was gone. What he did see was the wise old farmer, barely a silhouette in the pending dusk. Each man waved, and Kane knew, as he suspected the old man did too, that this tiny hamlet in the Tibetan Himalayas would never be the same again.

Kane jumped on the moving bus, which Chan had already started easing along the dusty lane, and took a seat next to Ridley. A minute later, they were speeding back west along the highway to Ngari.

As the bus finally disappeared out of sight a mile down the highway, darkness descending upon his tiny village, a glowing moon emerged large and bright from behind a cloud. The frail old man smiled in satisfaction, knowing it would be the last time he ever saw either. *At last*, he thought, *I was finally able to do something useful.* He continued standing there in that darkness, a slim silhouette and its long shadow cast by the huge moon. He wasn't surprised to hear the roar of vehicles coming towards him from the mountain trail across the highway.

With their headlights bathing the farm entrance in a blinding white light, old Tenzin Choedrak never flinched as three military Jeeps skidded to a stop in front of him. He was eighty-three years old. He remembered the wonderful, peaceful life in the valleys here before the Chinese came, and the memories were as golden as the sun on the first morning of an autumn harvest. Food was plentiful, the smiling, happy children running around without a care in the world. Teenage boys playfully chasing girls, just like he had done, and the girls teasing them back. They were good memories. His own smile was finally fading as he knew his time was ending. But that was okay for old Tenzin. He had enjoyed a good life, at least until the Chinese arrived. He was ready to die.

He remained still as the head of the Chinese hunting party stalked over to him, followed by a cluster of armed, angry men, shouting something in a language Tenzin barely understood, nor cared to. He had a final chance to do something good, something for his people. Something against the Chinese.

He pointed a bony finger back up the highway, east, towards the next big city. "Saga," he said. "To Saga." It was in exactly the opposite direction the bus had taken.

Tenzin Choedrak smiled his final smile and closed his eyes.

They shot him anyway, as he had known they would.

Chapter Fifty-Nine

Chan pushed the old bus hard along the G219 highway, angling northwest towards Ngari and out of immediate danger from any pursuing Chinese. If they could make it back to the tiny town and transfer the women and the waiting Tibetans into less conspicuous vehicles, Chan thought they might just have a chance of making it across into India.

There remained a possibility that the criminal group operating out of the Kailash caves would have already contacted the guards at the crossing into India. Hopefully, although they worked together in essence, the two groups were basically separate factions. Though essential to each other to maintain their operations, Chan knew that ultimately only one thing would make or break their passage across: money. It would be as it had always been... a simple case of just how much money they could offer. It was the only way across, anyway, and they would have to take their chances.

It was a long, tense drive but somehow they'd arrived in Ngari unhindered. They drove quickly to within walking distance of the safe house. After the obligatory security check, Chan and Kane rushed inside to speak with the Tibetans, who'd been waiting for their ride to freedom, no doubt afraid they were going to be let down. They spoke with the Panchen Lama, who listened on in horror as Chan relayed the terrible events of the last thirty-six hours. The biggest problem now was that they simply didn't have enough room to take everyone to the border. They definitely could not continue in an old Chinese military bus. The Panchen Lama thought silently for a moment, then spoke.

"I am so very sorry to learn of your ordeal and the awful situation to which those poor young woman were subjected. Of course, I understand we cannot all travel with you. If it were up to me, I would volunteer to stay myself, but for the benefit of Tibetans everywhere and for the future of all Buddhism, I cannot remain in Tibet. I hope you understand?"

Kane and Chan nodded that they did. Of course, the Panchen Lama had to go with them. His Holiness, the Dalai Lama, wouldn't live forever, at least in his mortal body, and Buddhism was currently in turmoil about who would replace him when he was gone. The safe return of the Panchen Lama, who for several decades many people thought to be dead, would put millions of minds at ease all over the world. Kane even wondered if it might even become the start of the end of the brutal Chinese occupation in Tibet. They simply had to take this man to Little Lhasa with them.

"Please, wait a moment," the Panchen Lama said. "Let me speak to my people."

He turned and in a calm, quiet voice explained the situation to the other Tibetans. Upon hearing about the girls, and about Lobsang and Jahm-Yang, they were clearly horrified. They had all known the young novice and were heartbroken to learn of his death. Consequently, for the next part, when the Panchen Lama asked for several volunteers to remain behind, every hand immediately shot up, and Kane admired anew the humility and selfless nature of the Tibetan people. Ultimately, all were agreed upon the eight who would remain behind, and they accepted it willingly and with grace. The others, a young family of four, another young married couple, and two orphaned boys also accepted the decision.

The Panchen Lama then spoke quietly with one of the safe house guards. He asked the man if he knew of any suitable vehicles that might be available. It was a small community in Ngari and everyone knew each other. A select few were aware of the safe house and the man knew of two who would do whatever they could to help, including donating their vehicles. With the Panchen Lama involved, he explained there was no doubt they would cooperate. The guard nodded, and he and another of the guards disappeared out of the house.

"We need to wait here only five minutes. They will return with the vehicles we need."

Kane and Chan looked at each other and smiled. Things were finally looking up.

Less than ten minutes later, after the two men had returned to the safe house, each driving a large and indistinct people carrier, everybody who had been on the bus and the eight Tibetan refugees, including the Panchen Lama, climbed into the two vehicles; Chan was to drive one and Kane climbed behind the wheel of the other. The whole unlikely entourage was soon headed west once more on the long drive through the night to the border.

Chapter Sixty

Chan feared they would encounter trouble at the crossing. After everything they'd been through; the kidnapped girls; Ridley and Sam with their injuries; the long-suffering Tibetans... all he could hope for now was a smooth passage across. As with almost all things, this depended as much on luck as the money they were offering. Chan knew that everything had its price, and that they would probably be allowed to pass.

His other concern was the Panchen Lama. No one really knew what he looked like other than those who had been his captors for so long, and Chan doubted the guards at the border would recognise him. However, it seemed obvious to Chan that all border guards would be on high alert in case the Panchen Lama ever tried to escape across into India. On the other hand, there was a chance the Chinese Government was so embarrassed that one of their own high-ranking officers had spirited their secret political prisoner away that they might best be served remaining silent about it. Of course, if they went public it was tantamount to an admission of guilt that they had kidnapped and detained him in the first place. They could never admit to that. So, Chan figured that if the Panchen Lama sat in the middle of the van, huddled in civilian clothes and wearing a hat pulled down to shade his eyes, and if he kept a low profile at the crossing, then it would probably be okay.

Ultimately, it turned out luck was on their side. It was before dawn when they reached the remote border crossing. As usual, Chan parked his vehicle a hundred yards back and approached on foot, and also as usual, the guards quickly summoned the main man. Chan hoped he'd been roused from his bed.

The old Captain approached the fence, his dishevelled hair swiftly stuffed under his military hat in a vain and pointless attempt at professionalism. He rubbed his eyes, but rather than saying anything, unlike usual when he reminded Chan in no uncertain terms how risky it was to keep doing this, he just held out his open palms.

This was better than Chan could have hoped for. He immediately stuffed the fat envelope into the Captain's hands. The old soldier glared at Chan for a moment, then looked inside. His eyebrows rose in surprise, then his eyes narrowed a little. Chan had given more than double the usual rate, hoping to have caught the man on a good day. His thought now was that the man was suspicious of him, and he breathed deeply, trying to hide his concern. Finally, the Captain nodded curtly, a smug grin crinkling his face. Then he turned and walked casually away, ten thousand dollars richer.

Chan returned to the van, and only once he was inside did he allow himself to fully exhale in a deep sigh of relief greater than he had ever known. Guards pulled the gates open, as the dawn cast its first dazzling golden rays of welcome light across the snowy peaks of the surrounding Himalayas. When Chan and Kane edged their vehicles through the gates and pulled away, Chan hoped beyond hope that all the people in those two vehicles were at last about to taste a freedom most thought they would never taste again.

Two days later, Kane eased his vehicle up the narrow, winding road towards their longed-for destination, the golden glow of a beautifully fresh Himalayan morning inviting them onwards the last few miles. Twenty minutes later, the random mix of refugees stepped from the vans, road-weary but in good spirits, onto the bustling main square of Little Lhasa.

"Good morning, good sirs and good madams," chimed a welcome and familiar sing-song voice. "It looks like you all need many cups of my famous and most delicious Little Lhasa chai, isn't it so?"

Kane turned, and was greeted by the wide and wonderful, heart-warming smile of Abhay Punyamurthula... Puny.

"It is so," Kane said.

Epilogue

For several days Kane and the others stayed in Little Lhasa. Ridley, Sam and the young women they rescued had all visited the hospital in nearby Dharamshala to assess their injuries. Ridley's were the worst, but Kayla had done an excellent job of stitching up the wound and the doctors commended her for skills she hadn't known she'd possessed.

They also used the time to help the girls arrange their transport out of India, which Chan Lee and Kane paid for between them. The Chinese guards had taken everything from the women, including cash, credit cards, passports and jewelry; they literally didn't have a penny among them. It was clear they could not have been more grateful; each woman insisted on returning the money as soon as she returned home. The Indian government assisted by fast-tracking new passports with their respective countries, and within three days all twenty of the rescued girls had left India behind. Kane suspected they would be forever haunted by their harrowing ordeal.

Ridley had become close to Kayla over those few days and they'd promised to stay in touch.

"You owe me a vodka, mate," was the last thing Kayla said to Ridley as she stepped into the waiting taxi. Ridley shed a rare tear as the cab pulled away.

Sam Stein had also flown home. In fact, he was the first of them all to leave. Chan made good on his promise and had paid for Sam's tickets to Hamburg. After a genuine, heartfelt apology, which Sam said in time he would try to accept, the two men shook hands. Sam thanked Kane and Ridley for helping him out that day, and for giving him a chance to help them back. He vowed he would never touch drugs again. They believed him. Sam spent his last hours in Mcleodganj with Puny. He would miss the chaiwallah, though perhaps not his jokes.

Chan Lee was the last to leave. He had one more duty to attend to, and he asked Kane for his help. Kane was reluctant to leave Ridley as she recovered, but she insisted it was fine and shooed him away. In truth Kane wanted to be certain Chan was as good as his word. So, while Ridley recuperated in the hotel, Kane drove with Chan back to Demchok to retrieve his vast stash of drugs and weapons. They then drove out into the countryside far from any settlements, and set about digging a deep hole in deserted, barren scrub land. Over the course of several hours they had, between them, dismantled every last gun and destroyed all the drugs. Once they'd discarded all the useless weapons and drugs into the deep, and refilled it with piles of earth until they were satisfied it would never be found by any human, they drove back to Little Lhasa. Kane believed Chan's solemn vows to never get involved in that despicable business again.

Chan Lee flew home to San Francisco a changed man.

With the wealth he had amassed, he soon set up a clinic for recovering drug addicts. It was on the main road in Richmond, not far from his apartment. Within a couple of months, Chan was spending most of his days visiting the clinic. Chan Lee had found his true calling, and as the months turned to years and the clinic expanded to help more and more people stay clear of drugs, the Chinese-American dared to believe he was at last balancing on the good side of karma.

Kane and Ridley spent one more day in Mcleodganj, attending one more of the Dalai Lama's teachings at the temple. That was, after all, why they'd come to India in the first place. Despite everything that had happened, they vowed to once more honour the memory of their friend, Evan.

Kane recalled Puny had once told him he knew the His Holiness Dalai Lama personally, a claim Kane found unlikely, at best. But that morning, on their way to the temple, Puny walked with them, a dazzling glint in the young man's eyes. Kane was mystified. "What's going on?" Kane asked. "What are you looking so pleased about?"

"You will see Mister Hiram," he replied, and his eyes shone ever brighter. 'You will see. By the way, I am so glad you both returned. I heard reincarnation was making a comeback... I am happy you did too."

Kane winced at the awful gag, but as they approached the temple, Puny surprised them by leading them past the long lines of eager tourists and pilgrims, then stop at a discreet door along a narrow corridor. The big security guard nodded at Puny, and smiled at Kane and Ridley as he opened the door for them.

Puny, smiling wider than ever, said, "Come in, there are some people who want to meet you, isn't it."

Kane looked at Ridley and knew they were both thinking the same thing. "No. Surely not. He couldn't—"

"Yes, he would. You did not believe me, isn't it," said Puny, "but you should have believed, because Puny is an honest Puny." They stopped at a second, internal door, and an elderly lady greeted them.

In English, she said, "Please, Hiram and Alexandria, do step inside." The pair shared another quick glance, then looked at Puny, his head doing its familiar wagging. Kane swallowed down his growing bewilderment and stepped through the door arm in arm with Ridley, Puny right behind. The lady opened another door, and Kane was stunned as His Holiness rose from behind a desk, opened his arms wide and flashed them a smile to match any of Puny's.

"Welcome to Tsug-lag-khang Temple, Hiram and Alexandria," he said. "It's so very good to meet such brave people." As he shook their hands, they fell into a stunned silence. "And hello again, Punyamurthula." Puny bowed deep and long.

"Hello, your Holiness," said Kane. Ridley followed suit.

His Holiness bowed lightly, then said, "Let me introduce you to my friend, Gedhun Choekyi Nyima, though I believe you've already met." His Holiness winked and his smile was broad.

"Um, hello again, erm..." Kane managed.

"You may call me Gedhun."

"Hello again, Gedhun."

"It's an honour to be here, your Holiness," added Ridley, "and hello again, Gedhun."

"Please, take a seat," said the Dalai Lama, and they all

sat on seats around His Holiness's desk. His Holiness and the Panchen Lama, however, remained standing. "Hiram and Alexandria, may I say, on behalf of myself and my family, and from Gedhun, and on behalf of all the people of Tibet and followers of Buddhism all around the world, from the bottom of all of our collective hearts, we thank you. And I wanted to share these words with you. Maybe they will help you move forward from these... awful events. There is a saying in Tibetan: *Tragedy should be utilised as a source of strength.*"

The Dalai Lama smiled at them, and said, "In short, I think that means that no matter what sort of difficulties, or how painful experience is, if we lose our hope, that's our real disaster."

Next in The Hiram Kane Archaeological Thriller Series

vinci-books.com/island-enigma

A deadly treasure hunt that threatens the peace of the world.

Lured out of hiding by an enigmatic stranger, adventurer Hiram Kane finds himself on a treasure hunt spanning across the globe. As the hunt turns lethal and not everything is as it seems, Kane must outwit ruthless adversaries determined to claim the prize at any cost. With the future of trans-Atlantic relations hanging in the balance, the adventurer must confront his own demons and outwit his enemies to prevent catastrophe.

Turn the page for a free preview…

The Oak Island Enigma: Prologue

Off the coast of Nova Scotia, Canada

November 27th, 1814

Captain Wesley gazed out across the surface of the foreboding ocean surrounding his ship as evening crept towards night. The bruised sky was darkening rapidly and very soon all would be black. The ship was the *HMS Fantome*. Wesley loved the *Fantome*, and it had been his life's honour to have captained her for the British Navy on numerous voyages up and down the eastern seaboard between the Chesapeake and Canada. It had been rewarding, important work. Yet, he considered this sailing, *HMS Fantome's* final voyage, by far and away the most important of them all. Wesley knew it might result in his death, and the deaths of his small, dedicated crew. Yet if it came to that, it would have been a worthy sacrifice and one that would be a fitting end to half a century of loyal service to The Crown.

The captain sighed. It was almost time.

"It is done, Cap'n," said First Mate Chisholm, trotting up to him on the bridge. "The hull is loaded with so much gun powder she'll be blown all the way back to Washington." The young first mate leaned over, panting from exertion.

The captain smiled. He loved the kid, as loyal a mate as he'd ever known, though he knew that loyalty was as much to The Crown as it was to him. It was a loyalty they shared. He hadn't had children of his own. The ocean was Captain Wesley's mistress and had been since he'd first boarded a fishing boat out of Penzance in 1763. He'd never married, and his only legal union was to the Navy, a bond that would never be broken.

He and the kid had been through a lot together since the boy had first joined their ranks in ought-six. He only hoped the kid survived. Once this was all over, he'd have a hell of a story to tell. Which of course he never would. Their mission was of the utmost secrecy, and of such national importance—international importance—that to mention it beyond this wheelhouse even once was tantamount to signing one's own death warrant. It would be to the gallows for them both. For them all.

"Good work, son," the captain stated. "Now go, and load the rowing boat with enough supplies to last two weeks. That should see us around the coast to Clam Harbour."

"And if it isn't?" The kid's eyes widened, and the captain saw in them a mix of pride and fear.

"It will be, lad, don't worry. But if it isn't, then we'll succumb knowing we've done our duty, and that is always enough. Now go on, son, get to the boat."

The first mate saluted, then bustled off below decks to prepare the supplies.

The captain sighed. This was only the first part of the mission. He knew he would need an unlikely amount of luck and good fortune to complete the second leg. Though a God-fearing Christian, Captain Wesley wasn't naturally a praying man. He'd seen storms toss ships around as if they were driftwood and knew Mother Nature was far more powerful than any revered human deity. Nevertheless, despite himself, the captain had indeed prayed, for his success could not depend upon good luck and fair seas alone.

He let his eyes drift once more at the flotilla of other ships that formed their convoy. He knew that on board those boats, the other captains would be having similar conversations with their crew and first mates. The *HMS Fantome* was one of only six ships on the mission. They had all been loaded with unimaginable riches looted from the Whitehouse several weeks earlier in a daring raid that had seen the Whitehouse destroyed, but not before the soldiers had stripped it of everything of value. Treasures from the colonies in South and Central America, including Aztec and Incan gold, and artefacts from the Mayan civilisation, once procured by the Conquistadors several centuries earlier then later claimed by the Americans. Jewels. Silver. Paintings of the Founding Fathers, Presidents and other noblemen and dignitaries. Now it belonged to The Crown.

But only Captain Wesley alone knew that the treasure wasn't the most important cargo aboard the *Fantome* and the other ships. He subconsciously placed his hand to his breast, feeling the small scroll tucked into his jacket, a scroll that contained secrets so important that they would need to be kept secret for a thousand years, lest the world descended into chaos and outright war between the New World and the Old.

With a final glance around the wheelhouse, the Captain stared out at the horizon, now fading as the storm descended, just as he knew it would. There he stood, and saluted, more proud in that moment than he ever had been in decades of servitude. Then he stepped down from behind the wheel of *HMS Fantome* for the very last time as a distant flash of lightning and a roar of thunder in the heavens above heralded in a new era.

Captain Wesley and first mate John Chisholm rowed swiftly and silently away from the *Fantome* on a dark surface that was chopping up as the wind grew beneath a burgeoning storm. The shadowy bulks of five other rowing boats traced their arcing route away from the flotilla, and when they were a hundred yards away, they drifted to a stop and waited. Only one smaller boat had remained, bobbing within a musket shot of the ships. Corporal Miles Smythe, the best marksmen in their ranks, stood aboard, musket in hand.

Captain Wesley couldn't see the young shooter but knew he was there by the faint glow of the oil lantern sitting beside Smythe on the bench. He also knew Smythe wouldn't fail them, even though the surface was beginning to rise and fall in blossoming swells.

Lightning continued to flash in the distance, but the thunder rumbled ever closer. It was a fitting scene for what was about to occur, but no accident. They had waited days for the storm to come, and it was finally here. *Perfect.*

The flash of a distant musket glowed momentarily, but the captain heard no retort. A second flash followed, then a third, then the oil lamp began moving slowly to the north as Smythe rowed the boat closer to the three remaining ships.

Suddenly a massive, concussive boom echoed across the surface, immediately followed by another and a third as the *Fantome* and two of her sister ships exploded in a mass of flames and splintering timbers. The booms were so loud Captain Wesley felt them in his chest, and again, his hand unwittingly moved to his breast, checking for the twentieth time in the last hour that the scroll was where it should be. Where it had to be.

He felt only a little sadness that the *Fantome* would soon be nestling in broken pieces on the shallow floor of the North Atlantic Ocean, alongside the other destroyed vessels. It was his solemn duty, and what needed to happen.

Within just twenty minutes, Captain Wesley and his fellow captains from His Majesty King George the Third's Royal Navy had successfully scuttled an entire fleet of ships. Just days ago, they had been filled with more treasure than had even been assembled in one place in modern history. That treasure was now somewhere else, somewhere even Captain Wesley himself was not privy to. That didn't matter. The tangible treasure was not his concern.

He had a more important duty now: transport the scroll to England and personally place it in King George's waiting hands.

When he awoke, it was to the sound and feel of sledgehammers pounding hard against his skull. The beat, he didn't recognise. Tommy Ramone? Nah, more like John Bonham. The pain was too familiar. Dhum! Dhum! Dhum! And annoying, like Phil fucking Collins.

Bile rose north towards the junction between his guts and his throat. It stung, and tasted like acidic shit. That, too, was familiar. He swallowed it down. His eyes watered. The pain rattled his brain. The throbs radiated, each one like a tourniquet on his mind, easing off like a receding wave, then crashing back down like a big one at Mavericks.

Drowning. *Am I drowning?* If he was, it was deliberate. Wasn't it?

Hiram Kane had seen enough. The deaths, so many of them. Worse than death was the dying. Dying was noisy. Death was silent. It was death he craved... silent death... Sometimes. Not often. Not yet!

In his more cognisant moments, Kane mused that in some ways he'd always had a bit of a death wish. That's what others had been telling him for years, anyway, and it made sense the more he thought about it. The more he reminisced. Is that what he'd call it? Reminiscing? *No, idiot!* At the very least, it was commiserating. With himself? Ruminating? Whining? Self-pitying? *That's a lot of gerunds, Kane,* he thought, ruminating some more.

"Too much fucking thinking mate," he heard himself say as he rolled over and puked on the floor. *Floor?*

Kane glanced around. He was indeed on the floor, the evidence proven by his rat's eye view. But whose floor? Where?

Instincts caused him to spin over, eyes suddenly wide and scanning left and right, searching for his killer...

Something jabbed him in the ribs. It felt like a stone dagger. That's what it felt like. The truth was a little less exciting. His phone. A few moments later, after both the bile and the fear had subsided, he took stock of his situation.

Alive? Yes.

Feel like death? Also yes.

In any immediate danger? Hmm... probably not.

Injured? Hmm... that will need further investigation.

With a hearty, fully fledged groan, Kane hauled himself up onto his haunches and dared a long, thorough look around. Ignoring the storm in his belly and the clash of imaginary titans in his skull, Kane worked out that he was in a dark corner of some quiet, apparently abandoned warehouse.

Hungover like a bastard.

Why? Why am I so wasted? What am I doing here? Where the hell is here?

Something metToullac clattered in the darkness and Kane spun, expecting the worst. He saw nothing, despite the hairs on his neck getting short-lived boners.

"What the fuck?" Kane muttered into the void. No one answered. *Why am I so edgy?*

Kane stood up wearily. With the palms of his hands, he undertook a swift evaluation of his physical state. He concluded that, while he was in one piece physically, mentally he was in several.

His eyes scanned the gloomy interior of the huge building again. The hint of natural light from a distant window beckoned him over. He looked down for any personal belongings. *Nope. Nothing here of mine.* He checked his pockets. *Wallet? Yep. Phone?* Also yep, but with no relief, as no one ever called. He also had zero expectation anyone would. No one. *Not even...*

He couldn't even say her name. Could barely stand to think it.

How have I let it get so bad?

Career? Relationships?

Life in general?

One minute I'm a famous explorer, working an important job for the British Museum, continuing the proud family name and... the next minute I'm nothing. No one. How? Why?

And then, Hiram Kane wept. The haunting sound of his powerful sobs echoed back at him from the dark, damp and featureless walls of an unknown building in an unknown town in an unknown country on an unknown continent.

"Jesus, where the fuck am I?" he muttered as he cuffed tears from his eyes.

That's when the shooting started.

The Oak Island Enigma: Chapter One

Rabbit Island, Cambodia

A Week Earlier

It was supposed to have been a new start. A change of pace. A great opportunity. A chance to do something good and positive. Something less dangerous.

Kane almost laughed. Almost. In truth, it wasn't remotely funny.

Things had begun so well. It was with great pride that he'd taken his position as leader of the Artefact Repatriation Committee at the British Museum in London. In his role, he only had one job to do: oversee the safe return of the Rosetta Stone to Egypt.

Just one job. And he had cocked it up.

Despite the fact that Kane, according to official records, had done nothing wrong, and ignoring the reality that multiple external forces had conspired against Kane and his

ARC team, he had embraced the failures as his own. He had been in charge. The complex operation had been his responsibility.

Kane had been recommended for the job by his grandfather, Hiram Kane Snr. He had humbly accepted the important responsibility, despite his own misgivings that he wasn't qualified and nowhere near up to the task. Higher-ups at the British Museum, as well as his grandfather, had convinced him he was perfect for the role, based on his experiences, his leadership skills, and above all, his world-renowned reputation of unrivalled integrity.

"Ha... how'd that work out for you? Idiot!"

"I'm sorry, sir?"

Kane glanced up as the barman approached.

"It's... sorry, it's nothing," Kane said, embarrassed. He hadn't realised he'd spoken aloud.

Kane looked around. A few other drinkers were scattered along the quiet bar. The afternoon had been long and winding, and of course lubricated. Kane had hardly moved from his seat at the far end of the long bartop, other than for an occasional visit to the loo. His flip flops lay empty in the sand beneath his bamboo stool. The palm trees above him swayed serenely in the gentle breeze, the fronds whispering an unknown tune. Modest waves gurgled onto a white-sand beach a dozen yards behind him.

It was an hour shy of sunset. Kane considered getting something to eat, something to line the stomach before commencing the evening session of sorrow drowning and misery seeking. He glanced at a waitress taking out plates of food to a handful of customers sitting on beach chairs. Nothing looked good. Nothing had for ages. He'd probably skip dinner again.

"A French 75, please," Kane heard someone say a

couple of yards down the bar. The words were English. The accent was French. Kane didn't bother to look up.

"Of course sir, an excellent choice. Celebrating?"

"Actually, oui, I am celebrating. So, I would like to get one for my friend here too, if you don't mind?"

"Certainly sir. Two French 75s, coming right up."

Kane knew the man couldn't be talking about him. Kane knew nobody on the island, and he didn't have any friends, at least not within several thousand miles. He glanced to his right. Standing two barstools along from Kane was a small yet well-put-together man. His colourful shirt was tight to his toned, tanned body. His winning smile was bright. His sunglasses were expensive.

"I hope you'll join me for a cocktail?" the new man said, his French accent barely noticeable.

Kane's weary eyes studied the man. Life had made him more cynical in recent years and he couldn't help being suspicious.

"No," he said, a little stronger than he'd meant. "No, thank you. I'm fine with the beer. Enjoy your cocktail."

"Please, forgive the intrusion," the Frenchman said. "I just wanted to celebrate. I don't know anyone else here, and since you're sitting alone, I thought I'd offer you a drink. Please forgive me. I will leave you to your beer."

Kane nodded and looked away. He glanced left. The sun was minutes from retiring for the day, and the sky was on fire with reds and oranges and pinks, the kind of cracking tropical sunset he used to appreciate. Kane didn't smile. He hadn't spoken to another human for days, other than the rotating bar staff and sometimes the mirror. *What the hell!*

"What is it you're drinking?" Kane asked quietly,

turning to face this newcomer to his commandeered corner of the bar.

"Ah ha," the Frenchman replied, his champion smile widening plenty. "It's a French 75, a classy mix of gin, lemon juice and sugar. Of course, the most important ingredient is Champagne. It is the perfect cocktail for a celebration. And, my new and only friend, I plan to buy you many of them on this perfect celebratory night."

The Oak Island Enigma: Chapter Two

The sun had long since set, dropping with surprising speed as it tended to do in the tropics. The only thing that had gone down quicker than the sun was the drinks Kane kept pouring down his gullet. Yes, it was thirsty work being a complete loser. *Perhaps not this thirsty*, Kane mused as he slugged the last of his sixth or seventh cocktail and signalled the barman for another.

"You like the French 75s very much," Francois said. "Almost as much as me."

"They are especially delicious in this climate," Kane agreed, slurring slightly. It wasn't just the cocktails. He'd only been drinking those since the Frenchman had started buying. It was more to do with the dozen beers he'd sped through in the afternoon. And the fact he'd skipped dinner. Again.

Kane rose unsteadily from his bamboo stool. "Back in a moment. Nature calls."

"I'll be here. There's a lot more merriment to be had,"

the Frenchmen stated, then added, "and when you return, I'll be ready with an exciting proposition for you."

Kane's ears pricked up. Exciting propositions made in southeast Asian bars came with all sorts of connotations, and usually a well-concealed manhood. He'd deal with that shortly. Not the manhood, obviously.

Now he just needed a piss.

Kane wambled—a combination of wandered and stumbled he'd coined for himself after recent experiences—down the beach towards the modest men's bathroom; basically a bamboo tiki hut with a hole in the ground. He thought about the other drinkers back in the bar. A few backpackers, drinking the cheapest things on offer; in this case, *Angkor* beer in a can. A few old-timers, European, perhaps in Cambodia for all the wrong reasons. He didn't want to think about that right now. Cambodia, along with many other southeast Asian destinations, had a gained justified and terrible reputation for sex trafficking and pedophilia in the eighties and nineties. Although the authorities had cracked down in recent years, Kane knew it still very much existed. He was on Rabbit Island. He knew that if he let that train of thought fester, he'd end up down a depressing rabbit hole—pun intended. He shook his head and focused on pissing in the hole and not on his bare feet.

Then there was the Frenchman. Well dressed. Plenty of cash. Clearly educated. And he'd sat next to Kane at the bar. Kane was unshaven. His hair had grown long. He hadn't washed his clothes in days. He probably stunk. So, why had this apparently classy Frenchman come to this humble, relatively unknown and totally random island off the south coast of Cambodia? This would usually set alarm bells ringing in Kane's mind.

Tonight, though, whether it was the cocktails, the

weather, the inactivity of the last few weeks—or, if he were being honest with himself, the total lack of action over those same weeks—Kane found himself intrigued.

"Proposition, huh?" he grumbled at a fly buzzing around the hole as he proceeded to piss on the sand next to it. At least it missed his feet. "I'll hear your proposition."

Kane shuffled back along the beach to the bar on the prettiest beach on Rabbit Island. A gentle breeze rustled his baggy clothes. The murmur of the sea as it lapped onto the island's shore from a million miles away promised everything, as it always did, and yet always delivered disappointment. He arched his neck and looked at the stars blanketing the vast empty blackness above, once again making Kane realise just how insignificant he was in the world. How small. Unimportant.

A drunk fucking loser.

"Fuck it," he mumbled to nobody. "Je suis tout ouïe, Français... I'm all ears."

The Oak Island Enigma: Chapter Three

"You see, the problem is, Mr Kane... may I call you Hiram?" Kane nodded. "I am not allowed into the United States or Canada, Hiram. It is because of... certain dealings with my, um, friend, Omar Abdel-Rahman. I believe you know him?"

Francois sensed Kane was suddenly on high alert. Omar Abdel-Rahman was a criminal, Francois had learned, now deceased. Before his death, however, online news reports had suggested he was actually a good guy who'd been corrupted by financial greed and the more powerful drug of collecting the uncollectable. He watched as Kane nodded almost imperceptibly.

Francois took that as his cue to continue. "In fact, it was Omar who recommended I contact you. But this was many, many months ago, before... well, you know, even before Egypt." Francois looked away, and he sensed Kane couldn't tell if it was out of sadness or guilt.

Francois eyed Kane, appraising him. In Kane's eyes he

saw questions: *What is your connection to Omar, and Egypt? Who the hell even are you?* It didn't matter, Francois knew, since it was all total bullshit. He'd never met the Egyptian. Never even heard of him until he'd selected Kane for the mission he was about to propose, and Google was everyone's friend when it came to procuring resources for one's important operations. The Frenchman turned back to Kane.

"It was with good reason Omar suggested I reach out to you. Your reputation... ahem... your former reputation, was unrivalled. The best modern-day explorer on the planet. The perfect man for the job."

"What job?"

"I will get to that in a moment. But I trusted Omar, so I did reach out. I tried to contact you many times. You are a hard man to track down."

Kane shrugged half-heartedly.

"You didn't receive my letters? I sent three hand-written letters and many emails, detailing everything about what I'm going to tell you now."

Kane offered another half shrug, and Francois sensed at least a little recognition.

"My fear now is that it is too late," Francois continued. "That is why I have made this special journey in person to find you here in Cambodia. It was too important not to."

"You got all the way here from... France?"

"Paris, oui," François confirmed.

"You came all the way here from Paris just to buy me cocktails on a Cambodian beach? Are you mad?"

Francois chuckled. He eyed Kane up and down, as if assessing the man's physical state. He looked about to say something, to confirm Kane's 'mad' assessment of him, but thought better of it. "No, Hiram, I'm not mad. I remain convinced this will not have been a wasted journey. The question is, though... who are you now, Hiram? Who is this man before me? Are you the famous explorer and philanthropist Hiram Kane, from the legendary Kane family, discoverers of Machu Picchu and Vilcabamba, and you, purveyor of many other great archaeological triumphs? Or are you a washed-up bum who doesn't see the need for shoes and clean clothes, and has forgotten what self-respect is?"

It was a gamble to be so forthright, but something told Francois it was the right approach. He glanced over Kane's shoulder, casually looking towards the line of palm trees that flanked the bar. He nodded imperceptibly, then turned back to Kane. The fact Kane hadn't punched him yet was a good sign, and he surged on. "I am only interested in offering this magnificent, once-in-a-lifetime opportunity to the better version of you." Francois eased himself off his barstool and took a few steps away, before turning back towards Kane, who now wore an expression that was somewhere between anger and shame.

Good, thought Francois... *that got his attention.*

"I intend on having a few more drinks this evening. However, after I leave later, I will be back here tomorrow morning at nine. I will wait only twenty minutes before I depart for Paris. I wonder, Hiram... not whether you will show up or not. I know you will. You will find it impossible not to after what I will tell you. I'll tease you with just two words. Then the only question will be... which one of you will arrive?"

With that, the mercurial Frenchman turned and made his way to the bar, pausing only to say "Oak Island" over his shoulder, smiling inwardly at how easy it was to land a big fish with a fake hook.

STEVEN MOORE

Grab your copy…
vinci-books.com/island-enigma

About the Author

Englishman Steven Moore grew up by the seaside, thus his first true joy was the great outdoors. His innate love of travel and a degree in anthropology, archaeology, and art history, help inform his fiction writing. Steven also loves painting, photography, and both playing and watching sport.

The travel bug bit the now perpetual nomad early, and to date Steven has lived and worked on five continents, and visited almost seventy countries. Steven combines an age-old writing adage; Write what you know, with his own mantra; Write where you know, and sets most of his novels in places in which he has either lived or spent an extended period of time.

When not on the road, Steven divides his time between Norwich, UK, and San Miguel de Allende, Mexico, which he shares with his rescue cats Ernest Hemingway and F Scott Fitzgerald (Ernie and Fitz), and his rescue puppy, Charles Dickens. Oh yes, and his beautiful travel writer wife, Leslie.

A lifelong love of food, wine, and beer, have demanded a new-found love of yoga and hiking in order to fend off the imminent arrival of middle age.

Acknowledgments

I don't know of any author who can finish a book of any kind without a lot of help and support, and I'm certainly no different. The assistance I've received for this novel and all my books has been both necessary and invaluable.

So, a quick shout out to these lovely folks—I couldn't have done it without you.

My gratitude to Anja Peerdeman, Michael Rhew and Tim Birmingham, my crucial BETA readers. Any remaining mistakes are my own. Thanks, guys.

I also want to thank the incredible team at Vinci Books for believing in me and supporting me on my journey. I appreciate you all.

And as always, to the one and only Leslie, my unstintingly supportive wife, I say thank you.

May you always be you!

Thank you!

Tibetan: Bka' druin che! བཀའ་དྲིན་ཆེ!

Hindi: Dhanyavaad! धन्यवाद!

Steven